Exquisitely Broken

A SIN CITY TALE

M. JAY GRANBERRY

"Maybe we'll meet again, when we're slightly older and our minds less hectic, and I'll be right for you and you'll be right for me. But right now I am chaos to your thoughts and you are poison to my heart."
—Unknown

For the imperfect lovers that believe in perfect love.

Prologue

Sinclair

"TIMES UP, KIDS. THE HOTEL IS EXPECTING AN ANSWER BY THE close of business today. I've given you all my reasons why this residency is a good idea, but if we do this, it has to be unanimous. For a band like us, a year is hella long. Have we ever spent a year anywhere?"

Adam Beckham, the lead guitarist of our band Sin City and my songwriting partner, asks as he paces the narrow path between the seats of the jet we boarded after closing a festival in Mexico City.

"Remember that time back in '02 in Mr. Cooke's class? That was a year, right?" Daniel Xu, our drummer, shrugs as he rips the top off a bag of M&M's and upends it into his mouth.

"Since when did a school year last twelve months? And bro, tenth grade was like fifteen years ago." Adam's voice is a low rumble barely audible above the hum of the engines on the opposite end of the jet.

"The point of that tickle to your memorables is to remind you that we have indeed been somewhere for a year," Dan says around a mouth full of candy.

Adam turns for the new leg of his next lap up the center aisle. "Tenth-grade band in Pahrump, Nevada, isn't exactly where I was going with this, but I feel you," he says, running his hands through his chin length blond hair and tucking it behind his ears. "I'm talking more about the grind. We've been in grind mode for so long, I'm not sure we know how to stop. Or if we even want to stop?"

"This constant touring shit is for the birds. Seriously. I mean when we were twenty-one, going to sleep in London and waking up in Belgium was an adventure, but now? Not so much. We're in our thirties. Three. Zero. Thirty. This one," Dan says, pointing a drumstick at our bassist, Miles Anderson, "is supposed to be my wingman, but since he put a ring on it, he's only interested in one set of tits and ass. And you two," he says, twirling the stick through his fingers, stopping the rotation to point first at me and then at Adam. "Get mobbed everywhere you go, and that is an even bigger cock block than his pussy pining. So, I get to go home, tap a whole new market, and make money doing what I love with my best friends."

"Speak for yourself. I'm only twenty-nine, asshole, and those tits are a masterpiece," Miles interrupts as he dodges the crumpled yellow candy bag Dan throws at his head.

"As I was saying before I was so rudely interrupted, my vote is not just yes, but ha-ha HELL YES!" Dan shouts loudly in the mostly empty cabin.

"Okay, that's two for the residency. What about you?" Adam asks with a lift of his chin toward Miles as he turns to walk down the aisle.

"Man, my wife and kid are in Vegas. My answer is easy. I've wanted to be home for a long time."

"I need to hear the word, Miles. Is that a yes?" Adam stops his pacing long enough to stare at Miles.

"Yes," he says with an eye roll worthy of a heroine in a telenovela.

"Good deal. So that's three for, and what about you Sin?" He starts moving again, his eyes boring into mine as he passes my seat. His blue eyes are still as piercing as they were the first time I saw him on the other side of the dinner table in the group home, and he took me under his wing and told me how my new home worked.

What about me?

No, I don't want to do a residency in Las Vegas. In not so polite words, fuck Las Vegas. What happens in Vegas needs to stay there. And live there. And never see the light of day there. I've avoided that city like it's ground zero of the zombie apocalypse.

Four years ago, I left on the first thing smoking, and although I've been back for a couple of concerts because the other members of the band have ties to people in the city, I only stayed long enough to get on stage and back to the airport once the show was over.

That shanty desert town means the world to the men that mean the world to me, and no matter how far I travel or how long I've been away, it's still home. How can I say no? Adam just got a notice from child protective services that his mother overdosed, leaving his sister at the mercy of a broken system that tried its damnedest to break us. Miles's wife is three months pregnant with their first baby, and although Dan tries to act like all he cares about is pounding his way through the female population, I know better. His entire family lives in Las Vegas, and his grandmother's Alzheimer has gotten significantly worse.

Saying no would be selfish and nasty in a way that I've never been. I've looked at this situation from every angle, and no matter how I slice or dice it I can't come up with a valid reason or at the very least a convincing excuse to decline the offer. Other than I'm afraid to see my ex. Just the idea of that man makes the hair on the back of my neck stand at attention.

Our breakup was singularly the worst thing I've gone through, and I've had my fair share of bad luck. Jacob Johnson tore me apart from the inside, inflicted a wound that no one could see, even though I was bleeding out. But when stacked against my bandmates' noble causes, my excuse fails miserably.

I can't deny that the money is good or that being on the road, if we can even call it that anymore with all the planes and trains that we travel on, is taking its toll. And I mean really what is the likelihood of me bumping into the one guy I knew once upon a forever ago in a city of millions?

Not very.

So, I paste on what I hope is a convincing smile and pull on my big girl panties. I can do this. For them, I will do a lot.

"Let's do it."

"The same rules apply to you too, Sin. I need a definitive yes," Adam says.

I close my eyes tight and throw out a silent plea to the universe. *Please do not make me regret this. Just a little grace. That's all I'm asking for.* I open my eyes to three pairs staring at me with varying levels of concern and expectation.

I clear my throat and with more conviction than I feel, I plunge headfirst into a decision I pray doesn't come back to bite me in the ass.

"Yes."

Chapter 1

Jake

I GLANCE DOWN AT MY TAG HEUER WATCH JUST TO MAKE SURE THE SECOND hand is still moving. These meetings are long, tedious, and a waste of my time. As chief financial officer of The Hotel, a newer casino on the Las Vegas Strip, my job is to oversee every account, secure funding for every project, and sign my name on the dotted line to make sure hundreds of employees are paid on time, every time.

Sitting in a meeting about the changes the beverage managers want to make regarding how they contact the extra board cocktail servers for a shift is not really my thing. Will the change improve customer service without increasing costs? Then do it.

I glance up at Dave, the director of the food and beverage department, as he collects his notes and steps down from the podium to make room for Aaron from marketing. As soon as Aaron opens his mouth, my already frayed nerves rip to the seam. He's animated and excited over minutia like an annoying cheerleader from high school still cheering when the team is losing by fifty points. No one is that happy at nine in the morning. Correction, only Aaron Martinez is that happy at nine in the morning. Maybe he wakes up seeing butterflies and rainbows.

I fight the urge to roll my eyes as I glance at my watch again. This is going to be a long meeting. We're not even halfway done and I already know I'm not making it through the whole thing. Connor Rappaport, my business partner and the CEO, requires all members of the executive team to attend quarterly meetings on the casino's goals and progress, but here's the thing: It's hard to fire the money man. Finding money, spending money and, more importantly, making money for this casino is what I do.

I learned from my father who learned from his father who learned from his father. My family moved to Nevada when Las Vegas Boulevard was still a two-lane dirt road in the middle of nowhere. My great grandfather got his first casino in a winning hand of poker and the second casino came as a pat on the head from the mafia outfit that was running Las Vegas at the time. Elijah Johnson was a hard drinker, a womanizer, a degenerate gambler but he was also a mathematical savant with a business acumen for gaming that multiplied my family's wealth and influence tenfold. In Las Vegas, the last name Johnson is nowhere near common. It is a gaming empire. A legacy that every man in my family has upheld. A legacy that is unparalleled by any other gaming family. The Johnson men are not just shrewd in business but we have a reputation for finding water when the well has run dry.

When Connor first approached me about opening an independent casino, I thought he was joking. Individuals almost never open casinos anymore. Contrary to its reputation, Las Vegas is no longer the Mafia's washing machine for dirty money or the hardcore gambler's playground. Vegas reinvented itself as a luxurious destination for playboy millionaires and socialites. *Thank you, Kim Kardashian and Paris Hilton.* Their type of celebrity helped kick off a new era, a changing of the guard if you will.

Connor was poised to take the reins. If my family are the rainmakers in casinos, then his family are the brains. Connor's father had the insight to bring big corporations to Las Vegas. Avery Rappaport is the leader of the pack. He sets the pace and dares everyone else to keep up. Conner, although he doesn't want to admit it, is the same. He's strategic and intelligent, always ten steps ahead of his competitors. He has a big enough ego to demand a spot at the table and enough self-confidence to own it. When his father began the process of retirement Connor was the only one capable of filling his Allen Edmond Oxford loafers. He quickly claimed a spot on the 'Executives to Watch' list in the local media and that was before he had the idea to open a new casino. Connor needed a little help to bring that idea to fruition and that's where I came in.

The first thing that any start-up needs is money. The capital needed to start a casino is astronomical. Even the most daring venture capitalists are leery about investing in a business that comes with the high degree of risk associated with gaming. That's why most of the casinos on the Strip are publicly owned and traded. It's easy to convince many investors to give a small amount versus getting a smaller number of investors to give large sums of money.

Connor personally invested fifty percent of our capital. Getting the other fifty took six months, give or take, and I worked my ass off for it. I tapped every connection my family had and some we didn't. Many of the investments came as a personal favor to my father and others came with strings loose enough to give us room to hang ourselves because a favor owed to you by the Johnsons and Rappaports in this town is better than money in the bank.

Second, we had to reinvent the wheel. Consumers are no longer interested in Steve Wynn's Vegas. His world of themed casinos that depend on gimmicks to get people in the door are a trend of the past. They want the opulence of the Waldorf combined with the nostalgia of slot machines and poker rooms. They want great food and the chance to be very important in an environment where anyone willing to spend money is important. Now people come to Vegas for the experience. A chance to say they walked on the same street where they filmed *The Hangover* or they threw dice at the table where Bugsy Siegel lost his bankroll. They want to sit in the showroom that hosted acts like the Rat Pack and Elvis and have a chance to play on the golf course where notorious mobsters out smarted the FBI.

When we finally made our move, we vowed to do it different. Do it with fresh eyes and on our terms, which is the main reason we decided to name our casino *The Hotel*. The name doesn't promise a tropical paradise or a trip to another country, but in a market saturated by the biggest, the flashiest and the gaudiest, it was our way to stand out, and it worked.

It's been a crazy ride, but if I could do it all over again, I'm not sure I would. There was a brief time four years ago when I thought I could walk away. Turn my back on everything. Seventy plus years of familial obligation and the weight of becoming a pillar to a community that already made my knees buckle under its weight. But I fucked up my chance, let her slip through my fingers, and the trappings of the life I'd wanted so badly to escape are now the only things I have left.

I check my watch again. Ten minutes later, Aaron is still going. It feels more like twenty. They have five more minutes then I'm out. If Connor has a problem, he can come find me. Truth be told, he has no more interest in this banal meeting than I do, so we'll see if he comes looking.

Aaron is at the podium. His slight frame a wisp of color behind the heavy wood. The room erupts in applause, and I realize I've blocked out everything he was saying. He waits for the clapping to die down before he continues, too pleased with himself.

"As many of you know this is a huge deal for The Hotel. Landing an artist of this caliber for a residency finally puts us in a position to compete with some of the larger corporate hotels on the Strip."

I've seen the list of local bands under consideration for the residency, but there was definitely no one of caliber and nothing to applaud over.

"Sin City is *the* local band, and according to most critics and fans, they're the architects of the "Las Vegas Sound." All four members are native to Las Vegas, but Sinclair James and Adam Beckham have to be two of the brightest stars this valley has ever produced. We'll be holding a press conference Friday immediately followed by a reception."

I jolt forward in my seat. The news like a cattle prod to my spine. Sin City? As in Sinclair James's band. I rest shaking hands on the table, intently focused on Aaron. There is no way in hell I missed a memo about Sin City. I'd just met with Connor a couple of days ago to final-ize the budget for the upcoming residency, and he hadn't said a word. If the CEO didn't know, they must have just confirmed.

Sin City is coming back to Vegas. Sinclair James will be back in Vegas, at my casino.

I dated Sin forever ago, long before Connor moved back to the States and we started The Hotel, way before I chose to conform and assume my father's role. Hell, for most of our relationship, the band was a lounge act. What my mother took great joy in calling the Las Vegas equivalent to a factory worker and I was still trying to forge my own path instead of following the one that had been laid out at birth.

It's been years. Four years… since I've seen or spoken to Sin. The last time I had any real connection happened a couple of months after we broke up. A video of her singing at a studio in London went viral on YouTube. She was breathtaking in her pain, and I took comfort in the fact she was just as miserable as I was. That I still made her feel something.

When I finally got past the visuals long enough to listen to the song, I was sick. Disgusted with what I'd done and how I'd broken us. That goddamn song was awful. All my missteps, all the regret, all the heartbreak laid bare for public consumption. I must've heard her sing "Exquisitely Broken" every day for months, and that was before the official video came out. One that featured a man who looked exactly like me caught in a twisted web of his own making, just like I had. I remember it like it was yesterday. Sitting on the sofa watching my TV doppelganger act out the worst day of my life. I just kept think-ing, *This isn't a game, it's my life*. Even though the listening public didn't know TV guy was supposed to be me I felt exposed. Flayed open in the worse possible way.

The single went platinum, and so did the EP that followed. I watched her star rise just like I imagined it would, but the higher she rose, the farther she moved away from me. There wasn't only time and space between us anymore. There was media and fans. There was persona and security. There was a completely different life I wasn't privy to and that reality sucked.

Through the years, I've followed her career. Year one post Sin, I turned into a low-key stalker. She avoided the valley, which meant I had to find her. I'd *coincidentally* end up at signings. I created dummy social media accounts to follow Sin City's posts without alerting Sin or the band to my presence. I listened incessantly to local radio channels. I would show up at concerts and try unsuccessfully to get backstage. I read all her interviews and watched every TV appearance. When she started modeling for high-end designers, I bought fashion magazines just to feel a little closer to her. That was a low point, but it was all I had so I took it.

It was around that time that the articles started to shift. The interviews didn't focus on Sin's heartbreak anymore or the asshole, me, who broke it. They focused on her current love life. Not a day went by I didn't see a headline linking her with tortured artsy types, from actors to pro athletes, and then I saw the picture of her with the ultimate, tortured, artsy type Adam, her so-called best friend and the lead guitarist for Sin City. The picture was taken backstage at a concert. From the look of the image, they had no idea a camera was present. His forehead rested against hers. He had a hand on either side of her face, and that connection that I'd always felt between them was palpable from the pages of a magazine.

Now I get to see her again. The only woman to ever hold my heart. The one that slipped through my fingers taking a part of me, the best part that only existed in her presence. Sin City will be working for my hotel, and I'm pretty sure Sin has no idea I work here. I don't know if the universe is finally throwing me a bone or if it's a rare combination of factors setting up the perfect storm. Whatever it is, years of curiosity will be satisfied. I want to know if there are vestiges of the girl that I met ten years ago and the woman that I have never stopped loving. The girl I knew craved passion and creativity. She exuded a social magnitude that drew me in from the first encounter, and we were in love. If that girl still exists, if there's a chance, no matter how far-fetched, I'm taking it.

"We're requesting that all senior management be present for the press release and reception that will immediately follow. Before the media arrives, we'll have a less formal meet and greet where you all will get an introduction to the artists. After meeting with them multiple times, I guarantee you all will be just as excited as we are to have them with us for the next year. Are there any questions?" Aaron looks around the room expectantly.

The meeting lasted another forty-five minutes after that bombshell. I was supposed to be gone forty minutes ago, but here I am, sitting at the conference table and watching my colleagues file out when Aaron places a hand on my shoulder.

"We came in almost fifty grand under budget, man." He moves my shoulder back and forth in his excitement.

"That's… uh… really great. So, you said Sin City will be here an entire year, huh?"

He puffs his chest with a sense of accomplishment. "Technically it will be two weekends a month, a total of forty-eight days spread over fifty-two weeks. Since they're local, we won't have to put the band up in the hotel, well at least most of the band. That's one of the ways we were able to come in under budget. Ms. James will be on property, but everyone else will be staying in personal homes."

Aaron, being in entertainment, understands hotel profits a little better than most. He gets that gains do not negate or impact the budget allotted for a project because the revenue earned is not immediately available. We track everything down to the cost of replacement light bulbs needed to light the stage. Eating the cost of a hotel room that we could otherwise book is a loss. Sure, it balances in the end but in the meantime, it ties up funds allocated for other functions. This is definitely a W for his department.

"I'd heard that the lead singer and the guitarist are a couple?"

I try to slip that question in without sounding too invested in the answer. My life is distinctly divided into pre-Sin breakup, and post-Sin breakup. If you weren't in my life before the breakup, and no one at The Hotel was, there would be no indication that I'd ever known Sin. I don't go around telling all who will listen that I once upon a time dated a pop singer who at the time wasn't famous. I've known Connor since grade school and with him going to undergrad on the East Coast and grad school in England, I don't think he's put the pieces together. When our relationship ended, Sin exited stage left. She didn't pass go or collect two hundred dollars. It was the damnedest trick, like magic. Now you see me, now you don't. She became a ghost, only existing in fractured memories and phantom touches.

In the years since she's been gone, I've done my best to relegate her presence to the times when I'm alone where I can recall the exact texture of her skin and the husky timbre of her voice. This time was mine, *she* was mine. I could reminisce. What we had was unique and maybe once in a lifetime.

So yeah, I asked a question. The one thing I probably shouldn't. The one thing I have wanted to know for years. Are Sin and Adam a couple? While we were together did they… did she ever… If they are a couple one room would suffice, and one bed, and one shower. My pulse kicks up thinking about the two of them taking full advantage of all the amenities in our hotel rooms. *Together.*

But on the slim chance I'm wrong, that hundreds of publications are wrong, I wait for Aaron's answer. Sin was always so adamant they were friends. God, if they're not together… I can't even let that thought percolate. I'm not saying I'd do anything stupid, but I'm not saying I wouldn't either. There is no telling what fool thing I'd do if given another shot. It would sting to get confirmation that she went from me to Adam. Okay, that's bullshit. I don't need a definitive answer for it to sting, but it still doesn't change the fact I want one.

I stand up, collecting the few papers I have on the table, trying to feign disinterest like we're discussing the weather, but every molecule in my body is zeroed in on his answer.

"I don't think so." A slight frown creases the skin between his eyebrows. "The couple of times I met with them, they seemed more like siblings, and they wanted to take the residency because their base guitarist is expecting his first baby. They all just seem like a close-knit family."

A firework of emotion burst through my body and the papers I'd been gathering into a neat pile with deep focus fall from my flustered grasp as his words sink in. *Fuck yeah! Those words are exactly what I needed to hear.*

I'm not a cup-half-full kind of guy. I don't pray regularly or hope for the impossible, but this whole situation seems like something bigger than me at work. What is the likelihood of Sin and I being in the same stratosphere let alone the same hotel for a year? I'm a finance guy who sits behind a desk, and she's a rock star who travels the world. For the first time in a long time, I let the idea of reconnecting with her take root.

Aaron pats me on the shoulder as he makes his way toward the door. When the door shuts behind him, I'm the only person left in the room.

"Thank you," I whisper to whatever's out there that brought Sinclair James back into my life.

Chapter 2

NOW

Sinclair

OVER THE LAST FOUR YEARS, I'VE TRAVELED TO EVERY MAJOR CITY around the world. Paris, Milan, New York, Los Angeles, and Prague to name a few. Traveling introduced me to a world so much bigger than my childhood dreams could have conjured. It's sumptuous and vast. Each place uniquely fascinating on its own but still strangely connected through the familiar, such as a Starbucks coffee shop situated on a random corner or a couple walking down the street with their fingers entwined.

In my case, that connection comes through music, my love language. It's how I carved out my place in a world that had little use for a girl with no pedigree and even less consideration for an artist.

When I'm on stage, the music feels like a blissful tremor rippling straight through me. It touches each person in the audience, and for a couple of hours nothing hurts. Everything wrong in the world falls away and it's just them and me, uncomplicated and in the purest form. We don't always speak the same language or come from the same background, but when I sing, every single word comes from the heart. They feel it and feel me in a way that transcends our differences.

With all the places I've seen and people I've met, Las Vegas is the only place I've ever considered home. Even when I ran away. Even when the sight of stylish neon and gaudy gold made me recoil.

Now that I'm back, it seems silly to have stayed away for so long. From the backseat of the limo, Vegas is a lot more gloss and not half as much grit. I'd heard from the guys in the band that the city finally finished the 215 Beltway and added casinos to the Strip at Harmon Street. But seeing the changes to the streets I'd walked and the skyline I loved is jarring. The new editions stick out obnoxiously. The new casinos are garish and dominating. Instead of billboards advertising tawdry shows and cheap meals, LED signs flash with designer labels and eighty-dollar gourmet buffets. How is that a thing? Gourmet is the antithesis of buffet.

The limo plunges into darkness as we come to a stop in The Hotel's underground parking garage reserved for high rollers and celebrities. The goal is to minimize the crazy that surrounds me as much as possible. I'm still not completely used to the circus. It wasn't that long ago Adam and I pounded the pavement, trying to get one hotel, any hotel, to give us a shot.

Now I'm arriving in a limo provided by The Hotel. Living in a penthouse suite, also provided by The Hotel. Performing in residence in an event center that rivals Madison Square Garden that four years ago we could have never filled.

I don't have to eye the people waiting at the entrance to know Seth and Aiden, my personal security, are waiting and have taken the time to check the route to the suite. Venetria McCullough, my publicist, is also somewhere in the melee. She scheduled a quick trip to inspect the appearance of the advertisements and promotions before our arrival.

The band's image is a carefully cultivated menagerie of music, social media, and endorsements that has taken years to perfect. Ven's job is to make sure The Hotel stays in line and seamlessly integrates with our current marketing visuals. Anita, my stylist, might be down here too, but I'd bet money she's already in the suite setting up racks of clothes.

Out of the sea of faces I know only three or maybe four people. The rest are a mix of hotel security and staff. I miss the days when I could melt into a crowd without worrying I'd be attacked by haters or hurt by fans. Don't get me wrong I love what I do. All I've ever wanted to do is create music. There was never a plan B. I know there are a million people around the world who would switch places with me in a heartbeat.

But I miss the old me. The one before the fame. The girl who didn't think twice about driving the 215 Beltway around Las Vegas and hopping out of her car at the top of Lone Mountain because the sprawling view of lights inspired her. The girl who frequented hole-in-the-wall bars because famous musicians, not celebrities or stars, would be there to jam for hours and she wanted to learn everything. Fame has its rewards, but it's hard. A quid pro quo. You must be willing to give something to get something. I just didn't bank how much that something would cost.

The bodyguard driving the limo is Joey. His backup is a new guy, one I haven't met, who rotated in last minute. They met me at the aircraft, so my personal team could secure my suite. As they exit the vehicle to open the door, Seth and Aiden immediately crowd in close. Seth leans forward ducking his head inside, his soft brown eyes take inventory, sweeping the empty benches and bar before coming to rest on mine.

"Good trip?"

"Nothing to complain about here. You guys okay?"

He nods his head and runs a hand over his cropped hair.

"Just a heads-up, Sin. One of these hotel fuckers let it slip"—his fingers twitch with annoyed air quotes—"that'd you'd be arriving to-day. So, it's pretty gnarly in there."

"Fans or paparazzi?"

"Both."

"Do they know I'm living here now? Or do they think it's sound check and prep?"

"As far as we can tell, they're all here to get their shots and autographs and go home. Once you're settled, one of the guys will get the luggage so no one will be the wiser."

"Okay, thanks, Seth. You touch base with Adam yet? Is he already home?"

A flush creeps up his neck, staining his cheeks, and his eyes drop to the empty space beside me.

"We…" He clears his throat and looks back at me. "I haven't talked to Adam for a couple of days. I'm sure he's fine. You ready to go?" He stretches out his hand, wiggling his fingers.

I glance between his wriggling digits and flushed face before I place my hand in his and step out. "I'm not letting that statement go that easy, Seth. And just so we're on the same page… I swear on my life if you break his heart, I'll bury you in the desert."

"It's not his heart you have to worry about, Sin," he mutters.

Before I can delve further into that statement, the sliding glass doors open and people cascade out with a jarring wave of noise. Seth and Aiden, close in tight as we walk forward. The Hotel security rushes forward to form a box around our little group, and we barely move a foot before the first paparazzi tries to break our ranks. Aiden runs closer to the edge of the square leaving me with Seth, to stiff-arm the person between the shoulders of two hotel guards.

"We gotta move, Sin." Seth's voice booms close to my ear. I pick it up, moving at a jog and trying to perfectly mirror Aiden's steps as he clears the path a couple of feet in front of me and Seth falls a couple of feet behind to cover our six. The crush of humanity around us is suffocating. We finally make it into the lobby when a slender hand wraps around my wrist, and a youngish girl trips forward and almost takes us both out.

The people around me are still plowing ahead with no consideration for the girl they're about to trample.

"Aiden stop! Hold up a sec!" I yell before turning to the girl.

"You okay?" She gives me big eyes, but nothing comes out of her mouth. So, I try again. "What's your name?"

It takes a second before she says, "Kasey with a K."

"Nice to meet you, Kasey. Sin." I wave the guys back as they start to approach us. Over the last couple of years, my instincts are pretty spot on when it comes to identifying the crazies from the fans, and this girl is a fan.

"OMG… you're like really here and actually like yourself."

"I hope so," I say on a chuckle. "How old are you Kasey? Shouldn't you still be in school?"

Her fingers drop from my wrist, and she tosses a worried glance at the two men flanking me. They probably look like cops from where she's standing. Then she squares her shoulders and looks me dead in the eye.

"I ditched. If my dad finds out, my life is so over. But it's worth it. I didn't think I would actually get to meet you. I just wanted a picture or something. But we're for real having a convo."

"Where's your phone?" She holds up a new smartphone with a picture of my guitar as the screen saver.

"Let's get you that picture so you can get back to school." Her eyes light up as she fumbles to open the camera app. I step in close to her and throw up devil horns as she snaps two or three pictures.

"These are f-ing lit," she squeals scrolling through the pictures. "My friends will probably think I photo shopped you in."

"It was really nice to meet you Kasey, but I gotta go."

"Oh, right. I know that. You're probably super busy with the show and stuff." Her careless charm and genuine adoration strike a chord. I used to be this girl. Tracking down artists that I loved. Doing anything to be just one foot closer to stardom.

"Yeah, something like that, but why don't you come to the first meet and greet? I'll leave tickets for you at will call. What's your last name?"

"Are you serious right now?" She bounces up and down, clapping her hands.

"I am, but I need that last name."

"It's Fairley."

"Gotcha. Kasey with a K Fairley. See you opening night."

Our group once again moves forward, leaving an openmouthed girl gaping behind us. I smile at her dazed look.

That was nice. See, Vegas isn't so bad after all.

Chapter 3

"**S**IN, I LOVE YOU!"

The screaming and chants get louder the closer I get to the venue The Hotel secured for the press release. Aiden immediately puts his hand on the butt of the gun attached to his hip. Checking for a threat, Seth scans the insulated bubble we walk in surrounded by hotel security. He quietly speaks into the communication device and signals to Aiden that we need to hurry up. The entire group moves double time until we get to the lounge.

Hotel security falls away once we get to the designated press area, it's lined with heavy gold stanchions corralling the reporters into civilized groups. They come to attention as soon as they see me frantically pushing against the ropes. Multiple cameras start to flash as they all press forward.

I stumble back on my four-inch heels in surprise when a grungy man jumps over the velvet rope. His meaty hand landing on my waist as he attempts to pull me into a hug. I look into crazed green eyes as I forcibly push against his hold.

"Sin, I'll fix what he broke!" Spittle lands on my shoulder as he rasps the harsh words.

Security immediately pulls him away, but his desperate screech as they wrestle him to the ground unsettles me.

There is no mistaking the stringy dark hair or the too tight T-shirt of Sin City from our first tour or the anguished declarations of love.

I've been dealing with Ian Foster for as long as I've been performing. I haven't seen him in a while because we've been overseas, and he only follows the tour when we're in the U.S.

I'll have to remind Seth and Aiden to give the hotel security a heads-up. Being in one place for any length of time is going to give him more space and opportunity to get close. In the past he has been relentless. Showing up at the airport or hotel. Last tour he actually followed the tour bus for days until his old Chevy broke down. He's always been creepy and weird. I stand off to the side to watch the big men in matching gold sport coats cart him off the premises. I don't breathe a sigh of relief until they've completely disappeared from sight.

Shake it off, girl. Stalkers like that are par for the course.

I toss a glance over my shoulder just to make sure Seth and Aiden are close. "Miss James… over here." A photographer calls to me as I walk the gold carpet. I stop once again with my hand on my hip, head tilted to the side, and my lips in a slight pout. Cameras repeatedly flash as I move toward the door. Every so often I stop and pose because if I play nice, they stay respectful.

Adam seems to pop up out of nowhere. His natural gait just as recognizable as his face. True to form, he's wearing jeans with holes in the knees and a Van Halen T-shirt layered under a plaid button-down shirt. He calls the reporters by name and asks about their kids and spouses as he makes his way to me as if he doesn't have a care in the world. I know different, but I've always admired his ability to show only the things he wants people to see. When he reaches me, he slips an arm around my waist. He presses his cheek tight to mine, and we both smile big as the paparazzi move in closer.

We've been playing the *are we or aren't we a couple* game with the media for as long as I can remember. It started as his way to protect me when I was too weak to do it myself and as my way to keep people out of his personal life. As time went on and we read all the outlandish articles the magazines printed, we taunted them with casual touches that could mean more and subtle kisses that might lead to something else.

His hand slips under the fall of my hair, and his nose brushes up my cheek. "Let's do this. You ready?" He says directly into my ear.

I nod, and he laces our fingers as we walk with purpose into the lounge. The event is the pre-media shindig that will welcome us as headliners at The Hotel. After years of struggling to get recognition, I don't take it for granted that they want us here or that they believe that people are willing to pay on a consistent bases to sustain a residency over the next year.

The doors close behind us, and the shift in energy is jarring. The paparazzi are always manic. It's like every minute is a battle to keep and maintain boundaries. However, the lounge has a smooth 1920s vibe with low light and jazz playing in the background. It's clear that most of the people in the room are here for business versus pleasure. Most are wearing dark suits and sensible shoes. Half of them look like they are still on the clock, watching the seconds tick by until they can leave. The other half are all about my age and happy for the free drinks and food.

Adam pulls my hand, making me stop short. "Did D tell you he wasn't coming tonight?" He quickly scans the room, frowning when he doesn't spot Dan.

"No, but he'll be here. You ever known him to pass up free food or free booze?"

"Not once, but you know he doesn't take anything seriously. We're already short one because Miles and Kat had the baby scare."

"Take a breath. He'll be here. In the meantime, work this room with me so we can get out of here and finally hit up In-N-Out."

"That right there is why I love you." He smacks a kiss on my cheek.

"My need to satisfy your craving for cow?" I arch an eyebrow.

"Do not under estimate the power of beef. It has the power to bring a man to his knees."

"Are you speaking from experience or…"

Adam rolls his eyes with a shake of his head and abruptly changes the subject. "You good by yourself in here? The young'uns seem to be chomping at the bit." Sure enough, some of the younger employees are organizing themselves into a line, glancing our way.

"I'll be okay. They're not a mob."

"Who's not a mob?" Dan slings a lanky arm around each of us. "The group of ladies standing over—" I turn to face him and almost bite a hole in my cheek to stop a burst of laughter. Dan's wearing gray shorts that stop right above his knee, a vest completely buttoned over a white shirt, a neon pink skinny tie, and a fitted gray sport coat.

"I see you dressed for the occasion," Adam quips. Laughter replacing the worried frown from a moment ago.

"Sin-a-sticks isn't the only one who cleans up well." He steps forward and spins on his heels. Popping the collar of his jacket as he completes the tight revolution.

"Indeed. I'm sure you'll be beating them off in that outfit." I flick a piece of nonexistent lint from his shoulder.

"I can pull the ladies in with my tighty-whities, a layer of funk, and day-old scruff. This dapper ensemble is strictly for the cameras."

"That's right, big guy. Keep telling yourself that." Adam ducks from under Dan's arm.

"I'll take the left."

"You"—he points at Dan—"take the right and Sin hit the middle."

"One hour?" I say.

He nods and walks off, winking at me over his shoulder as Dan does a bad imitation moonwalk in the opposite direction.

Aaron, the entertainment director, walks up to me with a big smile plastered on his face. From our very first meeting, his energy and excitement to book us has been unmistakable.

"Ms. James, we're beyond happy that Sin City has arrived and to have you all here for the next year. Did you get situated okay?"

"It's Sinclair or Sin, please. No one calls me Ms. James but my lawyer." I smile. "And I did, thank you. The villa is stunning."

He looks at me with big appreciative eyes as a warm flush moves up his neck to stain his cheeks.

When I arrived earlier today, I was escorted through a maze of identical hallways which eventually led to a private entrance of a luxury boutique hotel tucked within the larger resort. I've heard of hotels within hotels, but I've never actually stayed in one. The rooms or villas, in this case, are invitation only, reserved for high rollers. I'm not talking about the Michael Jordans of the world. I'm talking the sheiks of Dubai who don't think twice about leaving hundreds of thousands of dollars on the table as a tip. That kind of money is still no more than a drop in the bucket to them.

The Château is made of twenty-nine oversized individual Parisian themed villas that resemble extravagant private homes. All settled in and around a huge mansion in the exact replica of an actual eighteenth-century mansion near Paris. At least that's what the butler said when he gave me the grand tour, which started with my three-bedroom villa and ended with the menuless restaurant, salon, media room, study, exercise room, and massage room.

"Villa?" he repeats. A confused frown crinkling the skin at the corners of his eyes. I lean in closer, dropping my voice even though all the people here probably already know about The Château.

"I'm in one of the three-bedroom villas at The Château."

"I didn't…" Aaron shakes his head a couple of times.

"I'm so sorry, Ms. Ja… Sinclair," he immediately corrects. "There must have been some mistake. We don't normally house entertainers… not that we don't value your contribution. It's just that area is reserved for guests that require a degree of…" His voice drops off in frustrated huff.

I was actually surprised The Hotel would give me what equates to a house for my stay, but when I arrived my instruments had been set up in the living room and my bags delivered to the door. I just assumed that because the other members of the band were staying in personal homes, off property and they only had to house one person they upgraded the accommodations. I guess I was wrong.

"No worries. It's all good. I thought it was"—*beautiful, gorgeous, exactly where I'd want to stay if I had to be in this dust bowl of a city*—"a little extravagant. Let's get through the next couple of hours, and then I'll move into the correct space."

Aaron visibly sags with relief. After years of staying in places where I had to use the cotton from my tampons to keep roaches from crawling up my nose or in my ears, I have a deep, heartfelt appreciation for swanky, over-the-top hotel rooms. When we first started out, we stayed in places where we had to fight the rats for space. I could have never dreamed of staying in some place like The Château, but I'm sure any of the suites at The Hotel are way better than some of the places I've been and adequate enough to give my team time to rent something else.

Smoothing a hand over his bowtie Aaron offers me his arm. "If you'll follow me, Ms. James," he says.

"Sin," I correct him, tucking my hand into the crook of his elbow.

"Oh. R-i-i-ight. Y-y-y-yes. A-a-ah. Sin," he stutters. "If you'll follow me, Sin, I'll introduce you to…" He scans the room. "The CEO, Connor Rappaport, is right over there."

My eyes follow his to a man wearing a quintessential black suit. I can't put my finger on it, but there is something vaguely familiar about the dark-rimmed glasses covering light-colored eyes, the perfectly quaffed hair, and his give-no-shits attitude. Standing in the middle of the Stepford executives, he exudes power, confidence, and wealth.

Where in the hell do I know this guy? It's right there in the front of my brain, dangling just out of reach. Our eyes meet, and his follow my movements as I approach.

"Mr. Rappaport, I would like to introduce you to—"

"No introduction necessary." He holds out his hand. "Ms. James."

"She doesn't like to be called that, she prefers…" Connor's gaze shifts from mine to Aaron's. He tilts his head to the side, studying Aaron with the same intensity that he just examined me. His presence completely dominating the other man. A flush once again stains Aaron's fair skin, and I fight the urge to chuckle. I guess I'm not the only person affected by the whole dominating CEO thing.

"Is that right?" His warm hand closes over mine as his eyes move up and down my body.

"If not Ms. James, what do you prefer to be called?"

"Feel free to call me Sinclair or Sin."

"Sinclair it is. On behalf of everyone, let me welcome you to The Hotel. If you need anything, don't hesitate to ask. Aaron and the entire entertainment department are at your disposal, and if that doesn't work"—he pulls out a gold business card, holding it between his index and middle fingers—"call me, anytime."

I pull the card from his fingers. He holds my gaze for another long beat when I hear Aaron's voice in the background making another awkward introduction. I break contact with Mr. Rappaport. My face immediately falls into default mode: light smile, friendly, minimal teeth, no gums, head tilted slightly to the side, and eyes open.

My hand is already reaching for the person in front of me before it registers that I know him. Not with the vague familiarity that comes with casual acquaintance but with stunning, vibrant, clarity. I'd know this man anywhere.

Chapter 4

Sinclair

I'M LOST. MOST OF THE PEOPLE AMBLING AROUND CAMPUS ARE LOST TOO, although there is a significant difference between them and me. It's freshman orientation and I'm here alone. No parents to help with luggage. No friends to nervously chat up.

It's not that the campus is huge or anything, but when I should've been packing and looking at campus maps, I was playing my guitar for tips on one of the bridges that connect casinos on either side of Las Vegas Boulevard.

Sweat trickles down the center of my back as I make my way across the quad, struggling with two guitar cases and an overstuffed duffle bag. I probably should've tried to figure out where my dorm room is located before trapesing across campus. Now, as a result of my poor planning I might pass out from heat exhaustion before I find my place.

I walk for a couple more minutes before I drop everything to the ground and shake my arms to relieve the numbness that set in from carrying the weight of all my measly possessions. Painful little pricks travel across my shoulders and down to my hands in a rush of relief as sensation returns.

This isn't rocket science. I'm supposed to be headed for the six-story white building, right? I blow out a frustrated breath and squint up at the sun as I grab the bottom of my T-shirt and flap the edge a couple of times to generate some airflow in the stifling heat. A quick look around tells me every building in the general vicinity is six stories and white.

This can't be as hard as I'm making it.

Once again, I pick up both cases and my duffle and start to walk toward the closest building. My newfound determination only lasts long enough for me to go haul my shit into the wrong dorm and get booted back outside by the nice R.A. who was kind enough to offer a map.

Irritated, I sit on one of the stone benches that line the courtyard in the center of the buildings.

"Shit!" I jump up immediately because it burns my ass. I think I hear my skin sizzle through my threadbare jeans. I know better than to touch anything that absorbs heat, especially during the summer in the middle of the day. Fuck this day. I am seriously over it and being lost and hot.

I bend over to pick up the map that fell when I flayed the skin off my behind, and before I can offer a warning, a guy tries to sit on the same bench. He jumps up just as I did, swatting at the back of his jeans like something bit him. I straighten to stand to my full height and my forehead smacks into his.

"Really? This is seriously happening?" I mumble at the same time he says, "Yeah, that hurt."

I try to back away from him when my feet tangle in the strap of the duffle bag. I yank my foot free but end up falling for my effort. I go down, hard. I hear an audible intake of breath in front of me, and I look up.

The instant our gazes meet, my body tingles with recognition, which is laughable. The person in front of me has private school and well-to-do written all over him. If I'm reading his head to toe designer clothes and retro Jordan tennis shoes right. I can guarantee where ever he's from, it's nowhere near my neighborhood.

But good God, he's pretty. His rich bronze skin glows in the sunlight and being this close, I can see the individual threads of blue, green, and brown that make up his hazel eyes and the dark brown freckles that dot bridge of his nose. When those full lips split into a smile, my breath catches in my throat and my stomach tightens. The feeling is visceral in a way that teases my insides and makes me want to put pen to paper and wax poetically.

His stare is unwavering, only broken by slow blinks. I watch his body extend toward mine in slow motion as he offers a hand to help me. His palm slides across my palm as long fingers curl around my hand, simultaneously pulling me up from the ground. I hit the wall of his chest and catch the subtle fragrance of fabric softener, soap, and something that is uniquely him. I open my mouth to once again to offer an apology, but when his arm tightens around my waist locking us together from hip to knee, the words evaporate off my tongue.

I lean my weight against his arm forcing it to drop from my back. I don't know if we're that in tune or if he is reading my body language or something, but he takes a small step away from me and gives me some much-needed space.

I just need a little breathing room, and then I'll be able to think straight again.

Then I make the mistake of letting my eyes travel down his tall frame, across the defined muscles of his chest and the thick thighs encased in fitted jeans.

Nope, space not working. I still have the urge to claim him for my own.

He studies my body with unconcealed fascination, matching me, look for look. In his eyes, I see a reflection of my own filthy thoughts. The desire to discover someone new, to touch and kiss, and taste and grind. I want to know if he's capable of everything that look is promising, and I want to dare him to do it. I rub my free hand against my thigh and casually try to pull my other one out of his grasp, but his fingers squeeze mine, stopping the retreat.

"Jacob Johnson," he says. The deep timber of voice sends goosebumps skittering across the back of my neck and down the length of my arms.

"S-Sin," I stammer.

He yanks his head back in shock. "Sin? As in the cardinal vices? Really?"

If I hadn't been so flustered, I would have given him my full name and totally avoided the name conversation all together. Now I'm annoyed and admittedly insulted by the derision in his tone. He's not the first person to comment on my name, and I can pretty much guarantee that he won't be the last. I love my name even if I was named after a character in a 90s sitcom.

I don't have a lot of memories of my mom. I can't remember her smile or the way she styled her hair. But I remember lying on her chest while she hummed me to sleep. She had a beautiful voice too. And I have my name. Odd to some but to me, it's everything, and fuck him very much for making fun of it.

"Sinclair," I say, yanking my hand out of his, "James." There's an ache to my voice I wince at hearing. I don't like to think about my family or the lack of one as it were. And I hate that his stupid question can make me feel less than.

"I didn't mean any offense. I've just never heard—" He stops short to clear his throat. "It suits you. It's… beautiful." His gaze bores into mine, all sincere emotion and sharp curiosity, and I like it. Really like it. It's as if he can see straight into the heart of me, and it leaves me feeling exposed right in the middle of the quad.

He is hitting buttons I didn't even know I had. I cross my arms over my chest because I need a barrier, anything, between my body and his.

"It was nice talking to you, Jacob, but I really need to go." I turn to walk away, grabbing the handle of one guitar case, but he reaches for the other one before I can get it.

"Don't go yet."

I hesitate.

Three little words.

That's all he said, but the tone of those simple little words resonates with a heady mix of seduction and longing. And dammit if I don't like being the focus of it.

"What dorm are you staying in?" He walks backward toward the buildings, holding my guitar hostage behind his back. I match him step for step, which successfully keeps the guitar out of my reach.

"Dayton South. Please, give me my guitar." I stop walking and hold out my hand.

A panty-dropping smile slides across his face and to my complete mortification, I have to fight the urge to take mine off and offer them up as tribute.

"Me too."

I smile in return and hear a low groan.

"She has dimples too. Fucking perfect," Jacob mumbles, or at least I think that's what he says. "Look, let me help you with all of this." He waves an arm at the duffle bag and hikes the guitar case in his hand higher.

"Not necessary. I'm good." *And not really that sure I trust myself to follow you to the dorm.* Apparently, my body didn't get the memo that we don't fall over pretty boys and rub ourselves over them like a kitten begging to be stroked. "If you could just point me in the right direction…"

He shakes his head and takes three giant steps that swallows up the space between us, picks up the duffle bag, and grunts under the weight.

"I gotchu, Sin. Just have a little faith."

"In what?"

He pulls the second guitar case from my hand, taking a backward step toward one of the buildings. "Me."

Chapter 5

NOW

Sinclair

JACOB JOHNSON IS IN FRONT OF ME. THERE ARE CLOSE TO A MILLION people in this valley. Why him? And why now? I could've gone another lifetime without seeing Jake again?

Aaron's effervescent voice is coming at me through a tunnel, saying, "This is the CFO of The Hotel,"

I see the man who broke my heart, the one who threw me away like day-old garbage. He's standing in front of me with the same haunting eyes and full lips spread in a sad smile. He reaches out to take my hand, and I'm trapped motionless by shock. He takes my palm. Just for a second, okay maybe like two or three seconds, I let myself bask in the familiar feel of his skin against mine.

"Jacob Johnson. Nice to…"

I jerk my hand out of Jake's, his voice breaking my trance like shattered glass. And because this day fucking sucks, I stumble over some yet to be identified object behind my heel. He wraps an arm around my waist to stop me from toppling over, securing me to his chest. Our lips are a breath apart. When he exhales, the scent of his cinnamon gum takes me back to hundreds of other moments like this one, moments where he was my anchor.

"No." I place hands on his chest.

Jake pulls his head back, his questioning gaze searching mine. I take that inch and push as hard as I can forcing him back a couple of steps.

He immediately moves forward, trying to reclaim that space.

"Can we just talk for a min—"

I slap him. Hard. The sound echoes around the room and every eye in the place turns in our direction.

"Fuck you, Jake!" An imprint of my palm blooms red and angry on his face. His fingertips tentatively touch his cheek, but he doesn't back down or slither away as it were. If anything he doubles down, frustration and determination warring for dominance on his face.

Oh my God, that felt good! For years, I've thought about this day. The day when the shoe would finally be on the other foot, and he'd be the humiliated one.

Satisfaction swells in my chest.

Then my head swivels around the room, and I fully grasp the reality of this situation and my utterly dumb-ass response. Was it justified? You bet your ass it was. But smart? Not even a little.

"I'm not asking for..." The muscle in his jaw tightens as he grinds his teeth before he starts again. "I'm just asking for a minute... one minute of your time... that's it. The last time I didn't get to say—"

I lower my voice and plaster a fake smile on my face, conscious of the eyes on us. In a fast, hushed whisper I say, "Do you not see all these people?" I signal around with room with a tilt of my head. "No, we can't talk. What is there left to say?"

I turn around, looking for the closest exit. I have to get out of here before I make an even bigger fool of myself. I walked into this room on top of the world. Leave it to Jake to taint even this. He steps in close behind me.

"Wait!" he rasps. The low timbre of his voice is almost drowned out by the noise around us, but I hear him. Oh my God, do I hear him. The rough sound skims across my nerve endings, making my nipples pebble into stinging points, and my frantic movements slowly stop. I stand there with my back to him. My mind screams at me to move, but my body begs me to reconsider, just one more time.

"Turn around." He waits for a couple of seconds, and when I fail to respond, I hear a whispered, "Please. I just want a chance to…" He places a hand on my shoulder, and my eyes flutter closed as I fight the urge to lean back into his warmth.

"Just have a little faith in—"

"Have a lit-little…," I stammer, as I turn around, bringing us face-to-face. He's lucky I don't hit him again.

Asshole.

He said the same thing to me the first day we met. And look where trusting him got me.

He straightens his suit coat and runs a hand down his tie. Finally taking in the shocked faces and semi-hidden cell phones. Jake takes a deep breath. I can see the gears in his mind working to grasp the severity of the situation while still pleading his case.

"I don't want to hear it. Whatever you are about to say… just don't. Do you remember when I told you I treated you with a respect that you didn't deserve?" I wait for him to nod.

"Well, baby, those days are long gone. I'm not your mother and contrary to what she may have told you, the sun doesn't rise and set on your ass. You don't get to ask me for time or understanding. You don't get to ask me for anything…"

"If you would let me get a word in—" He squeezes the bridge of his nose while the other hand closed into a fist against his leg.

"You still don't get it. I don't want your stupid words! Actions, remember that?" I close the space between us, poking a stiff finger in his chest. "It's all about actions, right? What did your actions say?" I look up into his face waiting for a reply. The only answer I get is his hand coming to wrap around mine, pulling my finger from his chest.

The venom just keeps pouring out of my mouth. I can't stop. *Why can't I shut up?*

"Oh, I got the Sin-ain't-shit message loud and clear. So, no I don't want to talk, and no I will not give you a chance. You can go straight to hell, Jake. And real talk? Fuck you for making me appear like the no class hoodrat your family always thought I was. Nice touch!"

I push against the solid wall of his chest and turn back toward the exits. This time he lets me go. But I don't know what door will lead me out of here, and every direction I turn there's a phone out recording. My well-groomed facade starts to slip in frustration. I haven't worked my ass off the last four years to end up the tail end of a joke on a late-night talk show. Hindsight being what it is, I should've smiled prettily and walked in the other direction. But now I can see the GIFs of me slapping him playing on a loop.

Maybe by some miracle the fallout won't be as bad as I think. The only people I have with boots on the ground here are the band members and security. Venetria left about two hours after we arrived with promises she be here for opening night. Our manager isn't set to arrive until early next week, a day before opening, because who could have anticipated that I would go reality TV on my ex at the release?

All the other people in attendance are employees of The Hotel, so it can't be that bad, right? But all I need is for one picture or video to leak.

I forgot all about Seth and Aiden, who stare at me in wide-eyed disbelief. If I weren't in the middle of what amounts to one of the worst days of my life, this whole thing would be comical.

But right now? *Not laughing.*

And then there's Aaron, the entertainment director, who has the power to cancel Sin City's contract before we even start. Who is standing a foot or so away with his mouth hanging open and his head whipping back and forth between Jake and me. While Jake is still standing close enough that I can feel the heat coming off his body, his hands balled into fists, chest visibly moving up and down with each breath and suddenly it's too much.

I walk around all four men and beeline toward the entrance. I'm a couple of feet from my target when Adam appears like the archangel Michael, by my side ready to do battle. But when he doesn't see an easily identifiable target, he pulls me in the opposite direction. I follow his lead, tailed by two bamboozled security guards and a still flustered Aaron. We all exit into an empty hallway and as soon as the door closes, my composure crumbles.

"What in the hell was that? I heard the commotion from the other side of the room. I thought something had happened to you. Where in the fuck were you two?" Adam advances on Seth and Aiden. His anger needing a target.

"He's here." I can barely understand myself, but he seems to have no problem.

"He, who?" He looks at Aaron for answers and then back at me. I still can't formulate what just happen. He turns back to Aaron.

"I introduced her to the CEO, Connor Rappaport, and his best friend and business partner, Jacob Johnson, the CFO." He shrugs because he has no idea what's going on.

"Did you just say Jacob Johnson? Jesus… fuck!" Adam bends at the waist and growls in frustration. That is how I know that we're in trouble. Adam is usually the eye of the storm, but if he's bent over in frustration, shit just got real.

"This is a goddamned mess." Adam stands upright, running agitated hands over his jean-clad thighs. "How are we just now finding out that Jacob works here?"

"There is still time for us to back out of this thing. Go somewhere. Hell, anywhere else." he says. "But I gotta stay in the valley, you know?" And I did. He has an appointment early next week with the Department of Child Protective Services. They're supposed to check out his house to make sure it meets their standards for housing a child, and if he passes, they'll grant him temporary custody.

"I thought you guys were happy with the deal. We… I… I went through a lot of trouble…" He laces his fingers behind his neck and stares up at the ceiling, looking for answers in the stark white paint.

My eyes fill with tears, and I blink to stop them from falling down my cheeks. I refuse to let one tear fall because of that beautiful, pleading asshole.

"No one is backing out. It's just… he… just caught me off guard is all."

"If I have to be the fucking Wall of China, I swear I'll keep him away from you." Adam grabs my face in his strong hands. Worry lines crease his forehead, and his eyes are tight around the corners.

I love the sentiment, but we're not kids anymore. I don't need Adam to fight my battles or block out the bad things in the world.

"I'm a big girl. If Jake knows what good for him, he'll stay the hell away from me. If he's stupid enough to come looking, I promise he won't like what he finds."

"There's my girl. You got this, Sin. You ready?" He has said the exact thing to me every time we've gone on stage, every showcase we did for labels, every photo shoot, and when we ran away from the group home for the bright lights of Las Vegas.

"Abso-fucking-lutely."

Chapter 6

NOW

Jake

WHEN I PICTURED SEEING SIN AGAIN, I IMAGINED THINGS GOING differently. Not sure what different looked like, but I'm positive it didn't include yelling, public humiliation, or getting slapped in front of a room full of people.

At the beginning of the night, I'd been talking with one of the other guys from finance. It had been mindless talk. Conversation for the sole purpose of filling up dead space and helping me maintain a certain level of calm.

For days, I'd been vacillating between an almost euphoric happiness at the idea of seeing her again and the ugly despair rooted in the understanding our breakup was more than one incident. It was the culmination of a hundred, minute decisions. The mistakes I made were the unforgivable kind. But that doesn't change the fact that I still crave her. Her light, her creativity, her beauty, her love, her forgiveness, her everything.

Sin entered the room on a wave of noise with Adam by her side, security orbiting around the edges of her personal space, and the not so subtle attention of every person in the room. And I froze. The circulatory system in my body suddenly failed to deliver adequate blood flow and constricted the oxygen in my lungs.

She's here. Here. Right in front of me.

For the first time in four years, my eyes had the pleasure drinking her in and my view was fucking perfect. I was able to simply observe her, take her in. Let my eyes trace the slope of her neck and the distinct bones of her clavicle. Down the flat of her stomach and over the flair of her hips. She was a vision wrapped in hot pink, a color that made her dark brown skin glow with brilliance, after years of having to settle for flat images that never quite seemed to capture her essence. I was overwhelmed in her presence and in my reaction to it.

At twenty-nine, I've seen beautiful women. I've pursued and dated them. I've fucked them seven ways from Sunday and enjoyed it every time.

Every. Single. Fucking time.

Every scrape of nails, every low moan, and high pitch wail. I've enjoyed it all but I never loved it. What I had with Sin was love, an emotionally deep, physically satisfying, all-encompassing love. The women I got lost in as I tried to forget her couldn't even touch the memory of Sin.

At the time I hated it.

Hated her for leaving me, for icing me out, for having the nerve to hold me accountable for my shit.

Looking at her now, so far removed from the girl I knew, I'm not sure what I feel. Gone were her rough edges, the sweetly insecure walk, and the contradiction that struggled to find the balance behind creative pursuit and performance. The woman who stood in her place had confidence in spades. Beauty that was a statement of fact. Like the way the sky *was* blue or water *was* wet. Sin *was* beautiful.

In that moment I got it, all the media attention, all the appearances on television and on magazines covers. I understood why everyone wanted a piece of her. Why from the moment we met I could never get enough of her.

I watched Sin walk across the room all graceful poise and swaying hips and my instinct went to war with my common sense. Conventional wisdom would say approaching her in a room full of people after years of resentment and hurt feelings wasn't a good idea, but as I tracked her movements, watched her with an intensity typically reserved for a lion stalking its prey on the Serengeti, I had to fight the urge to break her off from the herd and pounce.

I wanted peel her out of that goddamn skintight, pink dress and take inventory of all the things that had changed or stayed the same since we'd last seen each other. I wanted to wrap my hands in the springy curls of her hair and watch her eyes melt into mine as our lips met for the first time in four years. More than anything, I wanted to repent at the altar of Sin. Sink to my knees and beg forgiveness. Worship her body with my body. Remind her how my hands felt against her skin, and how much she liked my face pressed into her wet core.

While I zoned out, Aaron immediately apprehended Sin and made a beeline to Connor, who was only a couple of feet away from me. When Aaron looked at me over her head and started the introduction, I hesitated, unsure how to progress. Pretend as if I didn't know her? Go in for a hug? Act on my baser instincts, strip her bare, and reintroduce myself in the biblical sense?

Ultimately, I held out my hand. My fingertips sliding over her palm. And before I could fully register the exhilaration of touching her again, she'd snatched her hand out of mine.

At first, a look of confusion creased the skin between her eyes, but in the blink of an eye that look transformed into biting anger. Those wide brown eyes with specks of gold looked through me as if I was nothing. No, that look said I less than nothing and that shit burned. Hurt much more than it should. And when she jumped away from my touch as if it repulsed her, the pain that had been a pinprick of sensation in my frontal lobe grew to an aching pulse that I felt all the way down to my toes.

Even through the plastic smile and stiff limbs, I could still easily read her. Her body language was screaming, *Why are you here? What do you want? Go to straight to hell!* And that was before every foolish thing that popped into my head came out of my mouth.

I should've followed my first thought and forgot about the whole thing. This night was a first, not only for The Hotel but for Sin as well.

I should have respected that. Stayed in my lane. Then I remembered the split second her body was pressed against mine, and I wouldn't change a thing. Not even the slap that snapped my head back on my neck. I should've waited until I had a chance to talk to her alone, but something tells me it would've played out the same with only a slight difference. My shit wouldn't be hanging out in the wind for the world to see.

Not just my little corner of Las Vegas but the entire fucking planet. There had been pictures and videos taken. All of which have the possibility of being leaked. From a business perspective I'm screwed. Think about it, most people, even the people that work for the casino, have no idea who I am or what I look like. Why? Because you don't need me to successfully brand the business.

Part of the allure of casinos is anonymity. The idea that anything goes. That no one is watching or judging. For the right price, hotel guest can engage in their dirtiest, raunchiest fantasies with no one back home the wiser.

But when the hotel becomes synonymous with a person or a group of people there is a layer of accountability. Suddenly the forty-year-old soccer mom from the Bible Belt is a little reluctant to wear the miniskirt or the see-through top. The devout church goer thinks twice about dropping a grand at the craps table, all because they feel like they know you.

How many CEOs or CFOs of major chains on the Strip can the average person name? I grew up in Vegas, the son of one of the gaming moguls and even I can only up with four names, Benny Binion, Howard Hughes, Bugsy Siegel, and Steven Wynn. Of those four names only, the last one holds any real weight with the media in the post-mob-owned era. Gambling still has a stigma and the people that own these establishments, such as me, are viewed as pariahs in traditional business circles.

Becoming the story, the focus, doesn't come with one positive. Putting a face, my face, to an album described as a monolithic statement of heartbreak does not bode well for me or the business that I've helped build.

I run a hand down my face, hot irritation making me break out in a cold sweat. This whole thing just turned into a shit show. The employees give Connor a wide berth as he walks the few feet toward me. His presence is enough to make everyone in the room pretend they didn't just witness the most humiliating moment of both my personal life and professional career.

My gaze finds Sin's retreating form as Aaron and Adam move her through the crowd and into the service hallway. She's the only motion in the still shocked and unmoving crowd.

Connor cuffs my shoulder drawing my attention away from the now vacant corner of the room.

"So, I'm going to ask the million-dollar question. What in the hell was all about?"

"Not now, Connor." I push his hand off my shoulder and stalk in the opposite direction Sin had gone. I can feel eyes watching me, and if that isn't annoying enough, I have a shadow matching me step for step.

"You know you're my best friend, right?" Connor whispers through clenched teeth and a professional smile.

"Right."

"And you know I love you like a play cousin that lived next door."

"Uh-huh," I roll my eyes at his pacifying tone.

"But seriously brah I need to understand why the crown jewel of the entertainment department just went fucking *Love & Hip Hop* on your ass in the middle of our media blitz." He tries to stifle a laugh.

"Too soon, Con. Way too soon. This shit isn't funny."

"From your perspective it probably isn't, but from where I was standing, I'm highly amused. There is obviously a story that I need to know. Spill."

"No."

"No? That's all you have to say is no?"

"Yeah, that's all I have to say."

We walk through the casino toward the elevators that lead to the executive offices. I almost expect the people sitting at slot machines to stare at us as we make our way across the casino floor, but apparently, my world is the only one that had just tilted on its axis. The elevator ride is fast, but Connor is hitting me with question after question about things that I've held in for a long time. Things that are coming out whether I'm ready to talk or not. And just for the record, *I'm not ready*.

What more can be said? The "fuck you" from Sin was clear.

The elevator doors open on the thirtieth floor. The offices are dark except for the ambient light reflecting from the neon of the Strip. I make for my office and collapse in the chair behind the desk.

I lift a finger to my cheek and gingerly poke at the still stinging skin. Yep. That hurt. "She slapped the taste out of my mouth with that one."

"So now he's ready to talk." Connor lounges against a bookcase on the wall just inside the door. His gaze direct and his demeanor chill, as if we're here to discuss something as trite as the weather or our upcoming high school reunion.

I scowl at his unruffled calm in the face of chaos and open my mouth to speak but the words stay trapped behind my barely concealed agitation. He rotates his finger in a circular motion for me to go ahead with what I'm trying to say. I clear my throat and brush my thumb against the tip of my nose before I try to start again.

"Come on, man. It's…" I look up at the ceiling hoping to find an explanation on the tiles. I know I owe Connor something but… "Fuck, this is hard."

"Yea, she nailed your ass good."

Not what I'm talking about, but the slap complicates things even further.

Connor takes the seat across from me, unbuttoning his suit jacket as he lowers onto the cushions. "She was all sweet, and doe-eyed when she was talking to me. Your ugly mug shows up, and she turns into a wet cat. I was going in for the kill when you—"

"Don't go anywhere near her," I growl at him.

Connor doesn't have a type unless dime piece can be considered a category, and Sin is a ten by anyone's standards. The idea of him or anyone else, for that matter, having a real shot at Sin still pisses me off. Yes, I know it's irrational. Yes, I know she's probably been with other men since me. No, I don't care if it makes me an idiot. There is this tsunami of emotions dragging me under, rolling me over, and drowning me in feelings that are changing faster than I can feel them. I don't want Connor or anyone else near her. Sin is mine. At least she will be once I figure out how to get her to talk to me.

"And why is that again?" He leans forward, resting elbows on knees as he studies me under his broad forehead.

I reach into the bottom drawer of my desk and pull out a bottle of Herradura tequila and two shot glasses. I tilt my head silently asking if he wants one. He nods, still eyeing me like I'm few cards short of a full deck.

Maybe I am. When I'm around Sin it's like Mercury immediately moved into retrograde and the crazy streak my parents tried to educate, socialize, and threaten out of me burst through the surface. I do things on impulse without thought to the consequences like ask my obviously pissed of ex for a second chance.

I pour two shots and slide one across the mahogany desktop toward Connor. We both pick up our glasses and toss back the clear liquid. The slow burn in my stomach replaces the one on my face. I pour another and drink it just as quickly. My mouth is full of liquor when he starts the inquisition.

"So, it's that bad?" *Tap. Tap. Tap.* Connor taps his glass against the edge of the desk.

I look at him over the rim of the shot glass still pressed to my lips and nod as I swallow.

"Yeah." The other words in my head die off. This time it's not because I don't want to talk, it's that I can't. I can't find the words to admit how bad I fucked up. How wrong I was.

Connor knows me better than most. We bonded at eleven over our shared ethnic background. He thought I was mixed, like him, because of my light eyes and light brown skin, but my family was Creole by way of New Orleans. As the only two black boys in an entire school, together we navigated the waters of gangsta rap, wave caps, slang, and girls. Circumstance threw us in the same arena, but shared experience made us closer than brothers. So, when I hurt, he knows. When I refuse to talk, which I do all the time, he gets it. He knows when to back away and when to push. It's one of the drawbacks of knowing each as long as we have and as well as we do.

That's why when he comments on how the corners of my eyes are tight and repeats that he wants the story, a story that I authored away from him, the ultimate shame I hid from everyone including my best friend, I can barely piece words together into a sentence.

He's not going to let this go. If circumstances were reversed, I would be doing the exact same thing. Hounding him with hows and whys. Insisting he let me help. If nothing else, I'm persistent, something we both have in spades.

"That's all I get?"

"Yeah."

"Nah, I don't think so. Not after that spectacle downstairs. Go ahead and drink the whole bottle if that's what it takes. But neither one of us is leaving this office until I understand what went down, and what kind of clusterfuck I'll be walking into when this shit goes public."

Yep, bossy and persistent. Connor folds his hands and waits patiently. Watching me down two more shots as I try to find a rational way to explain who Sin is to me and why things just exploded.

"I'll end it right here by killing you myself. We run a multimillion-dollar company, Jake, not the set of *The Jerry Springer Show*. Just start at the beginning so we can get in front of this thing." He rolls the glass between the palms of his large hands.

"I still love her." I forego pouring the liquor into the glass in favor of taking a long pull from the bottle.

"What the fuck does that mean? You love her how? Like half the male population in the world or like—"

"Like I remember she prefers her showers lukewarm and her tea scalding hot. That instead of perfume, she uses oils that get more fragrant as the day goes on. I remember what it feels like to be balls deep inside her and the way her hands gripped my ass to keep me there. Like I know the particular taste of her pussy and the fact that she rode my face as well as my dick. Like—"

"Come again?" He waves both hands in front of his face. He gets up, storming around to my side of the desk, and snatches the upturned bottle from my lips.

"When did this happen? Where was I?" He frowns.

"At school and then you did those two years in Oxford. I told you about Sin." I'd told anyone that would listen about her. Especially when we first got together. Connor wasn't an exception.

"I remember a Cynthia, not a Sinclair."

"Sin wasn't short for Cynthia, dude."

"Is this the one who walked in the house and found...?"

"The very same," I grumble.

"Are you serious? You fucked around on Sinclair James?" He leans against the desk, arms folded across his chest and one eyebrow arched so high it's almost to his hairline.

I try to snatch the bottle out of his hand, but he pulls it out of reach. The tequila must be doing its thing. My reflexes are slower than usual, which is good. Maybe it'll help me forget that split second when I had her body against mine. Yeah... no. Not even tequila is that good.

"No. I just made a fool of myself for shits and giggles. I love being slapped in front of a room full of people. Good times. It was great fun."

"So, CliffsNotes version of this story is the ex-girlfriend you cheated on is now a headliner at our hotel, and by the looks of it, she had no idea you worked here. You still have a thing for her and, correct me if I'm wrong here, she does not reciprocate on any level. Why didn't you tell me this shit before she got here?"

"I didn't think it would be an issue. Other than tonight, what is the likelihood we'd run into each other?"

"True enough. The only way that you'd see her is if you make it happen. You get in at what seven in the morning?"

"Around there but I'm always out by three. I can't tell you the last time I did more than just walk through the casino floor. You know the midlevel execs take care of the day-to-day operations. Her shows will be at 8:00 p.m. and 10:30 p.m., long after I've left for the day."

"But a heads up would have been nice. Neither one of us is on the floor regularly but this residency is a little different. Once you found out she was here, it didn't occur to you that we'd have to do press and show our faces? You're one of the cofounders for fuck's sake. What a goddamn mess." He grabs the black cap off the desk and twists it tight on the bottle of tequila.

"We'll have to bring media in on this."

"We don't need media. I can deal—"

"Call Jeanine," he says loudly, talking over my weakly uttered offer to handle things myself.

"I'm not calling Jeanine," I attempt to say around my alcohol-thickened tongue. Jeanine is the director of media relations for the The Hotel. On a good day, and she's a fucking ballbuster. On a bad day she's a man-eater. I saw her bring one of the people from food and beverage to tears with stern looks and a brutal word. The only person I've ever seen her tone down the attitude for is Connor. No way in hell I'm calling Jeanine.

"Call her, Jake, and ask her to help you fix this shit." He pushes off the desk towering over me. "And for the love of God, pull your shit together. You're not Drake, brah. This crying in your tequila shit is for the birds. You're Jacob Muthafuckin Johnson. Act like it. You're smooth enough and rich enough to win any woman, even Sinclair James. Remind her of it." Connor refastens the buttons of his suit coat and raps his knuckles against the desk. "If you still want her, go get her. If you decide tomorrow that you're done, that's cool too, but you have to decide one way or the other.

She's going to be here for the next year. That'll give you time. I have your back regardless." He starts to walk out the door but turns around and points the bottle at me. "But the shit I just witnessed tonight needs to be a first and the last. Kiss her ass, say you're sorry. Do whatever the fuck you need to do to make this okay. You got me?"

"Yeah. I got you."

"*Vaya con Dios*, brah. I think you're going to need all the help you can get."

Chapter 7

Now

Sinclair

I OPEN MY EYES DISORIENTED. *WHERE AM I?* I LOOK AROUND THE UNFAMILIAR space and blink at the harsh summer sun bathing the room in bright light. The sun only looks like that in the desert, unfiltered by smog and clouds, free to scorch and burn.

That's right. I'm in Vegas. I came home for a residency.

I stretch and take inventory of my body. I wiggle my toes under the heavy down comforter. I take a deep breath and let the air seep out of my lungs. Yep, everything seems to be where it was yesterday: two eyes, one mouth, one nose. Everything is in place, but I don't feel like me. I feel like an old, outdated model complete with chips and dings.

The previous night's events trickle into my conscious thought and quickly flood my brain with *oh shit* endorphins. I bailed on a media blitz because I... because of... goddamn Jake!

This kind of shit only happens to me. Out of everyone in the music loving world, why him? Was it asking too much to enter the city like a conquering hero? I know, I'm not a hero, not by any means, but dammit for once I wanted the people in Vegas to embrace me. To be like *that girl is one of us*. Instead, I go all Nye County whorehouse and come out the gate swinging.

Would it have been too much to ask in the four years since I've seen him that he'd gained weight and developed a bald spot or sported a limp? It's like he hasn't aged a day. Everything about him is exactly the way I remember it. His tall frame, lean and muscled. His bronze skin so perfectly smooth it looks airbrushed. Expressive hazel eyes that broadcast every thought and every emotion. Even the stupid inadequate apologies were coming out of his beautifully shaped lips. How messed up is it that he's still beautiful to me?

I've only ever let two people close to me. The first one is Adam, who has never let me down. The second is Jake, who reached into the heart of me and devastated everything in his path. Coming face-to-face with him after all these years is like looking at the wreckage of a storm. I can still see remnants of beauty, but it doesn't cover the gaping holes or broken, jagged pieces of what remains.

I silenced my phone last night and turned it facedown so I wouldn't see notifications from all the trolls on social media. I don't need to look at the phone to know I'm getting hit with a barrage of comments on all my social media platforms. Outside of the he said, she said bullshit of social media, I don't want to see how my actions have impacted my sponsorships and endorsements. Every contract I've signed has an ethics clause. I'm pretty sure physical assault is not considered ethically sound judgement.

I'd started getting calls from companies I work with and interview requests even before I made it back to the villa. I pull the phone off the side table to see the damage. My closest friends have reached out in a group text.

Adam: R u ok?

Miles: Sin-a-sticks!!! I was peeping out the pimp hand? WTF!? Thank Gawd I wasn't there. I'd h8 to testify against u.

I guess it's safe to say someone or maybe multiple someones posted pictures or video of the incident with Jake last night.

Dan: DUDE, it was seriously epic. Errybdy in the room was like whoa, what happened?

Adam: I'll tell you what happened. He Who Must Not Be Named caught them hands.

Miles: Sin, you know I have your back BUT fuck I'm glad I wasn't there. Boys, next time try knocking-up your wives, it works like a charm.

Dan: You're the only one with a wife, dickhole.

Miles: Speaking of dickholes...

Adam: And this convo just took a detour south... way south... ha-haha get it... south.

Dan: *fist pounds* Adam

I can't help but smile at their craziness.

Sin: So far, so good. And here's a thought, can I go one day without hearing about anyone's junk?

Adam: Y wld we do that?

Miles: I can't speak for the other two, but I don't carry junk in my pants... I have THE almighty staff of life.

Dan: Staff of... bawhahaha

Adam: ☺ ☺ ☺

I scan the rest of my unread messages and cringe when I read one from my publicist. Ven has been Sin City's publicist since we released our first EP. The last thing she said to me before she flew out of Las Vegas was to keep my head down and make the easy money. *Well, there goes that plan.* I wince as a read her messages.

Venetria: I taught you better than this.

Venetria: You can't be this big of an idiot.

Venetria: Call me. NOW!

My stomach drops. Those last two text messages clear up any possibility I'll be able to push Jake into a dark corner and pretend that slap never happened.

I turn the volume up on my phone and almost immediately, it's dinging with alerts from Twitter, Snapchat, and every other social media platform I have downloaded. On Twitter alone, I have 10,008 new notifications.

PR 101 says don't read the responses. It doesn't matter if they're good or bad. Hiding behind a screen gives people courage. Regardless of everything I know, I open the app, curious to see what my Tweeps are saying about @*TheRealSinclair*, which has been trending for the last five hours. I click on my news feed and groan. The backlash is worse than bad. The first several messages are memes and GIFs of me slapping Jake.

@igottabe: bitch mode! @therealSinclair hostile much?!

@the1derful1: yaaaaas girl #slapahoe

@nativerider: OMG! You don't deserve him, he's hot AF

@BIGwillthethrill: You can slap me anytime. #slapthishoe

@economusik: @TheRealSinclair we see you girl. And the cops did too. #bougiebitch #wherethemhandcuffs

As I'm making my way through the feed, the tweets keep coming in. Most of which are stories about how I regularly walk around slapping people, or how this was just another example of my diva ways. All things that are untrue. I know I shouldn't care. Hell, I'm pissed that I do care, but at the end of the day, I'm a person with feelings and the whole gambit of emotions.

So what? I blew up at an ex. Shit happens, right? Says every celebrity ever, but I know better than this. I'm under a magnifying glass. Not just Sin the musician, but Sin the person as well. It's been getting more intense because of how well the music is doing. I should've walked away last night instead of lashing out in anger. But something about his stupid face just begged to be hit.

I blow out a breath and close the app, sliding the phone facedown on the nightstand.

An elegant retro phone sitting on the marble surface rings loud and shrill in the silence of the room. Good grief that's loud. I sit up snatching the thing off the hook.

"Hello"

"Hi, Ms. James. My name is Jeanine Williams. I'm the director of media relations at The Hotel. Mr. Rappaport asked me to reach out to you in reference the incident last night." A slight English accent makes her voice sound cool instead of cold.

"Oh, okay. I have my own pr—"

"As a contracted employee of The Hotel, it is in the interest of all persons involved that we launch a united media response," Jeanine says, cutting me off before I could finish that thought. "I have already been in contact a…" There is a long pause and the sound of papers shuffling in the background. "Venetria McCullough. We're both in agreement that the best way to approach this incident is head on. Ms. McCullough will be arriving on the first possible flight. In the meantime I have scheduled multiple interviews today for yourself and Mr. Johnson. There will be a mixture of local and national news outlets present, but I'm trying to keep the groups limited around six to eight reporters at a time."

Once again there is a long pause and the sound of papers in the background. She must have put her hand over the speaker because her voice becomes muffled. "Oy… I have no time for you and your numpty friend. Out with the lot of you."

"If you've talked to Ven, then there's no way you think you're running anything with regard to dealing with my response to the media, and there is no way in hell I'm doing an interview with Jake," I blurt.

"Apologies, Ms. James. What was that?" Her voice dropped a couple of degrees. I feel the frost through the phone.

"I said there is no way in hell I'm doing one interview, let alone multiple interviews, with Jake."

"That's completely up to you, but let's break this down, shall we? In the last seven hours, there has been a purge of information regarding you and Mr. Johnson's relationship. Your fans, yours Ms. James, have done a surprisingly good job of putting all the pieces together. The inspiration for your album is no longer conjecture. The entire world knows who he is and what he was to you.

"They have somehow unearthed pictures of the two of you from ten years ago up to what, I assume, is a date close to your breakup. According to your team, there are pictures of a check written to you by his mother for a large some. That one really started trending. The comparisons to Romeo and Juliet are amusing."

Did she just say amusing?

"Stop!" I say a breath below a shout. "I'm calling my own publicist." I slam the receiver down with shaking hands and immediately call Ven from my cell. I don't care that Jeanine Whoever The Hell Works For The Hotel, her job is not to handle me. I have my own handlers, and not one of them would ever talk to me like a wayward child that needs direction. It's essential I strategize with my team, people that have me and my band's image in mind before I deal with a representative of the company that can, in theory, hang me out as the sacrificial lamb. I don't know what Jake has at stake, but I have to assume his needs align with the company and mine, at this point. don't.

I press the number nine and the screen immediately lights up with a picture of Ven and I. The word calling flashes in time with the ringing. She picks up on the fifth ring, sounding out of breath.

"Hello, Sin?" I hear the noise of traffic in the background.

"Yeah."

"What in the hell happened? I expect this shit from Dan, but you?" I accept the tongue-lashing I knew I had coming. She lets out an ear-piercing whistle, and there is a pause before I hear her giving directs to the airport.

"I said keep your head down. I said get the easy money. What about any of this says easy?"

"I know. But, Ven, listen I got a call from—"

"If you're about to say Jeanine Williams, I've already spoken to her."

"She's rude as hell."

"Maybe a little chilly, but I'm guessing you haven't seen the gossip blogs and Twitter yet. It's bad, Sin. The slap is just the tip of the iceberg. Did his family actually try to pay you off?"

I squeeze my eyes so tight that white lights pop behind my lids, and I let out a long slow breath. "Yeah, but what does that have to do with anything that happened yesterday?"

"It spins the story, changes the motive. Up until this point, you've been squeaky clean. Celebrity news outlets would like nothing more than to *dirty* you up. And the small-town girl who is actually from Pahrump instead of Las Vegas, whose mother OD'd while working in a brothel, who has no father listed on her birth certificate, and was possibly paid off by her ex-boyfriend's family to leave him alone? That girl's story is gold."

I've been waiting for this day. The day when the façade shattered and every nasty thing that ever happened in my life comes to light.

"What do we do?"

Ven lets out a long sigh. "First and foremost, you play nice with the *cuntress* from The Hotel. Although she be cunty, she be good." She chuckles. "Next, keep your fucking head down. If you surrounded yourself with an entourage like every other pop star, this wouldn't be a problem. There'd be someone there besides two bodyguards."

"Keanu Reeves and Lady Gaga are both way more famous than me, and neither one of them travel with an entourage."

"They live in New York, totally different. New Yorkers by definition are rude and don't have time for anything, including celebrity."

"You know you're from New York, right?"

"Exactly. That's why I can speak on it. It would be so much easier if you had an actual physical person there with you. I don't think you fully grasp how nasty this thing can get."

"Why? Because I was born on the other side of a mountain? Or is it because Adam and I hit the streets of Vegas at seventeen and once they turned eighteen Miles and Dan moved up as well? So what, I don't know my father's name, and I never lied about my mother being dead."

"The devil is in the details, Sin. Celebrities, meaning you, like to pretend like you're still the same person"

"I *am* still the same person."

"To a certain degree, you are. But fame changes everything. Everyday people do not have a twenty-four, seven two-man security detail or a stalker that thinks he knows the inner workings of their soul."

"You made your point, Ven."

"I'm not trying to make a point, Sinclair. I'm trying to prepare you for the storm that's brewing when, up until this point, you've had nothing but sunny skies. You need to do these interviews, and you need to do them with Jake."

"I can't do this."

"You can and you will. That slap damaged The Hotel's brand, and you need to help repair it. Also, Jake has been catapulted into the spotlight because of his past with you. He's not going away. Questions about him aren't going away. You made him the story. The two of you need to show a united front and squelch the more outlandish rumors."

She continues to talk about the dos and don'ts of the interviews for a couple of minutes, and when she disconnects, I bite the bullet and dial the number she gave me for Jeanine.

"Jeanine Williams," says a brittle voice through the speaker.

"Hi, Jeanine. It's Sincl—"

"No need to reintroduce yourself. I'm well aware to whom I am speaking. Now, where were we?" Just that quickly, she's back in business mode. "I have housekeeping en route to your villa now. We will do the press release from that location. Venetria and I both believe it will be a nice touch. It welcomes them into your world, showing that you have nothing to hide. I will be round in approximately one hour to prep for the interviews. Do you have a stylist?"

It took me a minute to realize she's asking me a question.

"Of course, but I normally do my own."

"How quaint. It's up to you if you want to handle your styling. All I ask is that you stay away from anything overtly sexual. I'm looking for the hometown girl that made good, someone that people can relate to, get behind. No big sunglasses. No drug addict chic. No, I'm a big rock star glitter, sparkles, or jangles."

My anger threatens to boil to the surface and spill all over this woman. It's like she lacks the filter of common human decency. I'm sure she's good at her job, but being good at her job doesn't give her license to keep coming for me. If she keeps it up, I promise she won't like what she finds. I inhale deeply through my nose and exhale in a long steady stream. *Play nice with the cuntress. Play nice with the cuntress. I can do this. I can absolutely play nice with this fucking cuntress.*

"I'm sorry, Jeanine, was it? I'm not—"

"Oh and Ms. James, I will dig us out of this bloody mess. I've dealt with worse, and I look forward to meeting you." She hangs up the phone without saying good-bye

Exactly one hour later, three sharp knocks vibrate my door. I open the door to find an elegantly dressed, tall, slender woman with a short pixie haircut and bright red glasses perched on her nose. She doesn't bother to look up from her phone as she breezes by me through the doorway. The door automatically snaps shut when I let go of the handle. Her silence is almost as disconcerting as the phone call. After several minutes, she looks up from her phone, finally looking at me.

"Good afternoon, Ms. James" She holds out a hand. "Jeanine Williams, director of media relations for The Hotel."

"Sinclair." I take her hand in mine and give it a gentle squeeze. "It's nice to meet you. Thank you for your assistance."

She drops my hand and with a nod walks around me, one finger pressed against her lips in concentration, appraising me like a piece of jewelry. I keep turning in an attempt to maintain eye contact. "Are you wearing makeup? Your skin is flawless. Your color is quite pretty, actually. Not at all smoke and mirrors like so many celebrities."

"Um… Thank you. I guess. And no, I'm not wearing makeup yet."

"So, let me tell you what I know, and you correct anything that rings untrue." She drums her perfectly manicured nails on her slender hips.

"I've spoken with Mr. Johnson, and he has given me a brief rundown. You met in college. Blah, blah, blah"—she flits her hand back and forth—"began to date. Blah, blah, blah. One of you traveled, someone cheated, and the two of you broke up. You released an album titled *Exquisitely Broken* in which you detailed said breakup. You and Mr. Johnson see each again after a few years and boom, media catastrophe." She summed up my life in three sentences. *Ouch.*

"That's the gist." I turn my head toward the wall and count to ten. Play nice. That's what Ven said.

"I'm not big on Indie rock, but your speaking voice is lovely. All that rasp makes you sound like a young Kathleen Turner."

"Who?"

"She was a popular actress in the eighties. Never mind, I digress. You, I can work with, and the camera loves you. I have a complete media kit from Venetria—that one is a bit of a mother hen—but the pictures really don't have the same impact of seeing you in person."

There is another knock on the door, and Jeanine moves quickly to open it. Jake stands there. His eyes are hidden behind dark sunglasses, and even though I don't want to, even though a spike of adrenalin makes my stomach queasy and my hands tremble, I can't look away. He still affects me. Hits me in a place that is unsophisticated and raw. Even after four years of harboring hurt feelings, giving voice to his betrayal and physically lashing out, I'm surprised to feel our natural chemistry. To feel his gaze on me too.

Chapter 8

NOW
Sinclair

"Mr. Johnson, I thought I specifically stated no wannabe rock star craziness. Take the glasses off. Now."

Jake lets out a long sigh but removes the glasses. His eyes immediately find mine. At first, all I see is the color. The multicolored threads that give his irises a chameleon factor that are still as mesmerizing as I remember, but as I keep looking, I see him. Not some version of him. Not the caricature that I've made him, but him. The man with a heavy heart and a messy soul. The man who recklessly threw away everything, and I can't seem to summon the anger that has fortified me for years.

"Whew, the air is so tense between the two of you. I can practically see the emotion." We both turn to Jeanine. I hadn't noticed she'd taken a seat on the sofa or her head bouncing back and forth between Jake and me as if watching a tennis match.

"Cut the cute shit, Jeanine," Jake grumbled.

"Oh, Mr. Johnson, rest assured there is nothing at all cute about this situation. Let's strip it down to the brass tacks, shall we?" She pushes up off the couch and stands between us. "I have a job to do. Seeing the two of you, together in the same room, I know my job undoubtedly got that much harder."

The condescending tone of her voice is beginning to shred my tolerance.

"I've been with the two of you for less than a minute, and I know there's a story here. There is not a journalist alive worth their salt that will stop before they get pay dirt on both of you. So, we have to create a narrative."

Once again, she placed a blood red nail against her lips. Her gaze is distant as she works the problem out in her head. After a couple of minutes, she snaps her fingers, and I flinch at the sound. Jake rolls his eyes.

"The first and most simple explanation is reconciliation. We pretend the two of you are attempting to work out the kinks in your relationship. We ask for privacy to do that," Jeanine says.

"What's the second option?" I ask, vigorously shaking my head like the motion alone will present a better option.

"Ms. James, the second option is the truth. We go into the gritty details of your separation from Mr. Johnson. We say that you slapped him after all these years because he cheated on you forever ago. That you still haven't worked out your issues after what can only be called a therapeutic album, and let's not forget all the men you've been linked with since the breakup."

"What do you mean all the men I've been linked with? I haven't dated anyone since him." My throat is aching with a barely contained desire to howl like a wounded animal. Seriously, what is happening right now? One day back in this city. One day and everything goes to crap.

"Well, now, Ms. James, Google says differently. I don't know or follow you, and even I'm aware of the rumors linking you to Mr. Beckham. And who said twenty-four-hour news cycles are factual? Conjecture and hypothesis are all that's needed for a reputable station to run the story. No one will believe someone that sounds like you or looks like you, for that matter, has been single, rejected, and pining away for one man the last four years. It's not what you know, it's what you can prove."

"I haven't been rejected or pining away. I've been working. My last two albums went platinum." My voice shakes. I can't with this whole situation.

"Ms. James—" she starts, serving me a frigid look of bored indifference.

"For the love of God, please stop calling me Ms. James! It's Sinclair. Plain and simple. Nothing complicated about it."

Jeanine takes a seat on the sofa, crossing her legs with cool sophistication. She tilts her head, resting her chin on the curved fingers of her right hand, and for a long uncomfortable minute, she doesn't utter a sound. She studies me. Her eyes periodically leaving me to bounce to Jake before inevitably returning to my face.

"Sin-clair." She stresses both syllables of my name in her accented English. "That's where you are wrong. This is complicated, and you made it ten times worse by behaving like an ill-mannered child."

She's purposefully trying to push every button I have, every single one. "You know what? You can take your condescending bullshit and stick—"

"Jeanine, can you give us a minute." Jakes cuts my tirade short. I want nothing more than to use her as a target and take out the last several minutes of frustration by ripping her to shreds. She's been doing it to me all morning.

He grabs my elbow and leads me into the bedroom. The moment we step over the threshold, he lets my arm go and closes the door softly behind him. He leans his tall frame against the wooden surface, taking me in, his eyes hitting on different points in the room before roving my face, briefly meeting my eyes only to skitter away.

"You look different," Jake says.

I back away a few feet and sit on the edge of the bed, unsure how to act under his scrutiny.

"Good. But... different than I remember," he continues.

"I can believe that. You haven't seen me in four years." His eyes flit back to mine before dropping away again. "Everyone on the planet has seen you, Sin."

"True enough. I've gained some weight. Adam finally convinced me that cheese is like manna from heaven. Maybe that's it?" Where his gaze had been everywhere, but on me, his eyes finally find mine. He arches one of his brows.

"Adam got you to eat...? When we were together, you wouldn't even taste—"

"But we're not together anymore, so it doesn't matter. You want to tell me why you brought me in here?"

Between the slapping incident with Jake yesterday and the over-reaching Brit today, I've reached my limit, and I'm not about to sit here and play twenty questions with a guy I knew once upon a forever ago. I have an interview—no a series of interviews—to get through, and at this point my inner bitch is more than happy to take over.

And you know what? Fuck him. He doesn't get to stand there looking like a wounded *Playgirl* centerfold. I don't owe him conversation or understanding.

"Ah, so that's how it's going to be? I get to play the role of the bad guy, and you get to be the snarky superstar."

"You are the bad guy in the scenario, Jake."

"And you slapped the shit out of me in front of God and country, Sin." He drags fingers across his lips and jaw, unflinching, daring me to defend my actions.

When I saw him last night, every single feeling of betrayal and all the times I'd wondered why returned full force and I lashed out. At this point, I wish to God I'd done something different. Anything different. But what's done is done.

Four years ago, I made a clean break. Left without the typical fanfare of yelling and crying and tears, and I never looked back. My feelings came out in lyrics and melodies, and like every other person with a broken heart, mine still beat. I put Jake somewhere in the back of my mind.

"Look this isn't getting us anywhere. You called this powwow..."

"Stop, Sinclair... just stop! We haven't been in the same space in four years. Four fucking years." He runs a hand over his closely cropped hair and lets out a deep sigh. "Fuck, I just wanted… I just want…" His words peter out in a frustrated growl.

"Be careful, your privilege is starting to show."

"That's a low blow, Sin. You know I never cared about my privilege. Until this morning, I had no idea they offered you money. For me it was always about you. And I'm here, trying. I want to—"

"You want to what? Pick up where we left off?" A manic giggle escapes my mouth.

"Not where we left off, but I thought we could have a do-over." His lips twitch with a half smile. That had been our thing when we dated, do-overs.

I couldn't have said anything to that stupidity if I wanted to. Jake's infidelity ripped my world apart, and he wants a do-over? When two people have shared as much as we have, how do you even begin to pretend like the past no longer influences the future?

"Let me ask you something," he says with his head cocked to the side and eyes unblinking. "Did you ever love me? I mean were you ever in love with me?"

"Are you serious? How is this even a question?"

"How is it not one? I look at you, at everything you've accomplished, and I'm just so damn proud. When I saw you last night, it was like seeing you for the first time. You blew me away all over again."

"And you expected me to what? Fall in your arms? Pretend my last memories of us weren't tainted with images of you in the arms of another woman?" He pushes his weight off the door, stalking a few steps toward me.

"Honestly, I'm not sure what I expected, but it wasn't this. I know you Sin and you're not cold or distant. Behind all this pissivity you know the truth. We could've made it work. When I said that I made a mistake, and I was still in love with you, I meant it."

It would have never worked between us. No matter what Jake thinks. The writing had been on the wall for at least the last year of our relationship. Maybe longer, if I'm honest. We just didn't know how to call it quits. Then he made the decision for the both us, and the rest is history.

"I didn't want you to make a promise that you couldn't keep." *Or one that I'd have to honor when he did.* It was easier to walk away and pretend like he didn't exist.

"Fuck you, I wouldn't have kept it. How did you know I couldn't keep it?"

"Because, if you had any integrity, you wouldn't have destroyed my trust in the first place. Anyway, that's not why we broke up."

"Oh, so now we broke up? That's funny. If memory serves, you snuck out of our house like a thief in the fucking night."

"We weren't right for each other, Jake. After all this time you have to know that."

"No. No, no, no…" Jake shakes his head. "I don't know shit. Explain how we weren't right for each other? In what way was my love not right for you?" He lifted his hands in air quotes, his voice taking on a mocking tone.

"It became pretty clear when I walked in on you naked in our bed with another woman."

"YES, I CHEATED!" He throws hands up in the air.

I recoil as he takes off his suit jacket and throws it across the room. I've never seen Jake like this. His anger its own kind of animal, making his body twitch and move. "We know that, Sin. I'm an asshole, but you know what… so are you. Who moves out all their shit without even talking to the other person? Who does that, seriously?"

"Me, I do that." I raise a hand in the air like I'm waiting a teacher to call on me. "Sorry, I didn't read the rule book on how to end a relationship that was slowly suffocating me with its bullshit. I'm sorry, Jake. Is that what you needed to hear? Feel better now? But don't you think it was better to quit while we were ahead instead of dragging it out, knowing that it could never last?"

"That it could never…" He points a stiff finger at me. "That right there is your problem in a nutshell."

"Me, I have a problem?" I roll my eyes, curious to hear how his actions are my problem. This man is delusional.

"You're one of the strongest women I've met, but you just quit. You wouldn't even look me in the fucking eye and tell me you were leaving." He glares up at the ceiling, jaw clenched, fingers templed in front of his mouth.

"I quit? So, you in bed with any other woman was putting in effort and devotion. But me walking out the door was the actual betrayal. Yeah, that makes total sense."

"Now she wants to talk sense, ladies and gentlemen." His eyes drop from the ceiling, pinning mine. "Let's talk to the woman that threw away six fucking years. Six years," he says in a pained whisper. "Six years gone for a rando piece of ass I never touched again." He laces his fingers and squeezes them tight before releasing the tension and repeating the motion over and over.

"She wasn't random. She was my roommate for two years. A person that I invited into our home, that we partied with, someone that I trusted. The fact that you went there left me little options."

"And there is reason number three that you're a coward. You don't take risks."

"The whole life I cultivated with you was a risk. And we see how that turned out."

"No, Sin, the risk would've been staying with me, when everyone, especially the guys in your band told you to leave. The risk would've been trying to make it work."

"That's not fair. I couldn't trust you anymore. So, if that makes me an asshole or a coward…"

"Did you even try, Sin? Did you ever ask why it happened? Do you know that I hated myself for being the type of man that could do that to you? That I hated myself for putting you in a position where leaving would be so easy."

He stumbles back against the door, defeated. One hand wrapped tight around the knob like he's fighting the urge to leave the room. His chin rests on his chest.

"What's next for Sinclair James? We have these interviews, and you'll be living at the hotel I work in for the next year. Where does all of this leave us? You can't run away this time. Have to stay and face the music. Did you grow a backbone yet? Or are you going to slip away into the night again?"

"In all honesty, the only way you and I cross paths is if we're trying. You're the back of the house, and I'm the entertainment."

Jake looks up at me through dark lashes with a sad smile pulling at the corners of his beautiful mouth. "I know that I won't be able to stay away from you. I guess I should let the team know that sooner rather than later we'll need to start looking for your replacement."

"If that's a threat, let's be clear. I've never backed out of a concert or missed a tour date. Ever."

"Not a threat, sweetheart, but we've been down this road. With me, missing dates and running is what you do best. You hit a few potholes in the road, and instead of trying to navigate through it you duck and dodge and slink away."

"You still don't get it. Not everything is about you. I'm not in Las Vegas for you. I don't care where you work or how you feel about where I work. Sin City has a contract with The Hotel, not Jacob Johnson." Anger propels me to my feet. If he thinks I'm going to kowtow because of an empty threat, he doesn't know me half as well as he thinks he does.

I pace the length of the king-size mattress, pushing my hands through the curls that lay against the nape of my neck. I force myself to choke air through the irritation tightening my lungs. By the time I get to the third inhale my chest no longer feels like it's been enveloped in fire and brimstone.

I stop pacing directly across from him. "Look, why are we even rehashing any of this? It's all water under the bridge. Let's just let it go and focus on a healthy professional relationship."

"Professional relationship? Why'd you slap me, Sin? If you were the consummate professional, why after all these years did you let your anger put us all in a position that compromises the casino and future contracts with other artists?"

And there it is, my stupidity thrown back in my face. It feels like I've been sucker punched in the gut, and along with my ability to breathe, every word has disappeared from my vocabulary.

I see Jake's lips moving, but nothing he's saying can penetrate the white noise between my ears. For years I've fantasized about what I would say to him, how I would say it. How he'd be the one crawling down the hall crying this time. But I can't seem to tap into the righteous anger that rooted me for the last four years and exploded to the surface last night. I don't feel empowered or glamorous. I just feel tired, and I want this, whatever we're doing, over.

"Jake, let's just close this chapter and move forward, okay?"

"And what? Be friends? I can't be your friend, Sin." He takes a small step toward me, but jerks back against the door like it's tethered to the wood by an invisible cord. "It's taking everything in me right now to stay pressed to this door instead of being pressed against you. When I look at you, I want you. When I hear your voice, I crave us, and when you walk into a room. I want every fucking inch. Do you think we can ever be friends? Colleagues?"

The sad reality is *no*.

"Look," he says, scrubbing hands up and down his face. "I didn't bring you in here for this. But it needed to be done. You know? There is just so much between us." He pushes off the door stretching his tall frame to full height and closes the space between us. His chest comes right up against mine, enveloping me in his scent. He places his hand against the back of my neck.

"I didn't expect it to be so hard."

I search his sad eyes and that heat that always lived in the quiet moments between us sparks to life, sending a jolt of recognition down my body.

"Jake, be serious. After everything, do you genuinely think we could've made it work?"

He leans forward until his lips are an inch from mine. "I don't know, Sin, but I would've liked a chance to try." Moist air moves across my lips with his words. We let the silence stretch between us, but the pain and resentment that's been festering for four years overpower it. Time didn't heal this wound, and we just pulled the scab off, causing it to bleed all over again

"Sin," he whispers as his eyes search mine "If you don't believe anything else… believe that I'm sorry."

"Don't. I never needed you to be sorry." I try to push away, but his other arm comes around my back holding me in place.

"What… do you need?" He pushes air out of his lungs, his desperation blows across my face and singes the skin.

I close my eyes against his fixed stare. Willing my heart to accept what my head already knows. Jake is my brand of poison. But my heart, my stupid wanna-believe-in-happily-ever-afters heart has always wondered maybe. Maybe, I gave up too easy? Maybe, I'm the coward Jake is accusing me of being.

"Baby, look at me," he pleads as his lips move softly over mine.

I can't do it. I really, really want to, but… I can't. I barely recovered from the last time. A little moan that escapes my mouth and my hand tightens on his chest pulling him closer instead of pushing him away.

"Open up your eyes," he whispers, his voice breaking on the last word. "It's me. Me. You know me. I'm the same guy that took you to your first bar, the one that gave you your first real kiss. Let me be that guy."

"The guy I know. He left a long time ago, replaced by a punk-ass player that shattered us." This time when I push back, he lets me go. "I broke my own heart, trying to understand you. When I walked in that house, our home, and saw you with another woman. It was the culmination of a thousand tiny fissures that finally split wide open. You," I choke past the lump of emotion sitting in my throat. "Broke. Me." I wipe my hand over my mouth, blinking back the swell of tears.

"You want me to remember that guy, the one that gave me my first kiss and took me to my first bar? That guy is dead. That guy would've never discarded me like a piece of trash. I look at you, and I see nothing but hurt and rage. And I don't want to live there anymore." My chest hurts with the effort not to fall apart in front of him, but somehow, I do it. I push all those emotions down and inject some steel into my spine. A long time ago I loved a boy, and as fun as it might be to reminisce, that boy carelessly broke my heart. End of story. We're adults now. He's stepped into shoes that ten years ago he swore he'd never fill, and I have a career doing what I love, and it's enough for me.

"I don't want anything from you, Jake. Not your friendship or professional guidance," I whisper.

Our eyes clash across the sea of space that in distance is only a few feet, but in time and heartache is a chasm worthy of the Grand Canyon.

"You don't get to be here anymore. That's the point."

He turns his back to me, his steps echoing on the wooden floor.

I follow behind, relief and confusion battling for dominance in my head.

"Okay, Sin. I hear you. I'll do these interviews for my company because the CEO is demanding I play a role in fixing last night's catastrophe." He doesn't turn back around, but I can see him struggling with the need to say something else. His shoulders are tense high around his ears, and his hands shake as he reaches for the doorknob.

The hinges on the door squeak when he opens it and relief floods my system. The victory is bittersweet as I watch him step just over the threshold.

Chapter 9

Jake

I LOVE FRIDAY NIGHTS DURING FOOTBALL SEASON. IN VEGAS, THE WEATHER is still warm, but it's not the scorching heat of summer. Every time I go to a game, I regret not taking the scholarship UCLA football team offered, but that's not what we do in my family. Like a good son, I stayed home, enrolled in the University Of Nevada, Las Vegas. Johnson's thrive on academic prowess, not physical aptitude. I hung up my high school cleats and chose to double major in business management and accounting.

My parents are ostentatious, and wealthy, and overbearing, and impossible. Looking at them it's easy to forget my great-grandfather was a gambler, a whore-monger, and a drunkard. In spite of his vices he had an aptitude with numbers and the luck of the draw. His brilliance with the cards set his family up for life, but it also created an inflated sense of importance. My family didn't build this city. We weren't pioneers or inventors. We swindled the land from better men, and for the last eighty or so years we've been trying to prove Vegas is as much our as it ever was theirs.

So here I am. I caught the tail end of the game and decided to hit the after party hosted by Kappa Delta Psi. UNLV doesn't have the best football team, but it does have the best parties. Players and students from both teams convened on the Kappa house. People are everywhere, all over the backyard and filling every square inch of space inside the house. There is trash talking and drinking. Bodies grinding together to the hard-base rhythms of *A Milli* by Lil Wayne coming from large speakers.

I take a sip of beer from a red Solo cup, not really paying attention to the people gathered around me. I'm pretty sure only one or two actually like me but the rest? They know who my family is in this city, and they hang around hoping to reap some of the benefits, or at the very least, get a comp at Le Cinq, the Parisian concept hotel my father carefully cultivated into Vegas' new destination spot. Yeah, not happening.

The beer I'm drinking is room temperature and tastes like piss, but it's doing the job. My head buzzes from the alcohol. The pressure to be perfect, to succeed, and to assume the role of my father starts to dissipate. I down the remaining beer in one gulp and crush the plastic in the palm of my hand. I'm about to amble off to get a refill when I get a sharp elbow to my ribs.

"That's her," Evan, one of the guys from my econ class, drunkenly slurs into my ear.

I follow his gaze, and there she is—Sinclair James. She walks by me and I can't take my eyes off her. Her normally natural curly hair is straight tonight and hangs in soft waves down the center of her back. I want to tangle my hands in it. Mess up the perfectly place strands. I wonder what it would take to make her sweat. Make those straight strands revert back to springy corkscrew curls.

She's in a white crop top with large black letters that read RUN DMC. When she walks, the edge of her shirt plays peekaboo with the bottom of her red bra, and below that top is nothing but skin. Smooth, deep brown, flawless skin with a red jewel in her navel that twinkles in the light with each step she takes. I want to lick and kiss and bite her belly, watch the taut skin ripple as her muscles tighten under my touch.

This girl is under my skin. Has been since day one. The fact that I can't pin her down, ask her out, figure out her class schedule, or what she does when she's not in class makes it worse. Much worse.

"I'm going to talk to her. Check my breath." He blows a hot stream of air up my nose, and I jerk my head back at the offensive odor.

"Damn, man." I wave a hand in front of my face.

"It's that bad? You have gum?" He tries to straighten his wrinkled shirt.

"Nah, sorry, bro. You gotta find that shit on your own."

"Come on, Jake, help me out. She'll be gone by the time I get back."

"Then you better hurry up, huh?"

When he walks away, I turn toward Sinclair and follow her into the kitchen. The sway of her perky ass encased in a jean skirt just short enough to court my imagination mesmerizes me. She stops and leans her hip on the counter. Every couple of seconds her eyes flit from the blonde I hadn't even noticed at her side to the door, like she waiting for something or someone to arrive.

I pull the fresh pack of gum out of my back pocket, take out a foil wrapped piece, and quickly open it. I fold the piece into my mouth letting the fresh minty flavor coat my tongue.

My system suddenly floods with testosterone. A caveman impulse pounds in my head, telling me to get in there, claim her, and put my stamp on it, so that the only person she'll look for is me. The only entrance she'll anticipate is mine.

After the blonde finishes at the keg. I grab one of the red cups stacked on the counter next to her hip.

"There she is," I say in a low voice next to her ear. I'm standing well within her personal space, probably closer than necessary and way closer than I should.

Sin turns her curious brown eyes and an answering smile on me. Those fucking dimples carve out matching valleys in both her cheeks and, for the second time in so many minutes, my night grinds to a slow halt for this girl. Only because of this girl.

"I didn't realize I was lost. Were you looking for me?" She smiles at me, but her eyes slide over my shoulder once again looking at the door. *Who you waiting for, Sin? I'm here. Right here. In front of you.*

"I was," I say. "You're a hard woman to pin down."

"Well, you got me," she says. Her eyes drop to her phone before bouncing back up to mine. "At least for the next couple of minutes."

Boss up, Jake. If you have a couple of minutes. Make every single one of them count.

"Omigod... Jake, is that you?" The blonde next to Sin squeals, pulling me into a hug.

She's vaguely familiar in a *Vegas is a big small city and there is six degrees of separation between people in a certain age group* kind of way, but I can't place her.

"A yeah." I squint at her face. Her name is something with a T. Tanya. Tammy. Trina. I got it. "Tina, right?"

"Right." She beams at me. "This is my roommate, Sinclair." She waves a dismissive hand in Sin's direction. Completely oblivious to the exchange Sin and I just had.

"Yeah, I got that." I say. I can't hide the thread irritation making its way into my voice.

Sin's eyes once again move to the door. This time staying on it for a longer period. I'm envious of that door and, by default, the person she's waiting to come through it.

"Tina, I'm trying to convince Sinclair here to give me just a little bit of her time, and I could use your endorsement. Tell her I'm a good guy." I wink at Sin and finally she looks at me with something other than amused indifference.

"Who needs good when dealing with Vegas royalty?"

I roll my eyes at that comment. Vegas doesn't have royalty. There is new money and older new money, most of it is ill-gotten gains from every conceivable vice. Las Vegas high society doesn't necessarily fit in with the cotton kings from the South, the railroad barons from Colorado, or the industrial revolutionaries from Detroit. This city made its bones catering to immorality. We're upper society's dirty little secret. Everyone has been here, done the drugs, sampled the prostitutes, and gambled in the back rooms, but no one wants to admit they enjoy it.

"Jake, take my number. We should get together." There is no mistaking the invitation in Tina's words or Sin's waning interest as she fingers the edge of her skirt . I absently hand Tina my phone when Sin's phone rings, and she immediately answers. I shamelessly listen, greedy for information, anything that will give me an in with her.

"Hey Adam..."

Adam? Who is he? Her boyfriend? She doesn't have a boyfriend, right?

"Tina drug me to a party." She presses the phone tight to her ear and sticks a finger in the opposite ear, trying to block out the background noise.

"Twenty minutes? But that'll only leave us fifteen minutes to get there," she says. "Yeah. I'm dressed but..." She pauses to listen. "No, I didn't bring the helmet. I straightened my hair. That sweaty thing will..." She nods at something he's saying.

God I wish I could hear what he's saying? I bet its candy, sickly sweet, sticky bullshit. That's what men my age looking to get laid do. That's what I'd be doing right now if she wasn't on the phone.

"At the Kappa house." She says.

"I'll be outside when you get here." She smiles into the phone before saying, "Absolutely."

The only thing I understood from the one side of the conversation was she'll be here for at least another fifteen minutes.

"Here you go." Tina slides my phone into my palm, making sure to drag her nails along my skin. "Sin, I think Lauren and Stacy just walked in. I'm..." Sin holds up a finger dipping her head to catch the rest of what Adam is saying, and Tina walks across the room without a backward glance.

"Kay. Just be careful and get here as fast as you can." Sin presses the button to end the call. A slight frown creases the skin between her eyes, her full lips are drawn down in a cute pout, and those dimples come out even when she's upset.

"Boyfriend," I ask flipping the cell phone in my hand.

"Best friend," she answers.

I expel a breath. I can work with that. Now, I have fifteen minutes to take my shot.

"Want to dance?" I hold out my hand.

She looks between it and my face a couple of times before she says, "Sure."

But she doesn't take my hand as she walks toward the makeshift dance floor. I follow her lithe figure through the throngs of people that have doubled in the last couple of minutes, and I grab her hand before I lose her.

Black lights hang above the dance floor. The purple hue washes Sin's white shirt and light-colored jean skirt with an iridescent glow. She finds a decent spot in the middle of all the bodies and turns to face me.

It's too dark to see her expression, but when I place my hands on the naked skin of her waist and start a sensual rhythm, she rocks with me. We move together like it's natural, like it's the hundredth time I've had her in my arms instead of the first.

I pull her in closer and curve my body around hers, erasing the last couple of inches respectable distance. Her lips are an inch from my lips, her chest flush against my chest, and when her legs part to cradle one of mine, my dick takes notice and hardens at our proximity. I ease her hips away from mine, trying hard not to offend her and embarrass myself.

"Let me take you out on a date."

"I don't date."

"Because of Adam?" I run my fingertips along the dip of her spine, gently digging into the muscles of her back.

"Not even close." She lets out a sigh as I hit a spot.

"You don't like me?"

"I don't know you." She laughs with a toss of her head. Those dimples pop, and the ends of her hair tickle as the length skims my arm. My semi becomes full and heavy between my legs.

"Ask me anything. I'll tell you whatever you want to know."

She half sighs, half moans, leaning into me, giving me more of her weight. "You sure about that?" she breathes against my lips.

"I'm sure I want to take you out. So yeah."

"How will I know if your answers are the truth?"

"Faith."

Her lips slip into a small smile, but the dimples don't pop this time. I'm a little disappointed until she presses her soft lips against my ear, and purrs in a husky voice, "Given the choice of anyone in the world, whom would you want as a dinner guest?"

"That's easy. You."

"Is this where I have faith?"

"You tell me. What I just said was one hundred percent true. I want to know you. Everything about you. I would love to sit across from you or next to you and have your undivided attention for how-ever long you'll give it to me."

She pulls back, tilting her head up to mine. The whites of her eyes glow under the black light, but I can't make out her pupils. What is she thinking?

A new song starts, the base deeper, the rhythmic flow of the rap-per hypnotic. Sin's body does this sexy roll, her back muscles flex un-der my fingers, and I'm not sure but, fuck me, I think her pussy just brushed my thigh. Her hands slide up my arms and curve around the back of my neck.

"Would you like to be famous? And in what way?" There is a weight to her words, one I don't understand. I stare into her eyes and try to formulate an answer, but her body is the ultimate distraction.

"Um… No. I never pictured myself famous. I look at famous peo-ple, and I can't imagine living under that microscope. Opening my life up to ridicule and judgement. Instead of fame I want freedom. To live my life on my own terms. What about you?"

"Do I want to be famous? Or Free?"

"Famous."

"Sometimes." She tilts her head to the side.

God, I wish I could see her eyes. If only so I could guess what she's thinking.

"I sing in a band. Music and fame kinda go hand in hand. It's crazy, right?"

"Not at all." I can totally picture her on a stage with her raspy voice reaching out like a siren's call.

My forehead drops to hers, our breathing comes together in hot, short, spurts.

"Can I kiss you?" I thread my fingers into her hair, easing forward the last fraction of an inch between us.

Since the first moment I saw her wandering through the quad and helped her find her dorm room, I've thought about how her lips would feel against mine. If she's taste as sweet as she looks.

"No," she says, her lips close enough to tease but still too far to taste.

The slightest shifts in our position would definitely satisfy my question of if she tastes as sweet as she looks. And God, do I want to taste her. I trail my tongue along my bottom lip, begging her without words. *Kiss me. Just a hint of taste. That's all I need.*

Her coquettish eyes turn up to mine, and I know she's playing me or, at the very least, playing with me. The eyes, the dimples, the made for sin body. Her. Everything about her does it for me. Lust spirals through my body, bottoming out in my balls, drawing them up almost painfully tight. I'm leaking like a fucking preteen, and I can't make myself care. She's a fantasy in the flesh, a lucid dream. One that I want to take my time to learn and explore.

A high-pitched ring goes off close to my ear, and Sin leans back, the light from her screen illuminating the otherwise dark dance floor. I hadn't even noticed she was holding the phone. We both look at the screen. It's Adam.

"Don't answer that." I take a chance and place a single open-mouthed kiss at the base of her throat. The touch is brief but still enough to make my lips tingle with wasted lust.

"I have to." She untangles her body from mine, her hands smoothing out her clothes.

"Hey," she says into the phone, pressing a palm against the opposite ear. "You're already here?" She pauses for a second. "It's been how long?" She raises her voice on the last word. "Shit. Sorry. I'm headed out." Sin presses the red button to end the call. She turns to go and throws a muttered, "Sorry" in my general on her way toward the door.

"Hold up." I grab one of her hands, trying to pull her back to me, but her limbs are stiff, making it hard to maneuver through the bodies still dancing around us. "You're leaving? Right now? I thought we were having a good time."

"We were and now I have to go." She turns her back on me again, walking with purpose away from me.

It's taken me months to finally pin her down long enough to get this far. I'm not just letting her go. That leaves me no choice but to follow as she pushes her way through crowd. When we finally exit the house, she expels a relieved breath, and runs her hands subconsciously over her hair and down her skirt.

The sound of a motorcycle engine pulls my attention off Sin to the man straddling the bike in front of the house. He pulls the helmet off his head and from this distance, we look about the same height. He has long blond hair pulled into a bun on top of his head. A worn leather jacket covers a Notorious B.I.G T-shirt. Skinny black jeans and heavy leather boots round out the look.

"Sin, wait." She looks at me over her shoulder. Under the bright light of the full moon I can clearly see her studying me, but I still can't read the emotions in the depth of her eyes. Desire is definitely there. But there is something else. Regret. Maybe irritation. Fuck me. I wish I knew her better.

I close the distance between us, and she turns quickly to face me. She presses her hand solidly to the center of my chest. I place my hand over hers, letting the heat of her palm soak into my muscles and ease the rapid beat of my heart.

"I have to go, Jake. We're already late." The white boy on the bike revs his engine burning rubber on his back tire and once again, she goes to pull away. I tighten my hand over hers, keeping us connected. Even if in a small way.

"Can you cut out? Just this once? Just for tonight?" I ask over the noise of the motorcycle. My eyes flicker from her to the man behind her obnoxiously interrupting our conversation and successfully cock-blocking me.

"Not the way this works, Jake."

"Then give me some rules. I can't wait another two months to see you again."

"There are no rules. I just…"

I run my hand up the smooth skin of her arm and settle my palm on the sensitive skin between her neck and shoulder. I sweep my thumb over the ridge of her collarbone. Chemistry, or connection, or pheromones, or something uniquely us flares to life. She lets out a barely audible sigh, but she leans forward possibly against her better judgement. Her lips brush over mine in a touch so chaste and fleeting. It's better than every other kiss I've had before it. But it's not enough. I need more.

My fingertips find the side of her face as I go in to deepen the kiss. My tongue traces the line between her lips, dipping inside her mouth, chasing my new favorite flavor. I nip at her lips, trying to devour her. She pulls back on a shaky breath.

"Why do I have a feeling tonight just changed everything?" She says biting the corner of her lip as she looks up at me.

"Faith?" I try to laugh off the significance of her question, but it hangs in the air between us. As real as the moon over our heads, or the desert heat warming our skin.

"Let me go, Jake," she whispers. I know she means right now, but I hate the sound of those words, hate that she thinks it's even possible to let her go.

"No."

Sin smiles at that, but she entwines her fingers with mine and pulls my hand away from her face. She looks at our hands, unlacing our fingers, and she take a step back.

"Give me something," I say and I mean it. "A phone number would be nice, but I'll settle for a time, a place, anything."

Sin drops her head forward. The long strands of her straightened hair float over her shoulder, and she bites the corner of her lip.

"It's 555-0108," she finally says after what seems like a minute of silence. Her naturally raspy voice an octave lower.

"Is that 702?"

"Nah." She shakes her head. "It's 775." She takes a couple more steps away from me.

"I'll call you tonight so…"

"Call me tomorrow. I won't be around tonight," she yells over her shoulder. Sin throws a leg over the bike, wrapping a loose arm around the guy's waist, plastered to his back, as if she belongs there.

I watch them drive off, and I blow out a frustrated breath when they hit the corner and fade out of sight.

Chapter 10

NOW
Jake

EARLY THIS MORNING I GOT BOMBARDED WITH PHONE CALLS FROM both Connor and Jeanine. The message was pretty clear—do the interviews and clean up my mess. I knew going in it would be hard. That I would be sensitive and exposed.

I walked into her villa, the one I booked because I thought it would be more comfortable and had the bright idea to *talk* to her. That conversation turned into a disaster. She's just too set against me and everything associated with *us* to even try to find common ground.

I slip back into the room unnoticed since a million different people litter the space. Housekeeping sweeps the hardwood floors and polishes all the reflective surfaces. I recognize a couple of people from the marketing department staging furniture, adding pillows and flowers to the table tops, and vacuuming the rugs. Which is overkill because I made sure shit was tight before she arrived yesterday. I wanted her to have a space that felt like her own, even if she is staying in a hotel.

Instead of the villa looking like Sin's private domain, it looks like the set of a promotional shoot or a playpen for the pampered and frivolous. Four-foot-tall bouquets of flowers rest on every flat surface. The sofa and the chairs have all been adorned with plush pillows, some furry, others jeweled. There's one that has The Hotel name and emblem embroidered on it. There is even a stack of them on the floor. The only curtains that have been opened are the ones that display the Strip. There are cameras in every corner, wires crisscross the floor every couple of feet, and a large screen computer monitor has been set up on the dining table.

Sin opens the door and slips out of the room, skirting around me, but even with her head down and turned away, I can tell that she's been crying. She'd looked so unaffected when I was in front of her. So, why was she crying? I grit my teeth in frustration because I keep messing up, when the only thing I've wanted since learning she'd be in town again was to fix what I broke. At this point I've handled seeing her with the finesse of a sledgehammer.

Only when she stops in front of the mirror and fluffs her hair, do I realize she's changed clothes. Skinny jeans and bejeweled Jimmy Hendrix top that hangs off her shoulder have replaced the loose-fitting pajama pants and tank-top. I can tell that she's put on makeup, but it's understated.

Sin pulls a tube of something out of her back pocket and swipes it across her lips. Her big brown eyes meet mine in the reflection of the mirror and her movement stalls. I make a move toward her, but Jeanine walks into the living room area from the adjacent kitchen, and I stop short.

Instead of going over there and demanding Sin put us both out of our misery, I drop my eyes and study my shoes.

"Ah, I see you've both stopped hiding."

My head snaps up. "Jeanine," I say. My voice, little more than a growl.

"Did I strike a nerve, Mr. Johnson? Well you're in good company. This whole mess has irritated several of mine." She shakes her head to emphasize the words.

"Just so we're clear, I do not work for you," she mutters through stiff lips. "Or you." She whips around in Sin's direction. "I'm here be-cause I own ten percent of the stock for this hotel, which plummeted overnight thanks to your shenanigans. Connor specifically asked me for this favor."

Jeanine advances toward me and I actually take a step back.

"I don't take it lightly that the company I've worked hard to establish lost credibility and, as a result, I lost money because of you two. I don't appreciate being called in the middle of the night and asked to do damage control for a situation that was completely avoidable. This whole situation with the two of you is so far outside of my wheelhouse. I am director of media relations for a major hotel on the Las Vegas Strip. Read that to mean marketing and advertising. I am not some sleazy tabloid queen looking to stir the pot. I specialize in corporate branding. C-O-R-P-O-R-A-T-E." She draws the word out annunciating each of the three syllables.

"So that we're all on the same page, I think this whole thing is ridiculous." Her arm moves in a loop around her head. "Grown-ups, everyone in this room appears to be over the age of twenty-one and that does indeed make you an adult, do not handle their affairs or professions in this manner. The two of you are walking around like sad puppies and snapping at me like goddamn piranhas, and I have had enough."

She turns toward Sin, taking off her glasses, and rubbing the bridge of her nose. "You don't want me in your room or coordinating your media response? How about you don't assault people or run from a room tragically like Scarlett O'Hara."

Then she turns toward me. "Before you snap at me one more time, why don't you find your balls and admit that nine times out of ten sorry doesn't fix shit. Apologizing makes you feel better not the person you've injured. Do you want forgiveness, Jacob? Actions mean a whole hell of a lot more than your hollow words."

Blowing out a deep breath, replacing the glasses on her face and patting hair back into place that hadn't moved, she starts prepping us for the interview. After a couple of moments in silence scrutinizing us, I get a pinched frown.

"Mr. Johnson, is there a reason why you are jacketless?"

"No, Jeanine, there is no reason"

"Good. Please replace your jacket. Reporters are already staging outside." She rolls her eyes, looking at the ceiling for patience.

Without a word I turn and briskly walk down the short hallway into the vacant bedroom, and what should have taken a couple of seconds easily turns into a couple of minutes. Without Sin's distracting presence in front of me, I take in the space that even after one day is uniquely hers. The rumpled bed, silk scarves thrown over lightshades, guitar cases propped against the wall, and the sweet scent of almond that always seemed to tinge the air around her. I take it all in, answering four years of questions. At least about the simple stuff.

At the sound of Jeanine's voice calling me out from the other room, I eye my rumpled jacket against the wall and quickly opt against wearing it. I'm not a stylist, but even I know wrinkled clothes are a definite no for television.

Fuck me. I'm about to be on TV. The most intimate details of my life out there for public consumption. My pulse kicks up and a nervous sweat gathers under my arms. I walk back into the other room rolling the long sleeves up my forearms. Jeanine rolls her eyes at my action but keeps talking nonetheless, so I'm assuming she's fine with the wardrobe change. I'm sure there's a study out there researching the effects of how rolled-up sleeves will make the public view me as more approachable.

"Look at the camera, not each other. Do not get defensive. I repeat, Do. Not. Get. Defensive. You're only obligated to answer the questions you want. I didn't provide you with a list of approved questions on purpose. Rehearsed answers will only fuel the fire. Leave the wrangling of reporters to me. If they step too far out of bounds, I will address it. Understood?"

"We got it, Jeanine," I snap, my irritation needing and finding a target. This whole production suddenly becoming too much. In less than an hour my family and employees, hell the world, will be privy to details that up to date have been exclusively mine and I don't like— scratch that—I hate it.

"I could've sworn no longer than two minutes ago I stated I was quite tired of the attitude I'm getting from you. Tone it down before

I let the camera crews in here, or so help me God, I'll be the one slapping you this time."

One side of Sin's mouth pulls into a half smile and something in my chest loosens. I'll be the butt end of every joke if it'll get her to smile.

"Now, since you two have shown questionable judgement and an aptitude for violence…" Jeanine pauses to throw Sin the stink eye after that verbal jab. "Before I open this door for the first interview, do I need to explain the rules of conduct to either one of you?"

"No," Sin and I answer simultaneously.

"See there, the two of you can do some things together. The first interview will be the longest. Let's say thirty minutes give or take. All the other outlets get between three to five minutes. Make this first one count because, more than likely, it's the one that will produce sound bites and headlines."

Jeanine throws one more look over her shoulder before she opens the door and invites in the first news crew. They exchange a couple of words at the door before she leads the reporter over to me in the center of the room.

"Mr. Johnson, this is Jarrod Ocampo with Etcetera Entertainment," Jeanine says. He's maybe an inch or so shorter than me. His bald head gleams under the lights, and he's dressed in a three-piece red suit with no socks and wine-colored dress shoes.

The reporter extends his hand, giving me a firm shake and a slight but professional smile. "Jeanine said this is your first personal interview. I'll try to make this as painless as possible. Just relax and let it happen," he jokes in a low voice.

"You still using that tired ass line, Jarrod?" His attention immediately shifts to the sound of Sin's voice.

"It worked for you, right? Remember when you were a media virgin? I eased you in real slow, taught you my best moves, and now you're all pro." Jarrod tilts his head to the side and bites the corner of his lip. His almond-shaped eyes rake her body.

"I was a pro long before I met you, J-Rod."

"Mmm-hmm, call me J again," he says with a flirtatious groan, opening his arms to her. She walks forward and he pulls her against his body in a tight hug.

"It's been too long, Sin." The fucker actually lights up when she says his nickname. Don't get me wrong. I get it. Probably more than most. Sin live and in Technicolor is a sight to behold, but not for this *Rico Suave* fuckboy.

"Where were we the last time? Monte Carlo?" She pulls back, looking into his face with her hands still on his shoulders and her beautiful lips split in a smile. Those dimples I love are out and popping.

What in the fuck am I watching right now? My teeth clench with jealousy at how familiar they seem, and how easy they fall into a friendly banter.

"Nah," Jarrod says. "I think it was Prague for the Rhythms of Love Festival. Remember Dan—"

"Got molested in the bar by that really large woman that just wanted his—"

Did she really just finish his sentence?

"Semen," they say together bursting into laughter. They go back and forth about other interviews they've had and times spent hanging out in exotic places.

"So, what's up with the slap? I've never seen anyone get under your skin like that."

"Is this off the record, J-Rod?"

His eyes flit to me over Sin's shoulder before moving back to Sin. "That part is work, you know that."

"Then ask me later over drinks." She winks. She fucking winks at this guy before breaking contact with his body.

My jealousy wants to morph into anger, because for the six years I had with Sin, I don't know her anymore. I've never met the world traveler, who even dressed in jeans and a T-shirt, can command this type of attention. I've never seen her slip into superstar mode with a megawatt smile and carefully crafted half answers that allude to everything and nothing at the same time. I back away from the two of them to sit on the sofa.

Jeanine walks around the chairs and sits on the arm of the sofa right next to me. "Close your mouth, Mr. Johnson. Gaping is not an attractive trait," Jeanine whispers. I shut my trap, but I can't reconcile the image I've had of Sin all these years with the woman who slapped me to the woman schmoozing the reporter.

"Mr. Johnson, I'll let you in on a little secret. She's quite astonishing. People see her, and their interest is intense and immediate. I'd wager a pretty penny you had the same reaction when you first met her. The only difference between then and now is that where you were the only recipient of her attention in the past, presently the world sees her exactly the way you do."

"How do you know how I see her?"

Jeanine doesn't answer until I look up at her. "Because your heart is right there in your eyes for everyone to see." She pats my cheek as she stands.

"Oy." Jeanine claps her hands loudly, and all eyes turn in her direction. "Listen up. You are all in my sandbox. Play nice, respect others, don't do or say anything that you wouldn't discuss in the presence of your mother, and all will be well." She flicks her hands at the group. "Right then, back at it." She walks just beyond my field of vision.

Jarrod, of course, takes one of the chairs, leaving Sin to settle in next to me on the sofa directly across from him. The producer explains the different shots he will do down to the close-ups. The assistant cameraman starts a countdown. When he hits four, he flashes fingers instead of saying the words.

"I'm here with Grammy Award winning artist Sinclair James and the man of the hour, chief financial officer of The Hotel, Jacob Johnson."

I startle at his mention of my title and The Hotel. *This is it. Ready or not my life is about to shift from obscurity to the center stage, aaaand I'm about to have a heart attack. But on the plus side, if I die, I don't have to answer any questions.*

"Tonight, among other things, we're going to touch on the video that has been making the rounds for the last several hours. Sinclair, Mr. Johnson, thank you for joining me tonight."

I expected him to jump right in with, "So, Sinclair what did he do to deserve that slap?" But the first several questions are light and simple. He focuses on Sin City's hectic touring schedule and their other commitments. The list of responsibilities is long and extensive. I had no idea they had a music foundation for underprivileged kids here in the city. Or that they plan to fly to Mexico City and back to Vegas in thirteen hours. I'm impressed by the list of duties Sin can complete in the same twenty-four hours that I have. So, when Jarrod addresses both of us, I blink stupidly.

"How long have you two known each other?"

"Six years," Sin says

"Ten years," I say at the same time.

Jarrod lets out a chuckle. "That's interesting."

He directs the next question to me. "How did you meet Sinclair?"

"We met at freshman orientation in college. She was standing in the middle of the quad by herself. She had this huge duffle bag and two solid guitar cases that I offered to help her carry."

"And did she let you carry them?" He shifts in his seat. A knowing smirk lifting the corner of his mouth.

"She did. It took a little convincing on my part, but by the end of the day, she liked me enough to play me a song." I hadn't thought about that in years. It's as if when we broke up, my mind got stuck on a tragic loop of things that had gone wrong instead of the good memories.

"It sounds like you were a fan from the very beginning," he states.

"Definitely." I look at Sin, letting my eyes drift across her face. She doesn't turn her face toward mine, but her muscles turn stiff and her smile falters for the first time since we sat down.

"Would I be wrong in the assumption that the two of you dated?"

"No."

"Are you still dating?" he asks in a smug voice because he already knows the answer to this question.

"No"

"How long did you date?"

"Six years."

He looks a little surprised, some of his egotistical self-confidence faltering. Confusion creasing his brow. He stops speaking while he processes that tidbit of information.

"If we do the math your relationship ended…"

"Four years ago," Sin and I answer at the same time.

Jarrod clears his throat. "Okay, now I get your earlier answer. Your relationship ended around the time Sin City's first album *Exquisitely Broken* was released." He doesn't ask a question. Therefore, I don't give an answer.

"Sinclair, was your album a case of art imitating life? Was Mr. Johnson the muse for your best-selling album?"

"No, it was a case of first love heartbreak," she answers.

"And Mr. Johnson was that love?"

"In a sense. Did I take inspiration from things that happened between us? Yes. Did I put every detail of our relationship in the lyrics? No. At that time, I was really frustrated with where I was in my career and my relationship. I was trying to figure out my next move, ya know?"

She didn't stumble over the words, but even I recognize spin when I hear it. And the reporter calls her on it.

"In the first single "Cheated" from your debut album one of the lyrics says, *'Unfaithful heart and silken lies he found his happy between another pair of thighs.'* That doesn't seem ambiguous. In fact, it's pretty specific and very descriptive. Are you saying that he didn't cheat on you?" He holds Sin's gaze, blinking ever so often and seemingly waiting her out. There are no remnants of their earlier friendship or banter.

"I'm saying it was a creative expression of my feelings at the time."

"Come on, Sinclair, did he or did he not cheat?"

"Yes, I cheated," I answer the question before she can.

The journalist temples his fingers in front of his mouth. His expression, turning serious. "And does that have anything to do with the conflict between you two last night?"

I let out a sigh and fight the urge to crack the vertebra in my neck. "Yes and no."

"That sounds complicated."

"I wouldn't use the word complicated. The short and quick of it is, I fucked up… Shit… I mean I messed up." I see Jeanine snap to attention in my peripheral vision.

"It's okay." He encourages me to keep talking. "We prerecord the show. It'll be edited out. In what way did you mess up?"

"I was a kid," I start.

"Twenty-four is hardly a kid. Some men that age already have families and careers."

"True, but I wasn't one of them. I had a young man's mentality, and I resorted back to the stuff that worked with my parents. I felt like if I acted out enough, she'd focus on me."

"In what ways did you act out?" Jeanine steps forward just out of the cameras field of view and runs her thumb across the front of her throat silently telling me to cut it. So, I try to redirect.

"Like I said earlier at the time I was immature. Her star was rising." My eyes shift to Jeanine who flashes me a thumbs-up. "She shined so bright that it drew people in. They flocked to her in droves, and it was hard for me to share her light."

"As poetic as that sounds, it doesn't really address how the relationship dissolved."

"The same way they all do, I guess. I wanted her to fight for me, for us, and instead of fighting she left."

"How did that make you feel? Sinclair not 'fighting' for you?" I look at Sin again, and this time her big coffee-colored eyes meet mine. "Heartbroken," I say, willing her to feel the truth of my words. I hold her gaze for a couple more beats before I turn my gaze back to the reporter.

Jarrod dips his head, schooling his features into a thoughtful look. "Sinclair, why didn't you fight?" The reporter's gaze darts from mine to hers.

"There was nothing…" She carefully laces her fingers over her lap and clears her throat. I can feel her muscles vibrating with tension when she finally says, "…left worth fighting for."

I suck in a breath because… fuck that hurt.

"When the relationship ended did you stay in touch?"

"No, we didn't," Sin says. She doesn't mention that she froze me out, changing her phone number and, as I later found out, leaving the country.

"So last night was the first time you've seen each other in what… three or four years?"

I nod as Sin utters, "Yes."

"Sinclair, when you signed a yearlong contract with the hotel, did you know Mr. Johnson worked there?"

"Not at all. We run in completely different circles. I've never had a reason to keep tabs on Jake." And the hits keep coming. She's right, but for me, keeping track of her was a compulsory impulse. Something I did to stay on an even keel, and in her mind, I didn't warrant the most basic curiosity.

"Did you have a reason to slap him?"

She curls her hands into the soft hair at the nape of her neck. "Yeah I have my reasons."

"Any that you want to share?" Jarrod's mouth turns up at the corners.

"None that I can share," Sin says, injecting false lightness into the words.

"What about you, Mr. Johnson? After last night, do you want to reconnect with Sinclair?" His face splits into a Cheshire cat grin. "Don't let me put you on the spot here."

That's precisely what he's doing, but fair exchange is no robbery. I knew when I sat down for this interview that, at some point, my feelings for Sin would come up. Now it's out there in the open, not somewhere in the foggy past. Maybe saying it in this format will help Sin hear it.

"I'd move heaven and hell to make a paradise for her on earth if she'd give me another chance." For the second time since we sat down to do this interview, Sin turns her head to look at me.

That's right, baby, let me see you. Stop hiding behind the past and the mistakes. And let me in.

"You sound like a man still in love," Jarrod states.

I shrug. "Those are your words, not mine."

"SINCLAIR JAMES FINALLY REVEALS HER MUSE."
—*USA Today*

"HEARTBREAK AND HAND SLAPS. SINCLAIR JAMES GETS BACK AT CHEATING EX."
—*People Magazine*

"WHO IS JACOB JOHNSON AND WHAT IS HE TO SINCLAIR JAMES?"
—*Entertainment Weekly*

"JACOB JOHNSON DEFINITELY NOT HIS FATHER'S SON."
—*Las Vegas Review-Journal*

Chapter 11

Opening night in Vegas is always a big deal. It doesn't matter if it's for something as mundane as a medical clinic or as grandiose as a themed hotel. Show girls outfitted with glitter and feathers serve as goodwill ambassadors, the liquor flows, the cameras flash, and attendees get suited and booted to see and be seen.

Having Sin City agree to a yearlong residency with The Hotel elevates this opening. It marks our transition from wannabes to contenders. Shows the haters, and the supporters, we're serious about creating a legacy in our own right. It serves as a reminder that the large corporations that currently own eighty percent of the Strip aren't the only ones that can turn a profit. Tonight needs to be perfect.

After my media debut as the guy who broke Sinclair's heart, I need a win. Something to pull the focus back where it belongs, off my personal life and on the business. Things have somewhat blown over in the weeks since we did the interviews, but those first couple of days were rough.

I had reporters camped outside my house and waiting for me in the parking garage after work. They contacted my parents, the people who couldn't stand Sin on general principle because she didn't come from money or because her complexion was darker than mine. And because her talents didn't include knowing the ins and outs of entertaining. Because, because, because… the list is too long to name. If my mother didn't like her when they first met, then she damn sure can't stand Sin now with reporters skulking through her garden and peeking in her windows.

What a clusterfuck. I think she almost breathed fire when reporters showed up on the college campus, hounding my baby sister.

I'm still getting requests for interviews. The national outlets have all moved on to the hot new thing, but the local papers and news stations refuse to let the story die. If it's this hard and invasive for me, it must be twice as bad for Sin. As a person who, up until a couple of weeks ago, lived my life in the background, the spotlight is killing me.

Just yesterday while sitting in the employee dining room, which is a smaller version of The Hotel's buffet, I was privy to what can only be called a fascinating conversation by some of the dealers. From the sound of it, the employees fall into two distinct camps—those loyal to me because I sign their paychecks and those who hate me because of everything my last name represents in this city.

I sat in a far corner, hidden by the metal paneling of the drink station. It was nice to sit unnoticed and relax in the familiar cadence of hotel operations. When I heard the first voice, my fork stopped halfway to my mouth.

Dealer One: "My wife told me she read the article in the *RJ* about Sinclair James, and apparently, she and Johnson were high school sweethearts, but his family didn't approve. So, his mother paid her off. Made her leave town."

Dealer Two: "Nah, the article I read said that they met in college and he cheated on her. Have you heard the album?"

Dealer One: "Then why'd she slap him? One of the girls from food and beverage, who was actually there, said that she damn near slapped the color off his ass."

They both snickered after that statement.

Dealer Two: "I'm telling you, the article I read said that she walked in on him having sex with another woman and decided to end the relationship."

Dealer One: "For real?"

Dealer Two: "You know how these rich pricks are. We see them come through here all the time. They think they own everything including people. I'd bet you money she slapped him because he was probably trying to get her and the other woman together for a threesome."

Dealer One: "That's just wrong."

Their conversation jumped to something else before they exited the cafeteria and I sat there in a daze. Jesus, is that what people think about me? I get the stuff about my family, at least my mom and dad. They were brutal about my relationship with Sin, my mom is still unflinchingly so. Call it ignorance or naivety, but when I found out about the attempted pay off, I was dumbstruck. My parents made no secret of the fact they preferred I find someone more like them, like us, but paying her off was low. Even I didn't think they'd take it that far.

I immediately drove to my parents' house angry and demanding answers. The most prominent question I had was why? Why would they hurt Sin that way? Why would they hurt me at all? Why would they purposefully destroy the one thing in my life that came without strings? Why? Why? Why? Why? My mother's response to my questions was a hate-fueled monologue ripping Sin to shreds. It made me physically ill.

When I think about all the family functions I dragged Sin to I feel even worse. I still can't wrap my mind around Sin's silence. She never said anything. Never uttered a word against my parents or about the check. Instead, she gave the money to a halfway house that works with prostitutes trying to transition from the streets and kept it pushing.

I stroll into the Skybox Lounge, which will host tonight's event. It's on the top floor of the arena overlooking the stage and Las Vegas Boulevard. From this position, I can see the empty stage.

The roadies are scurrying around from one side of the stage to the other. I can make out their clothes—all black. The color of their skin—diverse. Their individual features are nondescript and blurry. I recognize Sinclair as she walks to center stage, hand in hand with a tiny little girl who has toasted brown skin and a mop of golden curls, and my body tenses. I squint as I try to zoom in on the child's face, looking for a similarity between the two, but all it does is distort the already tiny features.

She can't possibly be Sin's. I would know. The world would know if she had a kid. But the proof is in the pudding, and her pudding is fraught with a secret baby? My heart beats harder.

If Sin has a kid… who by the looks of her golden skin and tightly curled golden hair is biracial, a perfect combination of Sin and Adam. Pressure builds in my chest as reality sinks its claws into my neck. Sin and Adam aren't just dating. They have the whole package, the career and a family. Suddenly it all makes sense. Their sudden agreement to be in one place after years of touring. They want stability. Someplace their baby could wake up in the same place for more than a couple of days at a time.

The little girl tries to pick up one of Adam's guitars and tries to lug it over her shoulder. Its weight is too much for her slight frame, both she and the guitar begin to topple over. One of the roadies grabs them both up and swings them around. The little girl throws her head back and squeals with laughter. I smile at her infectious reaction even through the pain radiating down my spine.

I turn my back on the happy picture, unable to stand another minute. Part of me wants to snatch Sin off the stage and demand she talk to me. The other part is so damn proud because she did it. Everything we dreamed about as kids—a successful career on her terms, a family. I always knew Sin would be a star in all things. She's a supernova. Just watching her with the little girl, I can tell she's a great mom even though in my mind her kids would have been mine not Adam's.

I rub a hand across my eyes and do my damnedest to force thoughts of Sin from my mind. Thinking about what should've been ours hurts. I'd lost the right to love Sin, touch her, and care for her… It hurts.

She was supposed to be mine. The picture in front of me was supposed to be ours. Now I get the pleasure of watching her from a distance, and that space is frigid when I know what it felt like to live under her heat.

I walk to the bar on feet that feel like lead weights.

"What can I get you, Mr. Johnson?" The bartender places a napkin in front of me.

"Whatever bourbon you have. Three fingers. Over ice."

I watch him pour the amber liquid over perfectly circular ice cubes. He slides the weighted glass across the counter, and I down the bourbon with an eagerness that lives in the alcoholic gene I probably inherited from my grandfather. The bartender doesn't ask if I want another drink. He simply picks up the bottle and refills the glass.

"Jacob Muthafuckin Johnson," Connor's voice booms across the room. I look up to see him and my father walking toward me. They are both wearing dark-colored suits, but where my father is in a starched white shirt and a crisp navy-blue suit, Connor is in all black, the color of his shirt blending seamlessly with the jacket. This is the first time I've seen my dad since Sin came back. Looking at my dad is like having a sneak peek at my future self. We're identical in most things. Physically I have his height, his build, and his hazel eyes. But I also got his drive, ambition, and his innate money sense.

"Son." My father extends his hand as I stand in greeting.

Clasping his warm palm in mine, I greet him, "Pop."

He holds my hand for a beat too long and stares in my eyes. I drop his hand and return to my vacated seat. He and Connor settle in chairs on either side of me.

My dad orders a scotch and Connor, true to form, orders a shot of tequila.

"Damn, we're finally here. I must say the view is lovely from the top. You ready for it?" Connor tosses back the shot and slams the glass down hard on the bar.

"Yeah, I'm ready," I say through the tightness in my chest, trying to mimic his excitement. This is exciting stuff. Really exciting. The woman that I haven't been able to cry, drink, or fuck out of my bloodstream in four years has completely moved on. She has a man and a kid and a career. As far as I can tell, she's checked all the major boxes, and she did it all on her own terms without me. Yep, super excited over here.

The skybox is starting to fill up. Jeanine walks in. Her short blond hair is slicked back from her face, and her modellike frame wrapped in a knee-length fitted black dress. Connor vacates the seat on my right and with three long strides he's in front of her. His wide shoulders blocking most of her face. I can't hear the conversation, but it's heated. He touches her elbow, and she jerks her arm out of his reach. What in the hell is that all about?

I turn back to my drink. Connor and Jeanine have had their own thing for a long time. They'll figure it out. From the corner of my eye, I see my dad take a sip from his glass and swivel the chair to face me. His eyes brush across my features, but I keep my gaze directed on the polished mahogany bar.

"When you were a kid you were always so serious. I'd find you sitting in my office, frowning over some perceived issue. Your shoulders hunched forward with the weight of your own thoughts."

"Is that right?" I say around the burn of liquor going down my throat.

"I don't know if it's right, but it's true. And you know what else is true?"

"Nah, Pop, what?"

An uncomfortable silence stretches between us for the next several minutes. He's staring a hole in the side of my head, gearing up to say something, and I don't want to hear it. I love my dad, but I don't need fatherly advice right now. My game plan for tonight is to get through the next couple of hours. No bullshit. No Drama.

I finally roll my eyes up to his.

"Even in elementary school you had a special ability to see the trees through the forest, and you'll get there again. Give yourself time. Think it through. Not everything is logic, Jacob. Trust your instincts. If they're pointing you in the direction of Sinclair James, then maybe that's where you need to be."

He leans forward, his elbows resting against the bar, and I'm... confused.

"Pop, Sin and I... We... There's nothing between us anymore."

A smirk so similar to my own pulls up his lips. "Son, I don't claim to be an expert on women. But if you can still pull that kind of passion out of a woman, I don't think it's nothing. The opposite of love is not hate. Love and hate take the same kind of time. The same devotion. It's not over until the indifference kicks in," he says, staring fixedly at the glass in front of him. His words are weighted down with knowledge and something else, I don't know, maybe pain or regret? "I might be an old man, but from everything I've seen, that girl is not indifferent to you."

"Are you telling me to go after her? I'm surprised. I'd think after you and Mom tried to pay her off. You wouldn't—"

"I never—" he says, cutting me off, a flash of anger narrowing his features. "Not everything is as it appears, son." He takes a sip of his drink, swallowing before he says, "I know the position we put you in all those years ago. I'm ashamed to say I even knew about the check, but you're a grown man. Your mother and I can't tell you what to do, or who to go after." My father places a heavy hand on my shoulder and lightly squeezes. "What I'm saying as a father is that I'm only as happy as my saddest child. And what I'm saying to you as man is that you're a good one, son. Stronger than me, smarter than my father, truly compassionate. But you haven't been happy since that girl walked out of your life. I want you to find your happy. If Sinclair James does that. Then I want her for you."

"Pop, it's not a good time for this conversation," I say, turning my face from his.

"Jacob... I wasn't trying to add to your burden."

"Then don't, Pop." I bring my eyes back to his silently begging him to drop it. "Enjoy the show and the amenities. I'm fine."

"But for how long? How long are you going to pretend like you're okay? Four years is a long time, and you're still buried under the guilt and shame and hurt. When the relationship ended, I was relieved. I thought, 'Now he'll step into his destiny,' but I was wrong. I realized how wrong when I saw that interview of the two of you. You were in deep when it first started ten years ago and now? I think you're up to your eyeballs. I can't imagine the obstacles. But you have to be that kid again, the one who sees the trees through the forest."

My dad gets to his feet and I stare at him stunned. Where did this man come from and what did he do with my father? My dad had never hated Sin with the vehemence of my mother, but he wasn't our biggest supporter either.

He checks his watch. "Your mother and sister should be here any minute." His eyes sweep the room before turning back to me.

"Jacob?"

"Yeah, Pop."

"If she's worth it. It'll be impossible for you to give up."

He leaves me sitting at the bar, a glass of bourbon clutched in my hands, and infinitesimal hope sparking back to life in my soul.

Chapter 12

Ten Years Ago

Jake

I'VE NEVER BEEN THIS FAR OFF THE BEATEN PATH. MY LAS VEGAS IS THE world of country clubs, private schools, and posh hotels. Needless to say, The Bunkhouse Saloon, located downtown on the corner of Eleventh and Fremont, isn't a place that's ever been on my radar. The tiny building looks like it was erected back when Fremont was a dusty wagon trail, and people walked around in cowboy hats and shit kickers.

After driving laps around the building for several minutes, I snag a parking spot conveniently located three blocks from the front door, but I'm not complaining. It's better than the lot with vehicles stacked one behind the other. No one is getting out of there until the very last person who enters it decides to leave. Not that I plan to go early, but I'm not sure what I'm walking into here.

I've heard Sin sing. Of course, I've heard her sing. Music permeates every nuance of her life. She belts out tunes in the shower and hums while doing homework. When we're lying in bed watching TV, it's typical for her foot to tap out a beat while her while her fingers are play air guitar. Loving something and being good at it are two completely different things. I'll support her either way. She could sound like Roseanne Barr singing the national anthem, and I'd still tell her she fucking rocked.

In the ten minutes it takes me to walk to the front of The Bunkhouse the line at the entry has tripled. The crowd waiting out front is an eclectic mix of barely there teens and hipsters, all buzzing with almost manic energy. People stand three and four across wearing a slightly different version of the same outfit—dirty sneakers, ripped up or worn jeans, and T-shirts. My fitted joggers, Henley shirt, and retro Jordans get a couple of wary looks, but they could give two squirts of piss about me. They are here for Sin.

There are a couple of hundred people here easy. I hear her name repeated through clusters of groups as I make my way to the front door.

A big guy wearing a black T-shirt with security written in white block letters across the chest glowers at me as I approach.

"There's a line."

"I see that, but Sin said I'd be on the list."

"You and everybody else here," he grunts, dismissing me as someone from inside the bar hands him a clipboard with a typed list of names. He turns back to the crowd and bumps into me. The wrinkles on his forehead sink into a deep V as he eyes me.

"Please check the list. My name is Jacob Johnson."

He doesn't move for a long moment. I'm not sure if he's going to kick my ass or refuse to let me in just to be a dick. But after a stare off, his eyes drop to the paper.

"You got ID?"

I quickly pull the wallet out of my pocket and let one side drop open to show my driver's license. His eyes bounce between the list and my picture a couple of times before he wraps a neon pink band around my wrist and steps to the side letting me in the door.

It takes a couple of seconds for my eyes to adjust to the dim light. There were only a couple of people sitting at the bar, but guys in black shirts seemed to be everywhere. One is fiddling with buttons at the soundboard. A couple guys were taping down extension cords and rotating speakers on the raised stage.

I immediately spot Sin center stage, arm draped over the mic stand, and her head hanging low looking at the ground. Her typically natural ringlets are braided into two long French braids that reach the middle of her back. She has on another crop top, this time it's a picture of the Rolling Stones lips with the tongue hanging out. The top stops just under her bra and low-slung tight jeans hug her waist, showing off her curves and exposing just enough skin to whet the appetite.

I walk to the edge of the stage and stop in front of her. Her eyes meet mine, a smile splits her face, and those fucking dimples that I love dent her cheeks.

"You made it."

"I told you I would."

A brief frown flits across her features like she's not used to men following through on their word, but it's quickly tucked away, replaced by a grin. Sin drops down to a squat in front of me, bringing us eye to eye.

"I'm happy you did."

"Yeah?"

"Absolutely." She leans forward placing both hands on my shoulders and a chaste kiss against my mouth. When she tries to pull back, I tighten my hold on the back of her neck and give her a kiss, a real one. A kiss with a sliding tongue and the sting of teeth. One that should only happen behind closed doors with naked bodies. One that has her sighing into my mouth and bunching the fabric of my shirt between her fingers.

God, this girl. I want her. In every way. In all the ways. She's invaded every corner of my life, and I can't get enough.

With a groan, Sin pulls her lips away from mine. Her fingers come up to rest on her kiss-swollen lips.

"What are you doing to me, Jake?"

"Whatever you give me a chance to do, Sin."

"Sin, you ready to do this?" A male voice asks from somewhere at the back of the stage. I can't see the guy from this angle, but some primitive part of my brain immediately bristles at the familiarity in his tone.

Sin brushes another kiss against my mouth before she pushes off my shoulders to stand.

"Yep. But come over here right quick. I want you to meet someone."

I size up the guy as he makes his way to the edge of the stage. He's the guy on the motorcycle from the other night. His tall frame is lean. Bright blue eyes dominate his face, and his shoulder-length blond hair floats as he walks. If we lived in California, I'd call him a surfer, but since we're in Las Vegas, I guess skater is more appropriate.

He stops next to Sin absently picking up the tip of her braid and twirling the end with his fingertips.

What in the fuck? Did he really just push up on my girl right in front of me? He is acting way too familiar.

"Adam, I've told you about Jake. And, Jake, this is Adam. Best friend, bandmate, lead guitarist, and songwriter extraordinaire."

He jumps down from the stage, landing with a thud in front of me, and extends his hand. I grip his hand a little tighter than necessary.

"Hi, bandmate Adam. I'm Jake, the boyfriend." I put base into the last word, letting him know he's trying to skate with a broken wheel. Adam's eyes roll harder than a moody teen.

"Yeah, okay."

"What?" I growl, fighting the urge to crush his hand, yank him in close, and dare him to repeat it.

"Adam, play nice," Sin chides. "Jake's a good guy. You'll see."

He winks at Sin before looking me up and down and definitely finding me lacking. "Not holding my breath over here."

Suffocate bitch. "Nice to meet you too."

Adam drops my hand and pulls himself back onto the stage. "Wrap it up, Sin. We gotta start in two." He gently yanks the tip of her braid as he walks past and picks up a guitar, settling the strap over his shoulder. He fingers a couple of chords and the sound reverberates loudly through the speakers.

"See you on the other side," Sin yells to me above the sound of Adam skillfully fingering the guitar.

Chapter 13

NOW

Sinclair

I WATCH JEANINE WALK INTO THE DRESSING ROOM BACKSTAGE. I HATE TO admit it, but she has been a godsend the last couple of weeks. The boys and I all agreed years ago that we didn't want to be beholden to a label because it comes with too many strings and not enough benefits. Record labels are notorious for exploiting new artists. As independent artists, we have creative control and freedom. And more importantly we receive all the profits.

Where we fall short is distribution. We have no problem competing with major labels where our production and writing is concerned. But we need help getting our music to the one market they still have cornered, radio. When we signed with WBB, the independent arm of Hartter Music Group. It gave us access to label resources without having to commit to a traditional contract.

In today's era of 360 deals, where record labels claim the actual artist as intellectual property and not just what they produce, we own our name, image, and all branding associated with the band. We pay the label a fixed amount to get our songs radio promotion and play.

The downside of being independent and not having the *big* contract is that we're independent. We have to hire our own people. Our last manager, Rich, was awesome but he left after the last leg of our tour. We thought we'd have time to replace him and fill some of the other holes on the administrative side of Sin City, since we'll be in one spot for an entire year, but then I messed up and slapped someone in a room full of people.

Once Jeanine and I came to an understanding, things have been good. I might hate to admit it, but I need her. It took a little time to embrace her straight-black-coffee style, but now that we're on the same page, it's been cool, almost surprisingly so.

"Good evening, Ms. James. Are you ready to schmooze with the who's who of Las Vegas?" Jeanine asks, her fingers flying across her phone screen. Her signature red glasses standout brightly against her pale skin.

"Yes," I answer with a roll of my eyes because we're doing this whether I want to or not. We've been prepping for over a week. I know all the names and most of the professions of the VIPs.

Jeanine finally looks up from her phone and blinks at me several times, almost confused. Her eyes sweep over my red leather pants and Swarovski crystal encrusted top that shows more than it covers but creates a rainbow effect when I walk that gives me Diana Ross post Supremes vibes. I finished the outfit off with sparkling red shoes, red lips, and pulled my natural curls apart, making my hair big and fabulous. Like I said, Diana Ross vibes.

"I see you took my advice and wore something other than a concert T-shirt. You clean up well, Ms. James."

"A girl can try," I say, checking my reflection in the mirror one more time as I fiddle with my top.

Jeanine's gaze flicks up to mine in the mirror. "You should do so more often. Right now, you look like the girl on the magazine covers. They will all buy what you're selling when you look like that."

"That's the goal, right?"

"Indeed, Ms. James. So, quick rundown. Mr. Johnson will be in attendance as will his family. Should I worry about any further assaults?" Her eyes drill mine in the mirror.

"Not unless provoked?" I press the tips of my fingers together, popping the knuckles on several digits.

Agitation at the idea of coming face-to-face with the two female

Johnsons makes me grind my molars. Danielle Johnson didn't like me on sight. I was the girl with the wrong last name and from the other side of the mountain that had no pedigree or money. All she saw was me trying to corrupt her son. He was the one corrupting me, by the way, but that's neither here nor there.

Jessica Johnson was always a sweetheart. I loved that kid. Like seriously loved her. She was sweet and funny and so much like Jake it was comical at times. But his mother? Jesus, that woman and I in the same room was a recipe for disaster. Truly and horribly awful.

"Hardy har har, Ms. James. All the major players in Las Vegas will be here tonight. We cannot afford any missteps. You're our prize, and we need you make them all covet you. Understand?"

"Jeanine, we've gone through this multiple times in the last couple of weeks. I get it." I can't stop the agitation from bleeding into my voice.

"Aren't rock stars notorious partiers? Shouldn't this be your element?" Jeanine asks, noticing my tension.

"Your sarcasm is like a balm. Right here." I tap my hand over my heart. This is all part of the gig. I'm dressed. I'm going. When we get there, I plaster on the big smile, but in my dressing room, I'll pass on the false niceties.

She types several keys on her phone, but a slight smile drifts across her face.

Adam walks in holding his little sister's hand. She's one of the main reasons we decided to move back to Vegas. Adam and I grew up in the system. There was nothing nice about it. It chews kids up and spits them out.

So, when Adam got the call about six months back that his mom had relapsed and OD'd, leaving a three-year-old sister he didn't know that he had, he did what he always does. He stepped in to fix it. He's been jumping through hoops and rearranging his life to accommodate her. From what Adam has said, this is the third time in three years Child Protective Services had his sister in state custody, but they're dragging their feet and making it difficult for him to formally take custody of her.

Tori twists away from Adam and barrels across the room toward me, colliding with my legs.

"Shin!" she yells.

"Hey there, puddin' pop." She crawls up my legs until she's nestled in my arms under my chin.

Adam looks relieved to have a reprieve. I think stepping into this whole thing with his sister has been harder than he thought it'd be. When you grow up the way we did, family is a makeshift group of people connected by time and circumstance, not an obligation tied to blood and lineage. Don't get me wrong, he cares for his sister, but it's just not the cakewalk he thought it would be.

"Addy says we're going to a party tonight."

"I think it's a grown-up party. Little girls named Tori would be bored." A deep frown moves across her face, and her little shoulders scrunch up around her ears before dropping back down.

"Why come?" she wails in a high-pitched scream and I panic. I look at Adam over her head, and he shrugs like me trying to soothe a frazzled baby is just another Saturday night. I jostle Tori in my arms, making a shushing noise as I wipe tears off her cheeks.

"This is the sweetest thing ever," Jeanine quips, her dryness and sarcasm amped up for full effect. "But you were expected upstairs over twenty minutes ago."

I set Tori on her feet and she slips her hand in mine, pulling me over to Adam. "What's wrong, pretty girl?" He bends down to her level.

"Tori, got a little upset when I told her tonight's party isn't really appropriate for a three-year-old."

Adam looks up at me before looking back at Tori. "We talked about this earlier. I only have you on weekends. I'm not going to miss a second of that time on something as silly as a grown-up party."

"A grown-up party that started several minutes ago." Jeanine throws in walking toward the door.

We follow Jeanine through the tunnels that run backstage to an elevator. We are surrounded by four security guards, two out front and two pulling up the rear. Jeanine holds up a keycard to open the secure door, and we all enter the car. She presses the buttons for the Skybox Lounge and rattles off a list of attendees, the dos and don'ts of a VIP event, and all the other things she's repeated multiple times over the last couple of weeks. I nod, half listening, and stare at the red numbers in the display box, my thoughts racing.

Dan is already there, and Miles is likely wherever his wife is now. I love Kisha, I really do, but girlfriend does not wear pregnancy well. With Adam out of commission and Jake and his family all in attendance I have a growing sense of unease. It's churning under my skin like the waves of the ocean before a storm.

The doors slide open and the party is in full swing. Jeanine exits the elevator first. The loud music immediately assaults my ears. Bodies are swaying, lights are flashing, and ceiling to floor windows provide a breathtaking view of the Strip. Seating clusters of white sofas dot the room. It's way more nightclub than cocktail party. Not sure why I expected a much tamer affair. This is Vegas. It's how people here get down.

Tori drops my hand and cringes back into the elevator. Her sweet little face disappears behind Adam. He turns to me, wary. He wants to get in there, join the party, support the band. But he can't this time, and it's eating him up.

I step back into the elevator. The doors close and I see Tory's little face peek up at me from behind Adam.

"Addy, can we please go home?" she whispers, her little voice barely audible above the party on the other side of the door. Adam runs a hand down her tight curls and nods, although she can't see him.

"I got this," I say with a reassuring smile. "Take her home. This is no place for a kid anyway and it's getting late."

"Sin…" He rakes his hands through his hair, tugging at the ends. "I'd never leave you hanging if I didn't—" He cuts himself off again.

"I'm a big girl, Adam, I swear. I got this. Trust me?"

"Always," he answers immediately without pretense.

"Take this little one home, and I'll swing by tomorrow. We'll take her swimming or something. Kay?"

"You sure, Sin?"

"Absolutely. Get out of here." I press the button on the elevator to open the door and walk out. I turn to look back at Adam and Tori and lift my hand in a silent good-bye. The doors close and Jeanine moves to my side. For the first time in our brief acquaintance, she doesn't have her phone out, or her attention divided doing a million different things.

"I assume Mr. Beckham opted to retire?" Her gaze shifts around the room before returning to mine.

"Yes, this isn't the best scene for Tori."

"Indeed, Ms. James. Indeed. Follow me."

I follow behind her as she navigates the room, stopping here and there to speak to this businessperson or that city council member. I lose track of the names and titles as she parades me around the room like a show pony.

We round another tallboy table, she pats a woman on her back to get her attention, and I come face-to-face with the Jessica Johnson. Jake's little sister isn't the gangly high school student I remember.

She's still tall but there is nothing awkward about the young woman in front of me. Her frizzy curls have been smoothed straight, and her smile is metal free. After all this time she still exudes light and positive vibes. I'm genuinely happy to see her again.

"Miss Johnson, may I introduce you to—" Jessica pushes past in her excitement.

"Oh my God, Sin! Jake told me you'd be here." She grabs me in a tight hug and then pulls back, looking me over with hazel eyes identical to her brothers. "You look gorgeous. But you've always been gorgeous even before you were rich and dressed by designers."

"I'm not rich, Jessica." She probably has more money in her trust fund than I have after working my ass off for the last ten years.

She rolls her eyes at me, shaking her head. "Jake is going to die when he sees you dressed like this." At her words I feels a spark of something. It's not interest, but a purely female desire to be coveted by the man that didn't want me. "Why has it been years since I've seen you? Just because you broke up with Jake didn't mean you had to break up with me," she says, looking genuinely wounded.

"I-I," I stammer a few syllables before she moves onto the next thing. Jessica is a whirlwind. She tends to suck in everything and everyone around her.

"He told me how bad it was. I totally see why you needed a clean break, but it's been so long and you two were so good together. Did you have to slap him the other day?"

There you have it. I might have been the big sister she always wanted but I don't hold a candle to her actual brother. Jake had her loyalty at birth. No way to compete with that.

"Once again we all have the unfortunate pleasure of dealing with your tactless and uncouth actions impacting our family." That sweetly accented voice does little to cover the venom of the words. My spine stiffens as Danielle Johnson wedges her small frame between Jess and me. I don't think she's aged a day in four years. She's beautifully cultured and well-spoken, but as beautiful as she is on the outside, she's as ugly on the inside. You know how they say that the devil wears the most beautiful faces? Enter Danielle Johnson.

"Ms. Johnson, so good to see you again," I say, forcing the words past the knot in my throat.

"I'm a married woman, girl. It's Mrs. Johnson. I would think in four years you'd have learned the basic rules of polite society, but then again, you make your living writhing on a stage and moaning about your vast sexual history."

"Momma, don't do this. Not here," Jessica pleads.

The older female Johnson pats Jessica's arm in a there, there motion as she flashes a cruel smile to me. She knows every venomous word hit its mark, and no matter how many accolades I receive or how much success I attain, to her I will always be that girl from Nowhere, Nevada, the fatherless daughter of a whore. The one who corrupted her son. A girl who showed him a life outside family obligation. I open my mouth but close it just as quickly.

What is there to say or defend? She's right. I am most of those things. With one major exception. I never corrupted Jake. He was the one that taught me how to down a shot and smoke weed. With him was the only time I've ever thought about sex outside of four walls or used something other than my body to get off.

"Actually, *Ms.* can be used for either married or single women," I say through the fake smile I have plastered on my face. "As nice as this little reunion has been, I have to—"

Her cold hand clamps around my upper arm, holding tight enough to break capillaries. From the corner of my eye I see Jessica stand on tiptoe. Her head whipping back and forth looking for someone to help corral her crazy mother. Danielle Johnson leans in close to my face. Her eyes narrowed to slits. "You listen to me, girl, and you listen good. Stay away from my son. You drew him in ten years ago because you were different. But how long did it take before that freshly minted penny no longer shined? One year? Two? Do you really think he only stepped out once? A woman like you doesn't have what it takes to keep a man like him." She lets my arm go, but she cups both of my cheeks kissing first one and then the other. In my ear she all but coos, "Stay in your lane, *Ms.* James, and stop reaching above your station."

She pulls back to look me directly in the eyes before turning to Jessica.

Let it go, Sin. Do not let the wicked bitch of the west make you feel two feet tall and dumber than a box of rocks. It's not your fault that she hates you. Hate is irrational.

I pull in a shaky breath and sink my teeth in the corner of my lip. I gotta get away from them. I take a slight step back, but she walks away before I can, all poised grace and sophistication.

"Let it go. Please. You know how Momma can be," Jessica says, her russet skin flushed with embarrassed heat. She hugs me again, her embrace saying, *"I'm sorry but she's my mom."* But the apology coming from her mouth says, *"I missed you. I know Jake has missed you. We've all missed you, girl. You are my sister from another mister."*

Her arms fall away, and she loops on of hers through mine. "I'm still only twenty, but Jake lets me drink when I'm 'in a controlled environment.' " She gives me air quotes and drops her voice to imitate Jake's.

She half pulls, half drags me to the bar. "Can we have the seven deadly sins?" she yells at the bartender. "You get it, right? Your name is Sin, the band is Sin City playing in Sin City, and the signature drinks for the event are called the seven deadly sins. Clever, right?"

"Yeah, no." It is but I'll be damned if I give Jake credit for anything. He probably didn't come up with the idea, but whoever did works for him, so they are guilty by default. Yep, still a little salty over here.

"Come on, Sin. Don't be like that. Loosen up. K?"

The bartender sets a colorful array of shots down in front of us on a small tray. Jessica hands me a shot glass filled with red liquid.

"To the return of the prodigal son, or I guess in this case, daughter." She taps our glasses, and we both toss back the cinnamon-flavored drink. I push the encounter with Danielle Johnson to the back of my mind as we down shot after shot. Jake taught me well. Jessica orders another tray, and I glance down at our already empty shot glasses giddy and tipsy. I might actually be pushing the line of drunk.

After splitting another tray of shots, we make our way to the dance floor. My hands go up in the air. My body automatically synching with the hard-hitting drum beats and my eyes slide shut of their own accord. I miss this. The freedom to be in a crowd of people. Nameless. Faceless. Just another body carried by the beat. It feels good. No, good is not the right word. It's ordinary, typical even, and I love it.

The people on the dance floor are here to celebrate the Hotel landing a residency with Sin City. They either don't know who I am, or they don't care. No one has approached me to ask for an autograph or selfie. I haven't had that in so long. One song blends into the other, and tension I wasn't aware I was carrying eases off my shoulders with each passing tune.

Jess and I are in our own little bubble, oblivious to the people around us. Watching Jess catapults me back in time to the ten-year-old girl that used to try to teach me the latest dance moves in my tiny kitchen. I've missed her. By the time I broke up with Jake, Jess was sixteen and I assumed, maybe wrongly, that she'd be one of the people firmly on his side of the line.

The alcohol pumps through my bloodstream, pushing me closer to drunk than buzzed. When I feel a big body sidle against my back, I relax into it. I don't have to turn around to know it's Jake. I could go blind and drunk but every fiber in my being would recognize this man, his presence, his touch.

His tentative hands slide over my hips and the rational part of my brain bristles at the idea of him being bold enough to touch me after our sordid past and all the years and hurt feelings. The other part of my brain, the one that can't forget the pressure of his mouth on mine and still imagines, even now, we could live happily ever after... that part moves my body into his, closing the small distance he's keeping between us. I sigh with relief when his hands slip around my waist and his hips start a slow grind.

Jessica is still in front of me, and the smirk on her face tells me this whole thing is a setup, and I totally took the bait. Hook, line, and sinker. She drifts away, carried by a sea of people, but I can't bring myself break contact. I force my lids up. My lazy gaze sweeps the dance floor. Not one eye is turned in our direction. No cell phones collecting more damming evidence. On tonight's guest list we have the upper echelon of Las Vegas who have their own questionable proclivities. Being felt up by my ex on the dance floor doesn't seem to be garnering attention—good, bad, or indifferent.

Jake feels good, too good, like a warm blanket on a cold night.

All I want to do is snuggle in and carve out a place next to him that's perfect and mine. I want to stay in that spot, make myself comfortable, and get tangled up in him. In his heat.

I can't hear the music anymore. My brain is only capable of feeling the even rise and fall of his breathing, the thump of his heart against my back, and the motion of our bodies moving to the beat. We are like melody and rhythm, innately different, but both key components to the perfect song.

Jake moves the hair off my neck to drop a kiss on the sensitive skin between my neck and shoulder. It's a fleeting touch, a reverent caress that hits me deeper that it should, and I shudder, my eyes drifting closed. Just for a second, I let myself drown in a world colored by memories where this is where I belong. Where his tentative hands roving my body is exactly as it should be. A place where the rosy hue of nostalgia shows him as he was, the lover that seduced my mind and enticed my body. He's the man who ravaged my soul.

We never had a problem with this part. Me wanting him, the physical aspects of him like his reddish-brown skin, the magic hands that always find the right spot, and the seductive flavor of his intense kisses. It was all the emotional baggage we couldn't seem to unpack. There is so much between us, all these little hurts that led to a big rift we just can't cross.

How do I reconcile him touching my body like I'm the most valued treasure with the man who slept with another woman in our bed or the man who was bitterly jealous of my best friend?

It's been so long since anyone has touched me in exploration and growing passion. And it's Jake. I lean into the solid mass of his body, rocking my hips to his rhythm. Maybe the music has hypnotized me because with a quick flip of his wrist Jake turns me around before I can make any sense out of what happened. We're face-to-face and for the barest second, I forget to hate him. He pulls me in close until every curve of my body melds with his. He slides his hands down my ribs, toying with the waistband of my pants before cupping both globes of my ass. I can't bring myself to move away. He feels like everything I've wanted and nothing I need.

Instead of calling it a night, going back to the villa and practicing some self-love, I melt against him.

Chapter 14

NOW
Jake

I PRESS MY FOREHEAD AGAINST SIN'S AND CUP HER FACE IN MY HANDS. THE place in the center of my soul that snapped and burned without her, that grieved her loss, begged for her forgiveness, and longed for her return finally starts to calm.

The beat slows down, and she raises her arms, sliding her hands around my neck. After four years of trying to remember the exact texture of her skin, I remember how soft and warm she is. My body comes to life with a vivid confirmation that, yes, Sin is as good… no, better than any memory. My erection grows against her stomach and to the surprise of both of us, I'm sure. She snuggles in closer.

"Sin," I murmur, my lips brushing her ear. I don't know if I say her name as a question or a statement. All I know with any conviction is I want her in my bed. Now. A shiver rolls down her spine, almost like my desires just broadcast on a frequency only she can pick up.

"Jake?" She glances up at me. Instead of anger, a different type of heat lines her voice. I lean back to look into her eyes, and I see a hedonistic mix of skepticism, apprehension, and excitement. Sin is excited—for me. We still have all our underlying issues, but for right now… *Sin is here.*

I let that thought settle into my mind. She not a fevered dream or a ghost I conjured from my past. For now, she's mine. An opportunity I cannot squander.

"Mr. Johnson, Ms. James, it is in the best interest of everyone here for the two of you to give each other a little breathing room." I hear Jeanine's stiff English accent. Fuck me! Since Sin came back, it feels like the universe is conspiring to keep us apart.

First it was the slap. Then the bullshit interviews. Tonight, I had the hard realization that although my life progressed in some areas without her for the most part, I've stagnated while she's… well, she's her. What do I have to offer to the woman that has the world at her fingertips besides my fucked up self?

My first curveball of the night was the little scene I witnessed on the stage. The second was my mother and her displeasure with the situation. I don't know what my mother said to Sin, but the tension between them was palpable from across the room, and that was before she grabbed Sin's arm or Jessica's eyes found mine silently begging for help. I refuse to let the third ball leave the pitcher's hand.

Jeanine clears her throat, but I don't look away from Sin. I can't. If I blink, if I so much as breathe the wrong way, I'll lose her and I can't do it again. Not when she's open to me for the first time in four years. Maybe even longer than that. I grab her hand and lace our fingers.

"All I'm asking for is a little faith, Sin. Just a little." I repeat the words I said ten years ago the first day we met. Her eyes flutter and her fingers loosen around mine and my heart plummets. It fucking drops into my shoes. She going to say no. I don't think I can take another no from those lips. Not when I'm this close.

"In what?" she asks, a challenge in her eyes. The adrenaline rush I felt at her impending no spikes higher when her husky voice gives me what I'm reading as a yes.

"Me."

I don't wait for a reply as I clasp her hand tightly in mine and push through the crowd. Away from Jeanine and my sister. Away from all the very real reasons why we don't make sense. I move forward with determination toward a hidden door that leads to an enclosed patio. The area was kept closed tonight because it doesn't have the space to accommodate even a third of the people we expected and sits adjacent to the lounge making it invisible to the people inside once the door is closed.

But at sixty-four floors up, surrounded by hedges, it's perfect.

I press my code into a small keypad on the wall. A glass panel opens with a whoosh. I pull Sin through the entrance just before the door slides back into place, the lock reengaging.

Away from the hard-base rhythms and curious eyes, the air around us is hot from the earlier summer heat and abnormally quiet. The stars are blotted out of the sky by the bright neon that makes up the Las Vegas Strip, but the moon is full and bright, washing her dark skin with a blue hue.

Sin faces the closed door. She has her hands on her hips and her head hanging down, exposing the back of her neck.

What thoughts are going through that pretty head of yours? Acceptance? Resignation? Some fucked up middle of the road indecision?

Her shoulders rise and fall as she breathes deep. Sin is knee-deep in a battle between her heart and her head.

I recognize it because I fought the same campaign the night she slapped me. She's trying to convince herself she shouldn't be here, in this space and moment with me, while her heartstrings remain entangled with mine.

Do something. I have to say something before she leaves or tells me to go to hell.

"Don't talk," I say, closing the distance between us, bringing her back flush with my chest. My arm wraps around her body, stopping just under her breasts. I slowly pull down the top and expose her skin. Her body jerks at the action and I smile. Sin doesn't ask me to stop. In fact, she makes a barely perceptible move that erases any space between our bodies and nestles my dick between the globes of her perfect ass.

"Just listen." I drop wet kisses down the back of her neck, and she stifles a moan. "Listen to your body, Sin," I whisper against her ear, cupping her breasts, tweaking the nipples into a stiff peak.

A ruined sigh falls from her lips as her body arches, pushing farther into my hands. Her head falls onto my shoulder and exposes the slender column of her throat.

"Do you know how long I've waited for this?" I say, resting my forehead on the back of her head as I place my hand between her breasts and bring it up her neck to wrap loosely around her throat.

"To touch you." I run fingertips down the skin of her tight abdomen. "Kiss you." My lips ghost up the curve of her jaw toward her ear. "Taste you," I murmur as my mouth brushes the edge of her mouth.

Sin twists in my arms and we both pause, staccato breaths forcing our chests to touch. I lean forward, drawn to her by something innately us, a chemistry that has been there since the beginning. We kiss again, the touch of our lips is fleeting like the flutter of a butterfly wing. The second time our mouths come together, it's in a frantic burst of desperation.

I lick my way into her mouth using my larger body to press hers against the wall and the kiss explodes. Our tongues twist and our teeth nip and our bodies grind. It's damn near euphoric. Lust pumps through my veins but it's more than that. It's this primitive impulse to reclaim her. Reclaim what is mine.

She pulls her head back and we're both panting, fighting to pull oxygen into our lungs.

"I get it. I do," I say against her lips. My tongue flicks against her full bottom lip. "I know you don't want to be here. That's that hardest part of this. The fact I know it's my fault. That my girl, the only girl I've ever wanted"—I run my nose along the length of hers and take a deep inhale of Sin spicy skin—"doesn't want me anymore."

Those midnight orbs study my face. The shadows obscure half her features, but I see enough of her expression to know she thinking too hard. Whatever this is between us isn't difficult. It just is. We just need to be.

"Jake, it's not a matter of 'don't want.' It's that I can't let go of—" She breaths out on a frustrated hiss. I don't let her finish that sentence.

I don't need to rehash the don't wants or the can'ts. I cut off her words with my lips, and she lets out a wrecked moan, grinding her tender nipples against my chest, and wrapping her hands around my neck.

"I know why you can't, Sin. Just for tonight let me remind you why you can."

I slide both hands into her hair and tilt her head so I'm looking directly into her eyes. I close the distance between our lips and devour her. She tastes like cinnamon and Sin, and she feels like… fuck, she still feels like mine.

Chapter 15

NOW

Sinclair

"TELL ME WHAT YOU WANT, SIN," JAKE MURMURS AGAINST MY lips as he draws me in. His tongue dipping between my parted lips.

Him.

Stripped down to its purest form I want Jacob Johnson.

It makes zero sense, like none at all. I can't even explain it to myself. How can I want a man like him? One who hurt me the way he did? No one held a gun to his head and forced him to smash another woman in our bed, no less. He made a conscious choice, a decision that reconstructed our future. It happened four years ago, but I still remember every stinging detail. Down to the color of the pink panties I was wearing when I crawled down the hall. Talk about a walk of shame. I was hurt and just so humiliated.

But seeing him again sparked a sense of recognition in my soul. And that was before he kissed me. I can't pretend like I don't feel the karmic connection because it's there. It's always been there, dragging us together from the first moment we met.

Right now, I don't know if it's the liquor swimming in my head or all the things uniquely Jacob Johnson. But I want to explore it. See if the memory holds up to the man, the reality.

I run openmouthed kisses down his jaw and his gruff moan stirs a passion I'd thought was buried a long time ago. It ruptures to the surface, pushing through every barrier I've erected against him.

All it took was a slow grind and one kiss. One sensual twist of his tongue against mine and I was done for. I close my eyes and let out a shaky breath.

Jake's mouth brushes over my mine. His probing tongue, tempting me to open up, to let him come in to play. I twist away from his lips, but he fists my hair, maintaining our position. His lips ghost over my cheek.

"Sin," he whispers with a possessiveness so raw my heart twists. "I'm not asking you to give me forever. Just give me now."

"Jake this only ends one way."

"And how's that?"

"With us—" *Back where we started. Raw and vulnerable. Lost in fantasy.* Until reality intrudes. I drop my chin, but his hands move around the back of my neck stopping the motion. Jake dips his head, his heated gaze unyielding.

"Together," he says in a voice that sounds like steel encased in the smoothest satin. "The way it was always supposed to be. Give me right now, baby. And the rest?" He lowers his head. "It'll take care of itself."

"Yes." The word rips out of me. Harsh and breathless, but he hears it, and it's like setting a spark to a flame. His lips slam down hard on mine, and he consumes me. His intensity casts a spell that pulls me down the rabbit hole.

"Fuuuuuck. I hope you're ready," he growls in my ear.

Oh, I'm ready. This night has been years in the making. Its possibility has lived under my skin and at the edges of my nonconscious thoughts since the day I left. I flatten my palm against the hard plain of his chest, letting my nails scrape against the indents of his abs and obliques. I palm his length through his slacks and jack him slowly.

One more time. That's all this is.

One. Last. Time. To let our bodies communicate the words we can't speak, to get the closure we didn't have four years ago, to finally work him out of my system.

Jake sucks in a sharp breath. His words are unintelligible, lost somewhere between frenzied kisses and thrusting the hard length of his erection into my tight grip.

He unsnaps the button on my pants and pushes the leather over my hips exposing already flushed skin to the hot desert air. His fingertips skim the newly exposed flesh, leaving a trail of goosebumps in their wake as he drops to his knees.

Jake wrenches off the leather pants in a swift move. My shoes come off with the pants and clatter to the ground. I'm so wet that the desert heat feels cool against my skin. "Jesus Christ, babe, you're seriously trying to kill me." He kisses my hipbone. "Since when do you run around without panties?" His hands curve around my ass as he eases my legs farther apart moving his thumb smoothly down my wet slit coating the swollen lips with my arousal.

My hips buck under his touch and a knowing smile pulls at his mouth. Soft lips graze the sensitive patch of skin right below my belly button and the edges of my vision blur, narrowing down to this man, and his mouth, and his touch. God, his mouth. I really, really missed his mouth.

I get no warning before Jake dives in, kissing my pussy with the same ferocity he kissed my mouth. It's hot and filthy and so fucking good. I scratch my fingers into the wall, searching for anything to anchor me because I'm spiraling down, down a long, dark hole of lust. I'm okay if I never see the light of day again.

He breaks the suction, and I look down the length of my body to find his eyes. "That's right, baby," he says right before he laps my slit in one long stroke "Give me a face full of that gushy. Ride my fucking tongue, Sin. Take what you want."

The vibration of his voice makes my clit throb. Sweat trickles down my back and I open my legs farther, giving him even better access. But it's not enough and I'm close. So close. If I could just move my left leg just a little more…

Did I say that out loud? Jake immediately reacts to my plea. He runs a hand down the length of my leg, wrapping it around my ankle. He lifts my leg over his shoulder, exposing every inch me in the most delicious way. Two fingers drag through my depilated folds, teasing the already sensitive skin.

I wrap my hands around the back of his head and guide him exactly where I need him, my hips moving of their own accord as I ride his mouth. I'm whimpering for him to give me more. Give me everything. All other thoughts are drowned out by the low buzz of lust.

Jake makes succulent wet sounds, groaning into my folds, gorging himself on me. He smacks my ass hard sending a shockwave straight to my clit, and then two thick fingers plunge inside me—the perfect counterpart to his soft mouth, and I pitch forward coming on a keening wail that sears my lungs.

I sag against the wall as Jake kisses his way back up my body. I'm too far gone to worry about what we're doing or what this means. Tomorrow. I'll think tomorrow. When my brain synapses start firing again and things like consequences matter.

But right now, the whisper of his zipper and the crinkle of a foil wrapper fills me with anticipation. When he slips his thick dick between the globes of my ass I go up on tip toe and arch my back helping him slip into the mess he left between my legs.

His hips pump just a little, easing the tip of his erection inside me, and we both groan. Jake shifts closer, pulling first one leg and then the other around his waist. The rough stubble on his cheeks sanding my own. "So fucking tight." He growls close to my ear. His voice a boom in the silence.

His hips retreat only to move forward again, pushing his shaft a little deeper inside. "I love you so much," he pants against my cheek and I melt. Even after all this time, those words from him make me feel special. Chosen. But no. No. No. No. He doesn't love me. He can't. This… what we're doing is closure. One. More. Time.

His tortured statement is enough to snap me back to the fucked up reality that is us. He brings his face to mine, softly kissing my lips.

I smell traces of my scent on his skin, and I taste us when his tongue delves deeper into my mouth. Jake's hips thrust again, this time seating him fully inside me. A look of sheer bliss moves across his face.

"I love you," he says over and over like a mantra as he finds his rhythm.

Where his body made me hot, his words chill me to my core. The last time he said those words to me, I believed them to the very essence of my being, and they turned out to be utter shit.

"Jake… stop," I pant, trying to knock his body off me with a shoulder. His movements still immediately.

"What's wrong? You okay, baby?" His voice is raw. Every word strains past his vocal chords.

"We never should've…" I start, pointing at my mostly naked body. "This can't happen. Off." I move away from his warmth, and I wince a little as he slides out of me. He staggers back looking confused as he stuffs his still wet dick back in his pants. His shirt is rumpled, and his chest is visibly moving up and down with hard breaths.

"Where are my pants?" I look around. My eyes sweep the small balcony locating the ball that was my pants close to the railing. With as much dignity as I can muster, I walk to my pants, shake out my shoes and wiggle to pull them up over my hips. Jake runs a hand over the back of his head, the muscles of his jaw ticking as he grinds his teeth into powder.

It takes me prolonged awkward minutes to pull up the top and grab each shoe and put them on under his heated stare, but once I've pulled my shit together, at least as much as I can in the face of blue balls and throbbing vaginas, I move across the balcony to the door. The closer I get to Jake, the harder my heart beats. I see a million questions in his eyes.

"Sin, just let me—"

"I don't need an explanation, Jake. For just a second, I was able to forget. It won't happen again." I'm not sure who I'm trying to convince more, him or me.

"All right, Sinclair," he says before he punches the code into the keypad and opens the door.

Chapter 16

Sinclair

I'M LATE TO MY MEETING WITH ADAM AND TORI. PART OF ME DREADS facing my best friend and knowing he'll smell bullshit as soon as I walk through the door. I'm a terrible liar, and he's been hyperaware of all the Jake related shenanigans.

I hate having secrets from Adam. He's my person. The one that I'd normally talk to about being naked on a balcony and staring in my own personal porno. Hands down the hottest night of my life.

In the light of day, I can admit maybe not my brightest idea. It should have never happened. I should have never let things get that far. Thank God no one walked out on that balcony and saw us. I can picture the tabloids now—Sinclair James Gets Pussy Demolished by Ex.

My mind wanders to Jake, and a phantom touch moves down my body. It's like I can still feel the strength in his hands as he gripped my ass and the roll of his hips as he fucked me against the wall. If my skin tone was a little lighter, I'm sure I'd be red with the flush spreading across my skin right now. I slow my approach, giving myself time to cool down before I ring the doorbell.

I run an anxious had over my hair and clothes. Almost like last night's sex left a noticeable stain or, at the very least, a hickey I didn't see in the mirror before I got here.

Adam opens the door before I press the button, his bare feet peeking from under low hanging sweatpants and an old Ramones shirt clinging to his chest and biceps. He's put his hair is up in a messy bun on top of his head in a way that accentuates all the sharp angles of his face.

"Sorry," I rush out before he can say anything. Adam leans against the door frame as his eyes rove over my face and reading me for fucking filth. He knows. He so totally knows. "I lost track of time. But…" I pull my writing notebook out of a messenger bag and wave it in his face. "I've been writing all morning. I think some of it can work."

"I was about to put the carne asada on the grill and make a PB&J for Tori," Adam says, walking down the hall toward the kitchen. "We'll eat first, and then we'll hammer out the music, yeah?"

"Absolutely."

I follow Adam toward the back of his three-bedroom house to the great room. His kitchen and den share one area. Tori is on her tummy on a shaggy rug in front of the TV. When she sees me, she hops up and runs over, wrapping her arms around my legs. Adam and Tori are twenty-eight years apart, but I still see him when I look at her. They share similar features, but where Adam is lean angles and fair skin, Tori is round cheeks, and her mixed heritage is evident in her golden cat eyes, toasted brown skin and golden curls. But when I look at her little face, I see Adam's deep-set eyes, straight nose, and full lips.

"Sin, Addy said that after we eat, we might go swimming. You'll swim too, right?"

"We'll see, sugar. I didn't bring a suit this time, but I might put my feet in the water and splash you." I squeeze her tight and can't help but smile as she squeals with happiness. She runs back to her spot in front of the TV, and I settle on the bar stool.

"So, you got anything for me to eat? You know I prefer my meals to be faceless and parentless."

"Yes, Sin, I'm pretty certain that after fifteen years together I'm well versed in what you do and don't eat. Carne asada for me and cheese quesadilla for you." He rolls his eyes with feigned annoyance.

We sit in a comfortable silence while he takes the meat out of the marinade and sprinkles it with seasonings "So… you gonna tell me about the song?" He wipes juice off his thumb while scrutinizing me.

I give him a blank stare. I'd been expecting him to say... I don't know what I have been expecting him to say, but that was not it. Where is the big brotheresque inquisition? Maybe the last eight hours was more than enough time to erase all traces of Jake away? Or perhaps for the first time in forever, his mind is on other shit like his sister and the pending court hearing for custody. He doesn't have time to worry about me and the hook up that should have never happened. I look over at Tori and smile. When I turn back to Adam, he raises his brows in question.

He looks me over more speculatively, like he's taking note. His gaze says he knows, but he's leaving it up to me to tell him. I drop his gaze and focus on my notebook instead.

Adam is the least judgmental person I know. He's the very essence of live and let live, but when it comes to me, to family, he can be a pit bull. Jake has always brought out every protective instinct Adam has. He doesn't need my very stupid confusion about a man the entire world knows is no good for me.

Adam leans forward and snatches the notebook on the bar. He opens the book, flipping to the last page, and quickly reads the lyrics. His gaze flips up to mine a couple of times before he says, "Good on you, Sin. This song is good. Rough around the edges but I like it. You got a melody yet?"

I cringe in my seat once again feeling the heat of an invisible blush working its way over my skin. His mention of the melody immediately takes me back on that balcony with Jake kneeling in front of me, his mouth working me over, tongue sliding over wet skin, thick fingers drawing out an orgasm. What I have in mind is a melody inspired sex, straight without a chaser, raunchy, up against the wall, skin slapping sex.

I clear my throat. "Yeah, I have a little something. Nothing set in stone though."

Once again catching my eye, he utters, "You want to tell me where the sudden inspiration struck?"

"No." I grab the notebook out of his hands feeling like a petulant child trying to lie to a parent.

"No worries. You thinking hard or soft?" His eyes bore into mine with way more understanding than I deserve. "Definitely hard. Maybe a little bluesy." He shakes his head. "Go get the guitars out of the studio. I'm thinking Jag and Hidalgo for this one. They're versatile enough we can play with some different sounds until we get it right. Ima throw this meat on the grill." He grabs the tray of meat and heads out the sliding glass door, but he stops just before the threshold.

"Sin?"

"Yeah."

"Whoever he is—" His eyes meet mine over his shoulder, and I know he knows. I don't know if he's letting me hold on to my dignity or work through this thing with Jake on my own, but my little act didn't fool him. "Just be careful."

I don't tell Adam that it was only one time or assure him that I won't let Jake and his asshole tendencies pull me so far into the abyss it'll take me another four years to find light again.

Embarrassment twists in my gut. I can't believe I let him do it again. Even knowing what he's capable of, I couldn't help but get sucked back in. What is that old saying? Fool me once and it's a warning, fool me twice and it's a lesson. I'm trying to learn, really I am, but that man is like catnip to me. More than anything I'm letting his presence erect something between me and the only family that I have.

Adam's position is clear. As one of the people who watched me fall apart last time and ultimately helped put all those pieces back together, he knows firsthand the damage Jake caused and I do too, which makes me an even bigger fool.

I jump off the barstool and head to the small studio he had built on the other side of the house. I need to do something to get my mind off my blast from a very dark past. His studio is neat like everything else in his life. I don't even have to look for his guitars. They are on the side of the room that has a mural of Clapton playing. Jag, his red and white Fender, is in a floor holder while his favorite, Hidalgo, a custom painted and crafted Fender, is in a case. The only time he comes out is if he's actually in use.

I carry both to the great room. Adam is back in the kitchen frying tortillas to make taco shells for dinner.

"We'll eat first and then dig in, yeah?" He throws me a look over his shoulder.

"Yeah."

This family is real. Adam and I making music while scarfing down tacos and quesadillas makes sense. Jake and I on a balcony with hundreds of people only a couple of footsteps away was insanity. I can't do it again. Despite how much I liked it or how good it felt, Jake may not be a bad guy anymore, but he most certainly is not my guy.

He caught me at the right place and time. *Tell the truth, Sin. You wanted him just as badly as he wanted you.* It doesn't matter. What I might have wanted last night is irrelevant because I can't have Jake. Not anymore.

With our meal done Adam and I settle on the floor, our backs against his large sofa, and guitars plugged into portable amps. I hum the melody that's been rattling around in my brain and try to make my fingers replicate it on the guitar. I usually write on a piano, but for this song I need to hear that high-pitched wail. Adam jumps in adding a riff here and a power chord there, and when I begin to sing the first couple of lines, his eyes close as his head bobs up and down.

"Fire, Sin. This song is sultry summer nights and the call for angsty sex," he muttered. And because I can't say, *"It's funny you say that, Adam. Just yesterday after all the drama and media scrutiny, I let Jake go down on me on balcony surrounded by sexy neon and warm air. And it was dirty, and raw, and everything that I missed from the one man I should stay away from."* Instead, I simply nod and get lost in creating.

When it comes to this part of writing, Adam has never asked me why. He doesn't need to because he already knows. I read somewhere once that your soul can have different kinds of mates. In fact, most soul mates aren't romantic. Their whole purpose is to challenge you. Help you get to the next level and that is Adam to a T. I've always known him. If our circumstances were different, I would've still found him. I feel the same way about Jake with one exception. Adam is my tribe while Jake is my other half. Correction, was my other half.

"It's different from all our other stuff," I say. "You think people will like it?"

"Of course, it's different, Sin. You're different."

Chapter 17

Four Years Ago
Sinclair

"LET'S HURRY UP AND FINISH LOADING ALL THIS CRAP," ADAM SAYS. I heft two guitar cases over my shoulder and move as fast I can under the weight.

We had a kick-ass show tonight. Wall-to-wall people came to see us, which is happening more and more. *Finally!* We're seeing a shift in the crowds. More people showing up to see us. Sporting our shirts and leaving after our set.

Tonight we got on stage late because of issues with the venue. And because of issues with the headliner we were able to perform every song on our set list, as openers we warm the crowd up for the main act, which is typically four to five songs.

After several trips between the venue and the bus we're finally loaded and ready to go.

"Is that everything?" I ask, peering into the cargo space, trying to take inventory, and making sure all the instruments are present, or at the very least, a case or account for each piece.

"I think so. Let me do one last sweep of the stage, and then we can go, 'kay?" Adam says over his shoulder walking away before I can answer him. I watch his retreating back for a solid minute before I pull the phone out of my back pocket.

My fingers curl around the edges and squeeze as I fight the urge to throw the damn thing as far as I can. I frown at the stupid blank screen. Pissed off because once again I don't have any missed calls or text messages. It shouldn't be surprising because lately Jake is cagey and distant.

He's stuck in Vegas, interning for his family's casino while he finishes up his MBA. He hates that I'm gone. I hate that I'm gone but this is the industry.

Music is hard. Way harder than I thought it'd be but that moment when I connect with one person, just one, in an audience of hundreds, the long nights, the hours of driving and lugging my instruments on and off stage, are worth it. I love what I do. I love my man, rock meet hard place.

This tour extended twice. What started out as a monthlong tour stretched to six months. We've crisscrossed the country, seven maybe eight times. I don't know anymore, but I've only made it home sporadically, a half a week here and a day or two there.

Things are finally winding down though. Three more weeks, that's it. Twenty-one days and I'm home. The distance and time won't matter then. At least I hope it won't.

I'm getting whiplash from dealing with his mood swings. Some days he's sweeter than molasses, his voice rougher than gravel as he whispers how much he misses me. How he can't wait for me to get home and all the nasty things he'll do to me when I get there. Other days I go without a word or a text. When I finally get him, he's speaking in monotone and rushing me off the phone. And I get this feeling of dread. Like he's over it. Me, us, the traveling, everything. I keep it buried deep, but I question if he's cheating on me. If in my absence I've been replaced.

I scroll through the list of names on my phone and stop on the entry with a small picture of us from a couple of years ago. I don't remember where we were or what we were doing, but we just look so happy. I like Jake and Sinclair circa 2008. The eighteen-year-olds that didn't have time to fight because we were too busy making love and having fun.

This new version of us is… I don't recognize it. We're so far removed from the people we were. Every day Jake shoulders more and more responsibly. Taking on the pressure of being the golden child. The one expected to do great things, to elevate his family to the next level, and God, he's trying. We're both trying

Is it too much to ask to hear his voice? That's it. I just want to hear his voice, change clothes, and sleep, in that order but after five rings, the call goes to voice mail. I sigh, disconnecting and sending him a text.

Me: Hey, babe. I tried to call, but u must be busy or asleep. How u doin? Miss u like crazy. See u sooner rather than later!! heart you.

As a second thought, I snap a picture and send that as well. I stare at the phone willing the damn thing to ring, but when it doesn't, I swallow the bitter taste of disappointment and tuck the thing back into my pocket.

Damn! Damn! Damn!

I promised to call earlier but then the show started late, and we stayed on stage longer. So now, I'm uber late, and once again I'm the jerk. The one that called too late, the one that's never home.

I drop my head in defeat, letting it hang on my neck. I just keep messing things up and sooner or later he's going to get sick of my shit.

A small voice whispers, *"He already is."* I rub my palm across my forehead in frustration.

"Sinclair! I love you!" someone screams, and the sound is jarring like a gunshot in the silence. I whip my head up, looking for the person attached to that shriek.

I don't have to look far. A couple of yards from me, a man barrels forward and for such big guy he's hauling ass. His pale skin even paler under the floodlights that surround the venue parking. His hair looks like it hasn't been washed in weeks and hangs in clumps around his face.

Both Dan and Miles move quick. Dan wraps an arm around my waist and hustles me up the stairs of the tour bus. While Miles, our resident hothead, pushes the guy back with a forceful shove that swiftly escalates into a scuffle.

I watch from the window as three burly security guards run from the building and pull both men apart. Miles is still yelling as one guard forcibly moves him to the side while the other two pull both hands behind the other guy's back.

The screamer is wearing a Sin City T-shirt with my signature on the front, and if that isn't creepy enough, I recognize him. He's been following us around for weeks, which was pretty awesome at first, because we finally had a bona fide groupie, but after talking to him a couple of times, shit got weird. I called it quits when he tried to cut off a piece of my hair.

But when I stopped talking to him, he really went cuckoo for Coco Puffs, doing his damnedest to get close to me. He's always front and center. The only still thing in a sea of movement with hair unkempt and wearing the exact same concert T-shirt every single time I see him.

The excitement of having our very own fan dulled quickly. Besides the crazy, sleep schedule, this part of being almost famous, freaks me out.

I turn my eyes away from his form being escorted away from the bus and watch Miles lope up the stairs. His T-shirt torn is at the collar and there's a new hole in his already tattered jeans. But his wide mouth is pulled into a grin.

"Does that mean that we're famous now?" Dan asks, flopping onto one of the captain chairs. His long limbs hang over the sides and the Bert and Ernie T-shirt raises just enough to expose his pierced navel. "Sin has her first stalker."

"I don't know how you can joke about this. That guy is getting weirder and weirder. I mean, did you see him tonight? It was like he was in a trance." My gaze shifts between Dan and Miles for confirmation that we've all been seeing the same thing.

"I think he's mostly harmless. If he got close enough, he might hump your leg, but he's not one of those dudes that'll boil your rabbit." But I see the worried look that passes between the boys before Miles, sits down next to me. As if they know something I don't, and for the first time since Mr. Crazy showed up, I'm a little scared.

"Nice, Miles. Thank you for that, really."

"Anything for you, Sin-a-Sticks," he sarcastically quips, slapping his big hand on my knee, causing an involuntary jerk.

"I can't leave you two alone for a minute without shit poppin' off," Adam says to Dan and Miles as he enters the bus, no doubt already aware of the incident with the stalker. Adam sits in the driver's seat and closes the bus door. We each take turns driving to ensure that we get where we need to go on time. I drove last night.

"Sin, let me holla at you for a sec." I sit right behind the driver's seat as he starts up the bus and pulls out onto the road.

"Our last four shows have been canceled," he says matter-of-factly.

"Why?" I squeeze the headrest behind him hard enough to break couple of nails. Every single time we break the surface, something pulls us back under. One step forward and twenty steps back. "What happened?"

"Indigo decided to call it quits."

"Like permanently?" How can she do that? She signed a contract with the promoter same as we did. As the headliner, Indigo is the one that convinced, her indie label to let us open for this tour. And now she's done?

"Yeah. I'm not sure what the hell is going on. Just got a call from John. So, it looks like you get your wish. We're going home," he says in a low voice. The disappointment is evident on his tired face. God, this sucks. Like really fucking sucks. Yeah, I want to go home but not like this. Not losing our ride or finishing what we set out to do.

"You okay, Adam?" I already know the answer, but I need him to do what he always does. Make me believe that Sin City can survive this. Convince me that one more set back doesn't equal failure.

"You know me. It's just... I'm just frustrated. We were just starting to get traction. Nah mean? It just feels like every time we get a little momentum, it grinds it to a halt. But when we get back to the valley, we have some options."

"This wasn't us," I tell Adam with a nod to drive my words home. But damn if it doesn't feel like it.

He looks at me for a brief second before rolling his eyes back to the road. "So, we'll sleep at the hotel tonight and tomorrow we head for home," he says.

"Home… God. How long has it been since we've been home?"

"For longer than a couple of days? Five maybe six months, I think." He rubs his thumb over the sharp edge of his jaw. His eyes once again flit up to mine before returning to the road.

"You gonna be good when we get back? I know stuff between you and your man has been…" He waves his hand back and forth in a so-so motion.

"Once I'm home it'll be better. We'll find our center again." We. Are. Fine. At least we will be. It'll all be fine. When I get home, everything will go back to normal.

We're going home!

"Hey, boys, we're going home!" I yell at the back of the bus at the other two.

"Vegas, baby!" Miles whoops.

"Vegas, baby!" The rest of us holler at the top of our lungs.

Chapter 18

NOW

Jake

I TOSS MY KEYS ON THE FOYER TABLE AS I MAKE MY WAY THROUGH THE hallway to the living room, dropping my suit coat across the arm of the old sofa, the only thing I kept besides a photo when I moved out of the house Sin and I shared together.

I've only seen her once since the balcony, and that was from across the casino with rows of machines and dozens of people between us.

I've never spent hours on the casino floor, skulking around corners, hanging out in front elevator doors hoping to catch a glimpse of a particular woman that somehow manages to avoid me even though there is only one entrance and exit to the villa within The Hotel, and she travels with two huge men and multiple security officers.

One stolen moment and all I can see are the intense stares, the searing body that melted like butter around mine, the silky tight fit while I filled her, and the earthy moans that fell from parted lips while I ate her pussy to my fucking heart's content. One reckless moment and I want to walk away from everything, leave it all behind. Be that guy, the one that didn't give a shit about what people thought or what his family wanted. Having her on that balcony was the worst kind of tease because it was just enough to remind me of what I'm missing.

I'm a simple man.

I like simple things.

At least I did until Sin reentered the mix. She's a loud reminder that complicated has its points too.

She left me with a wet dick and balls so tight they were aching for days. Then she walked back into that party with her shoulders back and head held high and so unaffected, I wasn't sure if I'd imagined the whole thing.

The chime on the front door goes off, signaling Connor's arrival. My mood is black, but that's pretty much been the case for the last month. I hear his footsteps coming toward me, and I sincerely regret giving him the code to my house.

We have these meetings every month. It gives us a chance to talk without all the politically correct, corporate bullshit hindering our words or worrying about the wrong ears hearing information we'd prefer to stay between us. At these meetings if I think he's spending too much money, which is often the case, I get say, *"Muthafucka, green don't grow on trees. Rein in that shit."* Instead of something like, *"We need to curb spending cost in that area."*

My department is tight. I don't question whether or not my employees are on top of things because I know they are, but they're not me. Money and I have always gotten along beautifully. I see things quickly that others just don't.

I know where to find money, how to hide it, and the right people to clean it. When you're a self-funded casino, not all the money that comes in is above board, and I had to reach far into the Vegas gutters to make this casino happen. The people we have to pay don't necessarily have offices or wear suits, and they don't accept checks from a corporate account.

We have another payment coming up at the end of the month, so we need to iron out some details. Shit doesn't stop because my life is in shambles. I silently yell at the ceiling, curling my hands into tight fists and throwing a couple of punches in the air. Nope, not irritated at all.

Connor comes in carrying a brown paper bag filled with what smells like Chinese takeout. The aroma makes my mouth water as soon as it hits my nose.

"Just for me?" I ask, batting my eyes at him.

Connor blows me a kiss as he pulls white takeout boxes out of the bag.

"No, jackass. I gotta eat too," Connor snaps but the smile on his face ruins the irritation in his voice. "You got the beer?"

Without answering, I reach into the fridge, pull out a couple of bottles, and slide one across the counter. I twist the metal cap off mine and take a long pull from the bottle. Connor tosses me a pair of chopsticks, and we both stand at the counter in silence, eating food out of boxes.

"So, what's up with you and old girl?" Connor asks me around a mouth full of food. "Did you finally man up and figure your shit out?"

I open my mouth but then close it because no, I haven't figured out anything where Sin's concerned. Where do I even start? I still can't get her to talk to me let, alone unpack our baggage.

Connor points a chopstick in my direction. "I take that as a no."

I shove another bite of my food in my mouth, taking my time to chew it into the smallest possible pieces while I let my mind go back to that night on the balcony. I know a couple of things.

First, is that physically we are perfection. Fire and gasoline. One feeding off the other to burn hotter, brighter. With an intensity that is immeasurable. Second, regardless of our past, we could have a future. Sin may not want to want me, but I live under her skin and flow in her veins just as she does in mine. Us is not a choice. It never was, it's inevitable.

"It's..." I keep my eyes focused on the food. "I don't know, complicated."

Connor grunts in disgust. I can feel him staring at me while steadily shoveling food into his mouth.

"Real talk. Did you expect anything different?"

"I don't know, man. But I didn't expect this."

"This?"

"She's icing me out."

"How so?" I finally look at him, and he shrugs. "Dude, I'm not trying to be an asshole."

"Then don't be."

He takes a swig of beer before he moves to open another box of food. "I'm just saying if you pursue whatever this is, you're about to stir up hella mess. Be ready for it."

"Meaning what?" I set my food down and brace my hands on the counter.

"Ever since she rolled up on the scene, you've been on edge, growling and snarling like a rabid dog." Connor picks up noodles with the chopsticks and shoves them into his mouth.

"It's not good or bad, just different. I was telling Jeanine the other day you need to get your shit together. Don't think I haven't noticed all the time you're spending out of the office. And even when you are there, you're not. You haven't messed anything up, yet. But I'm not used to your focus being divided." He tilts his head, eyeing me across the counter. "We owe bad people big money, J. I want you to get the girl, but I want to keep my legs in the process. Your heads gotta be in the game."

"I'm on it, Connor. I know a guy. A banker of sorts on the dark web that'll be handling the exchange in crypto currency. I got this."

"That's what I'm talking about. I should have known about this shit the moment you did."

I meant to tell him. He's right. I should have told him weeks ago. But I've been... fuck! I need to pull my head out of my ass. "Won't happen again, Con. I gotchu." I extent a fist which he taps with his own.

"I hate to bring this part up, but you also gotta keep that pretty mug out of the paper. I don't know too many people on the dark side that like that kind of publicity."

"I've never been the face of The Hotel, Connor, that's all you."

He smiles big. "This is true. But we, the two of us"—he moves the chopstick back and forth between us—"run this shit. So, man up. Daddy's name may have opened a lot of doors, but I guarantee it won't keep them open if we fuck this up."

I roll my head on my neck, trying to stretch the tense muscles in my shoulders. The vein next to my eye starts to thump as a headache creeps in. I'm trying to figure it out. Sin and I got turned upside down a long time ago, and I can't figure out how to get us right side up. While I've been trying to figure us out, I've haven't been as attentive as I should be to other issues.

"I'm good, man," I say. I'm not sure who I'm trying to convince more, him or me.

"Nah, your cranky ass attitude and bitchlike pussy pining says different."

"Don't make me kick your ass out of my house," I say halfheartedly because I can hold my own, but pound for pound Connor would kick my ass. Don't let the ten-thousand-dollar suit and the education fool you. He's a street kid.

His mother was the pretty showgirl that fell in love with the married casino boss. When she got pregnant with Connor, there wasn't a celebration or offer of marriage. There was a layoff notice and one-way ticket back to a small town in Louisiana.

I didn't know the woman, but according to Connor, people weren't too receptive to the pretty, dark-skinned single mom with a biracial child. She struggled to put food on the table and keep clothes on his back.

When he got old enough, he did what he could to help. First by helping neighbors with menial tasks and then by learning the hustle from some of the local thugs. Connor was smuggling drugs, guns, and fenced jewels through the bayou by the time he was ten. He never told me what happened, or why he had to leave but his mother shipped him to his father in Las Vegas to save his life. In all the years that I've known him, he's never lost that edge, that I wish you would try me that comes from making your bones in the harshest ways possible.

"You can try." He chucks a napkin in my direction. "But seriously, Jake, don't get amnesia now. Don't pretend like you don't know what we have to do. On that note, stop it with the, '*Why doesn't Sinclair James want me*' question. You know damn well why she doesn't want to touch your ass with a ten-foot pole. You got caught slipping. Now you're start-ing at less than zero. I myself like to sample a variety of woman, but if you want to stick with one flavor, vanilla or chocolate as the case may be, that's your bag. All I'm saying is make a decision and get it done because distractions can get us both killed."

"I already said we're fine, Connor. Let it drop. And as far as Sin goes—"

"I don't really care two squirts of piss what you do with Sinclair James—"

"Sin, Connor. You don't have to say her full name every single time."

"Nah, brah, I don't know Sin. I know the headliner of my hotel that created a media shit storm because of history with you. Ms. James and I ain't on friendly terms, and if she keeps distracting the one person I depend on to help me keep shit afloat, we never will be."

He carefully closes his now empty food container. "I didn't get the whole thing with you and her until I saw y'all at the party opening night. As much as I like you. I'm not willing to die because you're distracted by some repeat pussy." Without thinking I chucked a fork across the counter and hit something on the left side of his body. Connor presses both palms against the counter top and stands.

"You headed out?" I ask, surprised relief filling my chest.

"Nah, I gotta hit the head, but when I get back, I'm done. No more talk about the woman in your life unless you're giving me gritty details that I can add to the spank bank." He jacks his hand in front of his slacks. Asshole.

I stay silent as he walks out the kitchen toward the bathroom. There is no need to mention me on my knees with my face buried be-tween her legs a couple of feet away from him a month ago. That little video plays in a loop in my mind and is the cornerstone of my personal me time.

When he comes back, we finish our food in silence, but it's com-fortable, unweighted with the earlier irritation. Miraculously, I stay on track for the rest of his visit. When he finally leaves I unwind with a tumbler of bourbon and let my mind drift back to those sweet seconds when Sin was back in my arms, pulling me closer, trusting me to take her body over the edge of sweet oblivion, and then the cold reality of her shutting me out again.

I understand Sin even when she's hiding behind a mountain of hurt and anger. I get her because she's the same girl I fell in love with all those years ago. The same one who turns my stomach into knots and makes me afraid to blink for fear I'll miss something.

In my guilt, I let Sin runaway the last time, hide behind her career and her pain, and convince herself she couldn't love me. I'm done letting her hide. It's all still there, deep under the surface but I felt it. Now I need to remind her of what we had and coax her into thinking about what we could have again.

Chapter 19

Sinclair

MY FLIGHT JUST LANDED IN VEGAS AND, LIKE EVERY OTHER TIME I've returned, my eyes stay riveted on the lights and the sights of the Strip. No matter how many times I've seen it, the view never gets old. I don't know if it's that beautiful or if I'm reacting with a sense of nostalgia to the only place I've ever called home. Either way I love it.

The weather has finally cooled down, but even on the tail end of fall, it's still warm or at least warm enough to wear sandals and a light jacket versus a coat.

As soon as the airplane wheels hit the tarmac and the door opens, the entire band disperses, leaving me to my own devices for the rest of the night.

I could catch a movie or go shopping, but my bed is calling my name. I don't know what it is about flying, even short trips, that make me tired, a bone-deep weariness that's hard to shake for hours.

I stall at the airport because the idea of walking through the hotel makes my skin feel tight and itchy. I should have already been in my own place, but the villa is nicer than most places I'd find on the market, and honestly it feels like home with one major exception. A certain CFO keeps popping up. Almost like he receives a notification every time I step foot into the elevator leading to the casino floor.

If I got something off property, I wouldn't have to worry about that shit. I wouldn't have to find ways to blend into the scenery or sneak onto the crowded casino floor.

When I first realized Jake worked for The Hotel, I thought, *"He's a finance guy. He'll be working eight to four or whatever normal business hours are for a hotel. Why would I see him?"* Then I left the villa at ten in the morning and found him leaning against a slot machine. His hazel eyes studying each face exiting the elevator until they landed on mine. I hurried up and pressed the close door button before he could get on which worked that time, but I swear every time I hit the casino floor, he's somewhere in the vicinity.

This time I make it into my villa without a sighting, and it's a relief. I immediately get in the shower to wash away the long hours of travel. I unwind as the steam and warm water relax my muscles one group at a time. When I finally turn off the water and make my way back into the bedroom, I grab body cream and slather myself from head to toe. Just as I'm about to get clothes the phone rings.

No one knows I'm staying in this villa, and the few who do would use my cell. Please don't let this be a situation where someone has sold my information to *TMZ* or some other sleazy mag. I love the music, but I loathe celebrity. It's like people don't see me as a real person. I lost any vestiges of privacy when *Exquisitely Broken* released.

"Hello?" I say into the receiver, guarded and ready for whatever the person on the other end of the line is going to throw at me.

"Sin?" Except that. I know that voice. Remember all too well. "Hey, it's Jake. Are you busy right now?"

Am I busy? Why is Jacob Johnson on my phone once again, conveniently aware of my comings and goings? I really need to reach out to our new manager and make getting a rental my priority.

"You still there?" he asks.

I could just hang up. I should hang up but… I can't make myself do it. I flop down on the bed and wait for the flood of anger that generally hits me when anything Jake related comes up.

But I got nothing.

Maybe seeing him over the last couple of months has been a type of desensitization therapy? Or I'm tired and don't care about much right now. Either way we're apparently having a conversation.

I blow a noisy breath into the silent line. "I just got in. What's up?"

"Oh... I didn't know. I just thought since you didn't have a show tonight—"

"I had a festival in Chicago," I answer, cutting him off.

"Right, you're only here like two weekends a month," he mumbles almost to himself.

"Mmm-hmm. So, you called for...?" I say at the same time, a loud knock echoes through the villa.

"Open up," his voice says in my ear and I jerk upright into a sitting position. He did not show up here. Uninvited. But the second knock echoing through the villa confirms that he absolutely did show up without a request or invitation from me!

"Guess you wasted your time," I snap into the phone because what the hell? Who does he think he is? Before I finish the thought, I already know the answer. He's here because he can be, because I'm probably the only person in his entire life that has said no, and he doesn't understand that word. I'm not letting him in. Not for a repeat of the other night or to rehash a history I'd rather forget.

We happened.

Now we're over. End of story.

"Just give me a couple of minutes. I promise you won't regret it," his deep voice coos in my ear and rolls through me, tightening things low in my belly. My pulse kicks up just at the sound. How silly can I be? I took that gamble, years ago, and it didn't end well for either of us. The word calamitous comes to mind.

"Not a good idea, Jake."

"The best ones never are, Sin," he says, and a startled laugh leaves my mouth because the statement is so simple, and so Jake, and makes little sense in this context but it's perfect.

"Can we not and say that we did?"

"Where's the fun in that?"

He knocks on the door again. Much lighter than the last time. "Open up."

Then I hear a click in my ear. I stare blankly at the phone. My mind is working overtime to convince me to stay in my bed and ignore the man outside my door. Jake is a risk I shouldn't take, not now or ever again.

But I want to.

I want to know what brought him to my door at, looking at the clock hanging on the wall, it's ten. I should be over him. Done. But as I walk the short distance to open the door and see him there, wearing a light gray three-piece suit, hands tucked into his pockets and hazel eyes looking bluer today, I know we're so far from done.

We stare at each other for longer than is polite and in those few seconds, the air is heavy with the history of us. Not just the other night but all of it, the heartbreak and anger, the desire and fun. The remnants of our yesterlife live in the shadows of his expressive eyes and the tensed-up muscles of his shoulders.

"You letting me in?" he asks, his eyes dipping down my body to take in the oversized white fluffy robe and bare feet before coming back to meet my steady gaze. I step to the side and give him space, but he leans to the side to snatch something off the wall.

Jake strides past me holding a guitar case I recognize all too well. He gave me the 1958 Fender Stratocast for my twenty-first birthday. It's all scratched up around the edges with grooves in the handle from years of use, but I loved that guitar something fierce. Leaving it was almost as hard as leaving him. I can't believe he's kept it after all these years.

"Is this a regular thing for you now? Showing up uninvited to a woman's house, carrying a guitar instead of roses." I tilt my head toward the case.

"Nah, not regular but desperate times call for desperate measures." He sets the case down, leaning it against the arm of the couch.

"I can't believe you kept it all this time."

"I always thought you'd come back for it. I knew you weren't coming back for me. But this"—he pats the case—"had your heart in a way I never did."

Wow, there are so many things wrong with the comment, I don't know where to start. What does it say about me that my ex believed or maybe still believes that I'd pick an inanimate object over him?

"So, you just got in?" he asks. His eyes move around my space, stopping on the open suitcase to the pile of clothes I left in the middle of the floor just before I got in the shower.

"Ah… yeah."

Jake takes a seat on the sofa, unbuttoning his suit coat as he sits.

"Have a seat. Make yourself comfortable," I say sarcastically.

"I wasn't trying to overstep." He immediately stands and grips the back of his neck. "Why do I feel like I'm always apologizing to you?"

"Because since I got here, you have been." There's a second of silence, but then we both start to chuckle at the same time, and just that quickly the mood shifts to something a little lighter. He once again makes himself comfortable on the sofa and I sit on the arm next to him.

"So, you brought a bribe?" I nod to the guitar case.

"I was thinking of more of a peace offering." He bumps me with his shoulder, a smile playing around the edge of his lips.

"A bribe by any other name."

"Is it working?"

"Maybe a little."

"Go ahead, take it out. You know you want to." His words are subtle, seductive. Probably because since our moment on the balcony, thoughts of Jake and sex with Jake have been one in the same.

He grabs the guitar case and unsnaps the locks, pulling the guitar out by the handle. My hand immediately reaches out to stroke the smooth wood.

"Play something for me?" I can feel his eyes roving my face.

"This is an electric guitar. We were together long enough that you know it needs an amp for you to hear it."

"I was also with you long enough to know you have one some-where around here."

I roll my eyes because we both know that he's right. Any musician worth their salt has an array of instruments at their disposal at any given time. I don't do digital. I need to feel the vibration or keys under the tips of my fingers, and an electric blues guitar with its warm sound has always come first, second to my piano. I usually compose using a keyboard because the sound combinations are almost limitless versus a six-string guitar. In the privacy of my home when I sing for me, and a long time ago Jake, it was always the guitar. This guitar in particular. My fingers brush against strings, and I can't stop the smile that breaks across my face.

"There she is," he says. A smirk pulls at one side of his full mouth.

"Was I lost and didn't know it?"

"To me, you have been," he says, his voice is a decibel above a whisper.

I pull the guitar into my body, settling it on my lap. I tweak a cou-ple of chords.

"You still using the pocket studio?"

"When I travel. It's somewhere in my suitcase. If you want to wade through that mess be my guest."

He stands and walks to my bag. I hear the metal teeth of the zip-per, and in the blink of an eye, he's back with a small portable amp. He hands it to me, sitting so close I can feel the heat coming off his skin. I shiver as I plug it in. This time when I brush my fingers against the strings, the sound reverberates around the space, bouncing off the walls to surround us.

"Sing for me."

My fingers move of their own accord, and at first, I hum. Then I'm singing. Not one of my songs because I can't look Jake in the eye while I sing about us. Us when we were happy or us as the hot mess that we're right now. It doesn't matter. I opt for Rhianna's "Kiss it Better" before I can think wiser of it. The guitar dominates that song in a slow sexy rhythm, which isn't the atmosphere I'm trying to create. In truth, I don't know what I'm doing. Singing in such close physical proximity in this small of a space is more intimate than the act of sex. Whether I'm singing my songs or someone else's, it's still a mining of the soul.

If I feel it, I can make the person next to me feel it too.

And I feel this. Every damn word of this song is at once a taunt and a plea.

As the words pour out of my mouth his eyes drift up to mine. He doesn't blink. I'm not even sure if he breathes. When my fingers stop moving, the silence between us is pregnant with emotions that should've died when our relationship did. My desire so strong it propels me to my feet.

I place the guitar back into the case, taking great care to lock the top in place. When I straighten up Jake mirrors my position on the opposite side of the coffee table.

"Sin." His voice cracks.

"I'm gonna go throw something on. Give me a sec or are you heading out?" I'm already walking into the bedroom before he can answer. I feel raw like I've just exposed every single vulnerability I have to the only person that can destroy me. I know he can because he already did.

Chapter 20

NOW

Sinclair

I DON'T BOTHER WITH THE LIGHTS. THE CURTAINS ARE OPEN, SO THE bright neon twinkling in the skyline is bright enough that I have no problem moving about the space. I open the only drawer that has items inside. My hand is on the belt of the robe when a sense of recognition zings down my spine. I know Jake is behind me before I see his reflection in the large mirror hanging above the dresser. It's like we're magnets, our attraction a force that pulls us past common hurts and common sense.

I watch his approach with an almost trancelike fascination and jump when he kisses the tender spot behind my ear. Staring at his reflection I didn't realize he was so close.

Our gazes stay locked in the reflection. Jake's arms wrap around me, clutching my back to his front. We're close, pressed so tight that his pulse is a heady metronome.

Steady. Strong. Melodic.

Even with our sordid history and our uncertain future, at this moment we're perfect.

"Sin, don't say no... Not tonight." *As if I could.*

His softly whispered plea leaves me undone. I turn in his arms, sliding my hands up his muscled chest to his head, and I pull him down to meet my mouth. The kiss is no more than a brush of lips and an exchange of air, but Jake responds with a groan, pinning my body against the dresser. For a couple of seconds, we both still, and then his mouth fuses with mine and it's better than the sweetest love song. His hands move between us, untying the belt of the robe as he strips the material off my nude body.

Jake leans back. His eyes rove over my body from the top of my head to the bottom of my feet.

"If you don't want to do this tell me now, Sin. Because once we start, we're not stopping."

Jake

"Strip," Sin demands.

Her dark gaze is feral as I shed my clothes. When she looks at me like that, like I'm everything that she's ever wanted, I want to give her the world, or at the very least, multiple orgasms. When I stand nude before her, she attacks my mouth. Her taste is something I crave, but this kiss is almost manic with her urgency.

"Slow down," I whisper against her lips.

Sin shuts her eyes tight, and her movements grow stiff. I can feel her panic just under the surface, almost as if she's fighting her body's desire for me as much as she's fighting the idea of us.

"In these four walls, it's me and you. Don't be scared of that. I got you." I won't let her down, not in this. Before, I lost my way and steered us both into shark-infested waters, and we're still in survival mode. What we had… it was real. That's the only plausible reason it hit us both this hard.

Her eyes crack open to bore into mine. I dip forward, bringing us skin to skin, my eyes never leaving hers as I take her lips in a gentle kiss. My hands trail down her body, gripping first one leg, and then the other. Securing them around my waist as I walk us to the bed. I lay back against the mattress draping Sin over me like a blanket.

She pushes up on her arms and the panic I only felt a couple of seconds ago is written across her face now. I know that look. She's about to bolt. I grip the back of her stiff neck, leaning up to run kisses down her throat.

"Jake… I—"

"Don't say it."

She looks at me with startled eyes.

That's right, baby, we're not playing that game. Not tonight. I need Sin with me. Not fixated on the events of four years ago. But right here in the present with me. I suck on the skin just above her clavicle, and she arches into my touch.

"You set the pace. You make the rules." I run my hands down the curve of her ass. Gripping her thighs, I pull them wide, so she lands with her knees on either side of me giving me access to her soft core.

"You still like it hard?" I smack the rounded flesh of her ass, and she groans from deep in her chest. "Or do you want it soft?" I trail kisses down to her breasts, moving to lick the dark skin around her left nipple before I take the stiff peak in my mouth. Sin's hips settle against mine. She grinds her wet center against my shaft. "You can be loud," I say dropping wet kisses on her skin. "I remember I used to make you scream. You still a screamer, baby?" I peel her body off mine and retrieve the condom from the wallet where my pants lay on the floor. I tear the foil wrapper with my teeth and roll the latex down my length. I crawl on the bed between her legs, and with flawless accuracy, I sink into Sin. All the way to the hilt.

"Ah… Jake" She licks her lips, her back bowing in a sharp arch, hips rocking in my hold to take me deeper.

I get three or four shallow strokes before my hips jack up, kissing her womb, which rips a high-pitched moan from her mouth.

"Easy, baby."

I run a hand over the thud of her heart behind her rib cage. Her hips roll with mine, meeting me in the middle, and I need… more, now. Right, the fuck now. I want to go so deep that she'll feel me for days. I hold her thighs..

"Let me hear you."

I angle her hips and thrust hard, setting a languid pace that teases us both.

"Tell me how you want it," I murmur. My hips pull back only to sink inside her even slower this time.

"I want it all," she moans.

Yes! A satisfied pleasure bursts in my chest at her words. My hand ghosts over her beautiful face that has haunted my dreams. I tip her chin to bring her eyes to mine. I rub my thumb across her full bottom lip, and without breaking eye contact, I drop my head for another taste of her mouth.

Her eyes drift shut.

"Nah-uh, baby. You don't get to hide. Let me see those eyes."

She opens her eyes. They shine with unshed tears. "Jake." My name on her lips has never sounded so good. Tears spill over her lashes, but her eyes never leave mine.

"That's right, baby. It's you and me. You remember that?" I underline every word with a thrust. Sin curls her legs over my hips, drawing me in deeper, closer.

Our mingled breaths grow strained as we move together. Each thrust is coming harder than the last. I'm not sure how much longer I can last. My balls are already so tight, they hurt. I snake my hand between us and work her clit as I continue to pound into her.

"Let me feel it, baby. Milk that dick." My eyes try to close but I force them to stay open, to take in every inch of her. The deep hue of her skin, a striking contrast to my russet tone. She's flesh and bone, and willing woman, the answer to ever uttered prayer. And she's here. Her body joined to mine in a way that surpasses the physical. Together we're air and stars. Our connection, deep and vast, is limitless.

Sin gives me exactly what I ask for as the first flutters of her orgasm trigger my own. I keep going, my shaft throbbing as I jettison every drop of come into the thin latex barrier that separates us. I collapse against her chest, taking in heaping breaths. Sin's arms wrap tight around me.

The aftermath is as good, if not better, than the sex. The quiet moments where we can just be is all I want. I'm not sure how long we lay there, but Sin's breathing gets longer and slower, and her body sags into the mattress. I raise myself up onto my elbow, my fingers sliding over her high cheekbones and the cute button on the tip of her nose. I kiss her unresponsive lips just because I can.

For the first time in what feels like forever, I'm at peace. I roll to my side, gathering Sin in my arms and tucking her head under my chin. Right here is exactly where I want to be—where I'm meant to be. I don't know if I believe that soul mates exist, but if they do, Sin is mine. I'm hardwired to love her.

When she left, I thought this is just until I could gain her forgiveness. Until her heart was repaired. Until I could be the man she deserves, the one she needs. I messed up in the worst way a man can. I betrayed her trust and broke her heart. I know she's scared. I'm terrified but that scared feeling in my gut? That's how I know this is right. That Sin is the best... no, the only choice.

We lost years and I'm not willing to lose another second.

I finger the soft springy curls around her shoulder and snuggle in closer. Then I close my eyes to sleep.

Chapter 21

Ten Years Ago
Sinclair

WE'RE STANDING AT THE DOOR TO JAKE'S HOME, NO HIS FAMILY mansion. I knew he came from money, but I didn't expect... this. This house is big, like I couldn't see the side walls as we drove up big. Like we had to check in with the guard at the front gate big. Like it's in Anthem, one of the richest neighborhoods in the city, at the base of Black Mountain big.

"Babe, relax. My parents aren't that bad."

"I'm relaxed," I whisper shout, wiggling my arms at my sides to dry the stress sweat already gathering at my pits.

"Says the girl having an asthma attack." Laughing Jake wraps both arms around my waist and presses a soft kiss to my temple.

"This is me not laughing." Even to my own ears my voice is tight with anxiety. "Don't you have a key?"

The last thing I need is one of his parents overhearing our conversation from the other side of the that door and thinking that I don't want to be here.

I don't.

I really, really don't.

But they don't need to know that.

"Of course, I have a key, but I's trying to do this right, formally introduce you. Not bring you home like a playmate."

Formally? The only formal thing I have ever done in my life is high school graduation. Even then I was wearing a T-shirt and jeans under my cap and gown. I'm dressed similarly today. Different shirt, different pair of jeans, but the same me. The unwanted daughter of a Vegas call girl, who was raised by the system because my mother wasn't capable or interested, and finally because she wasn't alive. I normally don't care what people think about that. But today is different. The stakes somehow higher.

I care what these people think.

I want them to like me.

I want them to choose me for their son.

"Jake, I can't... You didn't tell me that you... that your family is." My words die down on a frustrated breath. "I'm not dressed, and my hair is—"

"Perfect. You are perfect just the way you are." I twist in his arms and meet his steady gaze, and he's looking at me the way he always does. A heat mixed of lust and something that just might be love. Like in his eyes I'm perfect.

Me—the poor girl from Pahrump whose mother made her living at the whim of men, whose father was a nameless, faceless good-time-guy, who spent more time unwanted in the home of strangers—at the home of the adored son of one of Las Vegas's richest families.

"I'm over reacting, huh?"

"I think all this worry is for nothing. Just a little faith, babe. My parents aren't bad." Dropping a soft kiss on my lips, he threads our fingers and depresses the doorbell button.

The door swings open immediately.

A slender woman with golden skin, eyes and hair, wearing an all-white pantsuit that looks like it came directly off a mannequin at one of the high-end boutiques in the Forum Shops at Caesars Palace is standing there.

Her eyes move from the top of my head to my Converse-clad feet, pausing... no staring at my hair, before lowering to Jake's fingers twined with mine. Her gaze sweeps back up to meet mine. And yeah... in a few seconds, this woman just sat as my judge and jury. Based on her grimace, I was found guilty.

Please Jesus don't be his mother. In the pit of my stomach I know she is. Why else would she look at me like my very existence insulted her? She looks from me to Jake and real joy shines in her smile.

"Son it's been so long I've almost forgotten what you look like." A rich Southern accent pours over her words, dipping them in syrup and coating them in sugar.

She opens her arms and Jake drops my hand to walk into her embrace. I feel alone and very much like the girl that used to show up at houses with my black garbage bag in tow.

I gotta get out of here. When I left Pahrump for the final time, I promised myself that I'd never do this again, be the unwanted burden people are forced to endure.

I take a step back, but Jake reaches out, his long fingers curling around my wrist. He's right next to me. When did that happen?

"Momma let me introduce you to Sin." He says pulling me forward. "And Sin this is my mom, Danielle Johnson."

"Nice to meet you." I extend my hand, which she doesn't take.

"I'm sorry? I must have heard that wrong. Did you just say that this child is named Sin? As in ugly acts that tarnish the soul?" Her gaze flits between us before settling on Jake.

"My name is Sinclair. Sinclair James but people call me Sin for short." I awkwardly lower my outstretched hand as I stumble through my explanation, but she doesn't look at me. Her eyes stay focused on Jake, completely dismissing me presence.

"Sinclair is a last name, not a first. People who have two last names cannot be trusted. Deception is weaved into their spirit at birth."

"Really Mom?"

"You're a grown man. Far be it from me to tell you what to do, but I will light a candle for you at mass on Sunday. Pray to the good Lord to protect you from Sin, as it were." She waves a hand in my direction before turning around to walk into the house. Jake steps into the house gently pulling me behind him and closing the door. His mother's retreating back is already at the other end of the massive house.

"She hated me on sight, Jake," I whisper.

"She doesn't know you, babe. My mom is… She can be a little pretentious, but she'll warm up."

He tries to walk in the same direction as his mom, but I dig my feet into the polished hardwood floors. He looks back at me curiously.

"I'm not staying. She doesn't l—" I back up until my back hits the solid surface of one of the walls.

"Give me thirty minutes. If you still want to leave, I'll walk out the door with you."

"Jake. Tell me you saw that. You saw that she refused to shake my hand or even look at me, right?"

"She's…" He looks away running a hand across the back of his neck. "I'm sorry about that. I'll talk to her, but you'll love my dad and my little sister."

"Thirty minutes? That all, right?" I ask searching his eyes. "Promise?"

"Promise," he says.

"Jacob," his mom calls down the hall. "Don't dawdle at the front door. Maria prepared your favorite, crab cakes for lunch on the back deck."

We both turn our heads to watch her walk through a sliding glass door. When she's out of sight, Jake drops a soft kiss to my neck. "How about we skip the whole meet the 'rents thing. We can go upstairs. I'll show you my old room and the bed in that room. I'm not in the mood for crab cakes anyway."

He drops a kiss on my lips. "But I could go for the taste of your sweet pu—"

I cover his mouth and stifle a laugh. "Oh my God, you are so nasty. I can't believe you'd even bring that up in your parents' house."

"Why? You think this place makes a difference? It doesn't. I'll be quick. You'll be more relaxed…" His hand drops to the button of my jeans.

"And your mom will hate me more than she already does," I say, pushing his hand away.

"She doesn't hate you." His hand drops from my button looping our pinkies. "Let's get this over with," he says, leading me toward the open door.

His mom and a man, who I assume is his dad, sit at a table with long stem wine glasses in their hands and colored fiesta plates in front of them. Jake pulls out a chair for me directly across from his mother and takes the one across from his dad.

"Jacob," his dad says once were seated.

"Pop."

"Your mother told me you'd brought a friend. We weren't expecting—"

"Sin, this is my dad, Conrad Johnson. Pop, this is Sin."

"Nice to meet you M-Mr.—" I start but I stutter to a stop when I hear his mother.

"Did you hear that name, Conrad? Didn't I tell you. Trash."

I drop my head to hide the tears that immediately well in my eyes.

"Mom, enough!"

"Do not take that tone with me, Jacob Johnson. This girl"—she tips her wine glass at me—"is a girl you have fun with. Not one you bring home to your mother. I could smell the trailer park, or is it ghetto, on her the moment I opened the door."

Jake pushes back from the table hard enough that the chair topples behind him. He pulls out my chair with a little less force.

"We're out."

"Son, your mother didn't mean to—"

"Yeah, she did, Pop. And you let her do it. I won't ask Sin to deal with this, and I'm not dealing with it either."

He offers a hand to help me stand and without another word, we walk out of the house.

Chapter 22

NOW

Sinclair

I'M HOT. I TRY TO KICK THE COVERS OFF MY BODY WHEN AN ARM AROUND my back pulls me closer to the source of all that heat.

"Hey," a gravelly voice rumbles under my ear.

"Hey, yourself," I say, pulling the sheet across my chest and scooting up the pillows. Shit! For the second time in so many days, I slept with Jacob Johnson. The first time didn't really count, but waking up in bed next to a sleep-warm Jake absolutely counts. There is no way around this one. The movie reel of last night's greatest hits start running through my head. Oh, Jesus, I let him hit it raw. The known cheater didn't use protection, and I...

"Stop over thinking it." Jake runs a thumb between my eyebrows, smoothing the crinkled skin back into place. Yeah, because that was possible. It is entirely realistic to forget the way this man owned my body. Jake touches my chin, tilting my face up to his, but I jerked out of his grip. He lets out a sigh, capturing my chin once again until my eyes finally flit up to his.

"What?"

"Why all the hostility when for the first time since you got back, we're good?" Jake frowns.

"We're so far from good, Jake." I let out a breath.

"But we're not. Seriously, Sin. I was there last night too. Hell, I'm here with you right now." He traces a finger down my cheek. That simple touch has my pulse leaping in my veins.

Is this hell or the sweetest heaven? Jake is right in front of me. His muscled body curved around mine. His beautiful eyes focused and penetrating. Every time we kiss, he injects a sliver of hope into my soul. That one speck of light on an otherwise dark canvas. With every thrust of his hips, that anchor I tried to yank out four years ago embeds itself deeper into my heart, filling the Jake-sized hole and strengthening our few remaining ties.

Laying in his arms makes it hard to remember all the reasons why opposites don't work. When we were together, Jake was the sky, boundless and towering. Where I was from, I had no choice but to stay grounded, a little more real. I used to think I gave him a bit more reality and he helped me shoot for the stars.

"Why can't we just be, Sin?" he asks in a subdued voice, his arm involuntarily pulling me closer.

"Because we have so much water under the bridge that's lapping at the sides and threatening to crush this thing into a million pieces."

"You're not that weak." He lifts my leg over his hip. "We're not that weak. What we have isn't water under any bridge, babe. It's just the beginning. We have so much more… so much."

"Jake I can't—"

"But you can. Choose me." His hand squeezes my thigh. "Do the unthinkable, and I promise you'll never look back." He seals that promise with a brush of lips. Jake is all intense conviction, and me? I'm teetering on the edge of crazy. I want to believe him. I want him to fix us. Erase all the heavy clouds the crowded my blue sky but common sense and a ten-year history says that in every situation, Jake is a bad bet.

"If we do this—" I start, but he shakes his head.

"When, Sin. The word you're looking for is *when* we do this. It's already happening. Give in, babe."

"Don't say that," I say, my voice cracking.

"Okay. Then what is this?" He shifts his body, dragging his skin along mine. "If not proof."

"Chemistry? Sexual attraction? I don't know. But this has always been the easy part with us. It's everything else that's hard"

"It's only as hard as we make it," he says playfully, bumping his hips against mine.

"Or as easy as I walked in and saw you with another woman." Just saying those words seems to steal the oxygen out of the space between us. I try to unwind my body from his so that I can take a breath, but his hand tightens on my thigh, keeping us sealed from our chest to our toes.

"That wasn't easy. I was… it was…" He blows out a hard breath. "The whole thing was fucked up. If I could change hurting you, if I could wave a magic wand and make it all go away, believe me I would, Sin, in a heartbeat. But I need you to stop pretending like that one horrible thing is the culmination of us. It's not true now and it wasn't true four years ago. I don't deserve your forgiveness but give us a chance. Give yourself this, and I'll spend every day for the rest of my life working for your forgiveness. Proving to you that you made the right choice."

The words tumble out of his mouth in a stilted cadence punctuated with an earnest desperation. I need a minute, or two, or thirty for them to sink in. But he keeps going.

"I'm not giving up on us. Not anymore. I know you and Adam are a thing now. That you have a kid—"

"What are you talking about? I don't have a baby." His muscles turn to stone under my touch. "And if I did have a kid, he or she would never be Adam's."

"I saw you, Sin. You and Adam and the girl. All of you. On stage the night the show opened. Just like four years ago I saw the Facebook post of the two of you laying on a couch backstage kissing."

"What in the hell are you talking about? What Facebook post? And that little girl you saw is his sister, Jake. Why would you just assumed she was mine?" I push back in his arms scrutinizing his face. He's serious. Dead serious.

"Start at the beginning because I need to understand this Facebook thing."

"Forget it."

"No! You just accused me of sleeping with Adam. Is that why you..."

He squeezes his eyes shut.

"It is, isn't? You thought I was sleeping with Adam. When I was on the road. Before I came home... you actually believed..."

His eyes peel open, and I wince at the pain in their depths.

"You were topless, laying on a sofa, kissing him, Sin. What was I supposed to think?"

"You were supposed to ask me. I would never... I never cheated on you. I remember that picture. I had on one of those backless tops and tripped over my shoe. Adam caught me. And we were most definitely not kissing," I say flabbergasted.

All these years he thought he'd caught me cheating. It explains so much. "Jake, Adam is... He's... Adam is gay."

He blinks once and a frown creases his brows.

"And his little sister is named Tori. She is one of the main reason's we're back in Vegas."

"Why didn't you tell me he was..."

"Because it's not my secret to tell. Because it shouldn't matter one way or the other. I told you who he was to me, who he's always been, and it should have been enough. Because he's not out. Shit I shouldn't have said that. You can't tell anyone."

"I wouldn't do that. Not to him or you."

"Please don't. If it gets out, he'll—"

"Trust me. I've been jealous of him since the first time I heard his name. I never guessed... but fuck, I needed to hear that."

He melts under my fingers, the tension oozing out of his body one limb at a time. I don't know what's more problematic, the fact that he thought I cheated with Adam and that we have a child, or the fact that he came here tonight with the intention of seducing me even

161

when he thought I was with someone else. No. Not just someone. He thought I was with Adam.

"How are you even here if you thought I was with Adam?"

"Because I'm over here fighting, Sin." He pushes both hands in my hair, dropping a hard, stinging kiss on my mouth, and even in his harshness, my body responds.

"And if I had a baby there'd be nothing to fight for, right?"

"Wrong. I'm all in. There is no plan B. So even if you had a kid with another man, it doesn't change that fact that I want you. And not just this…" He moves his growing erection through my slippery folds.

"I want it all. Your trust." A light kiss touches my lips. "Your body." His tongue plunges deep, thrusting against mine. "Your music." He rolls me onto my back, his body hovering over mine. "Your everything." This time when our mouths touch, it's the luscious meeting of two lovers reconnecting, the exchange perfect in its simplicity. He strips me down to my basest desires. The ones I've been afraid to even admit to myself.

Jake doesn't take his time. He's uncontrolled. Panting between searing kisses and barely coordinated thrusts of his hips. We both moan in anticipation when I reach down, my fingers wrapping around his shaft and guiding him into my entrance.

He enters me, thrusting hard. Forceful pumps that move us up the bed. I stretch my hands over my head pushing my palms against the headboard, to save my skull, as I rock my hips, taking him deeper. And God this man. Every single time is better than the last time. Good in a way I was sure I'd only imagined. If anything, my memory didn't do him justice.

Gone is my suave lover, but I like him like this. Emotional. Severe. Overpowering. His body is not asking for permission but instead taking, what he wants. Possessing me from the inside out.

He rears back on his knees, firm hands working my hips up and down his length. The new angle is almost too much. From this position, he's nearly too long, too thick. He leans forward tangling my hand with his. Our joined hands glide on my sweat-drenched skin to settle on my sex and move in slow circles around my clit.

"Show me what you do when you're alone and this insatiable pussy needs to be filled. Let me see how you make yourself come," he rasps.

He goes back to thrusting with abandon, and my fingers move around my sensitive flesh. At first, slow, tentative. I've never done this in front of any man, including Jake. Especially not while he's inside me. But it feels so good. My fingers strum my clit faster and holy hell... I explode.

The orgasm barrels into me like a Mack truck, starting in my chest and moving to the very tips of my toes. He gets in a few more unco-ordinated thrusts before he jumps off the cliff after me. He collapses against my chest, our sweaty skin sealed together, our breaths haggard.

My mind is blissfully empty except for one thought. What am I getting myself into now?

Chapter 23

NOW

Jake

THE LAST SEVERAL HOURS WITH SIN ARE THE CULMINATION OF A thousand whispered prayers and infinite dreams. The last four years weren't gone, but tonight I think we got from under the shadow. One night doesn't erase years of history and hurt, but at least there is a light at the end of the tunnel.

Sin makes me earn every touch and every kiss, and each time she lets me inside, every high-pitched moan and every stinging scrape of her nails on my shoulders is worth it. She brings out the Jerry McGuire feels. For the first time in four years I feel complete. Unlike the night on the balcony, she's not turning away or hitting me with an unaffected attitude that hardens her face into an unrecognizable mask. Tonight she met each kiss with equal passion, and that gorgeous body took everything I offered, and in some instances, demanded more.

As much as I wanted the sex. I want this. The intimacy that comes from lying beside her while she sleeps. The knowledge I'm the man that took her bed and put her asleep, the one she'll see first thing in the morning and the one she'll hopefully turn to in the middle of the night.

I run my hands up and down her spine and revel in the feel of her under my fingertips. Soft and taut. By the time I close my eyes the sun is peaking over the top of the mountains, casting a golden glow across the room, highlighting her dark skin to a copper hue. I pull Sin's sleep heavy body closer. And with her legs tangled in mine and her exhales synced with my inhales. finally I sleep.

Jesus who left the blinds open? The sun blazes its way over the top of the mountain and tries to singe my retinas even behind closed eyelids. I turn my face away from the window only to get a mouth full of hair.

I move her hair to the side and brush a kiss on her shoulder, and just because I can, I do it again. Sin shifts at my movement, blinking her eyes open. For five, maybe ten seconds, she looks at me like she used to with possessive hunger and tender devotion. But I watch her as the worship fades to confusion, her soft brown eyes become guarded and her body starts to hum with barely concealed anxiety.

She slips out of bed, eyes everywhere but on mine, uttering an excuse as she hurries to the bathroom. The door snaps shut, and the shower starts a couple of seconds later.

Don't do this, baby. Don't shut me out. Not after last night. Not when for the first time in four years we could be in perfect accord. I move stiffly to the edge of the bed. The late hours and multiple rounds of sex makes me sluggish.

Sin wants distance. Why wouldn't she? The last time we were together, really together, it didn't end well. I hurt her. Bad. The right thing would be to back off. Let her come to me. Give her the space she rightly deserves. I'm solidly on the wrong side of right. She knows how to freeze me out, did it for four years and I'm done being stuck in the cold.

I glance at the closed door for a full minute before I walk to the bathroom to test the handle. Unlocked—good sign.

The door quietly opens and there she is, behind steam-covered glass, warm water cascading over her curves. She doesn't utter a sound when I join her inside the shower stall or when my hands find the soapy skin along her ribs.

"You hiding in here?" I ask, pulling her farther under the spray.

Sin looks at me through eyelashes spiked with water. Her brown eyes glued to mine when she mumbles. "Not well."

"Not at all."

"We don't have to do this," she says, shaking her hands in front of her like she's shaking off bad vibes. "We don't. Now that we've gotten whatever this is out of our systems, we can go back to our respective lives. Let's not do the long, drawn out discussion." She tries to move away, but I use my body to back her against the shower bench.

"Last night was the first time in years that I felt normal. That I didn't feel like something was missing."

"Don't do that. Don't pretend like it's more than it is. That it's more than sex."

"It's more."

"I can't do another trip down memory lane."

"Me neither," I say gruffly. "I want to make new memories." I bend my head, brushing my lips over hers and gliding my fingers over the gentle slope of her jaw to turn her face. She lets out a shuddered breath. The first kiss is rigid. Her lips don't open under the pressure of mine or when my tongue tries to explore her mouth. "Kiss me," I say against her lips. "Kiss me and let the rest go." I drop kisses at the edge of her lips.

"Jake, we shouldn't—" she says in a breathy voice. Her shoulders sag and her head tilts at just the right angle so I can't see her eyes.

"We should." I use my thumb under her chin to push her face up to mine. "We absolutely should, and we already have," I say right before I kiss her again. My tongue flicks at the crease of her bottom lip. My hands shift down her body, and my thumbs instinctively rub her hardened nipples.

"Oh…" she groans. Her hips jerk forward. So, I do it again.

Sin turns fully toward me. Standing on her toes, her lips crash onto mine, and I open up, let her tongue inside my mouth. I offer no protest when she pushes me down on the bench and straddles my legs, rubbing her slicked pussy along the achingly tight skin of my shaft. I don't need a gentle seduction. I just need her, and at this point I'll take her anyway I can get her.

"Use me, Sin," I demand, wrapping my hand around the base of my dick. Standing the hard column up, the broad crown teasing her entrance.

Bracing her hands on my shoulders as she eases her weight down. Her pussy unfolds around my shaft, the lips perfect and silky. She's tight, so fucking tight. Sin sets the pace, a slow grind up, followed by a hard bounce down.

"Fuuuuuck, baby," I pant, leaning forward to wrap my lips around her nipple and laving the tight bud with my tongue. Sin arches her back pushing more of her breast into my mouth as her hands wrap around my head, holding me to her chest.

"Don't stop, Jake," she whimpers. "Right there. I'm right there," she says, moving faster. Her drenched pussy dripping down my balls.

My hand skims down the flat plane of her stomach to her clit. The barest touch makes her shudder.

"Ohhh…"

My thumbs circles that sensitive flesh, and it swells beneath my touch. Sin constricts around my length, her orgasm milking me in deep pulsing waves. I'm a man barely holding on to the edge of sanity, and each pulse pulls another finger off the ledge until I'm falling into the abyss with her.

We don't move for several minutes, our breaths ragged and our hearts beating hard in our chests. It isn't until the hot water turns luke-warm and then cold that I ease out of her. Sin stands and turns off the water. I grab her hand before she can walk out, and she pulls me into the bathroom.

She grabs two towels hanging on the rack, tossing one in my general direction. "Here you go."

I catch it and wrap the thick white cotton around my waist. I follow her into the room where we tiptoe around each other in a silence weighed down by the awkwardness of two people with a broken past and an uncertain future, who, over the last eight hours, have shared enough to make us vulnerable and uncertain how to proceed.

At least that's how I feel. Maybe it's different for Sin. Maybe she just wants me out of her villa and doesn't know how to politely ask. She keeps her back turned to me as she rubs oil into her skin and pulls on black exercise shorts that barely cover her curves and a Def Leppard tank top that does nothing to cover the fact that she didn't bother with a bra. Her skin is luminous and fragrant, and my dick immediately takes notice.

Not right now, you randy fucker. I take my eyes off Sin because even after the shower I want her again. Right now. But I'm not pushing my luck.

I should say something. Open my mouth and convince her to let me stay but the only time I get past the walls Sin is hiding behind is when I'm inside her. So instead of begging yet again, I locate my discarded clothes.

I take my time pulling on one rumpled garment after the other. Throwing glances her way hoping to catch her eye.

"I'm going to go ahead and go," I say fully clothed now. She doesn't object so I head toward the door. She follows a couple of paces behind me, and when I'm standing on the other side of the door, she finally meets my gaze. And nope. I'm not getting past those walls right now. We stare at each other over the threshold, waiting for the other person to make the first move. Like always, I cave first. I wrap my fingers around the back of Sin's neck and brush my thumb across the tip of her collarbone.

"You good?" I ask because what else can I say? *Sorry that I hurt you. Sorry that I cheated. Sorry that I'm still stupidly, head over heels, in love with you. But next time will be different. Just watch.* She knows how I feel.

"I'm…" Her head lowers to my chest before she brings her eyes back up. "Okay." Her tongue swipes her full bottom lip.

"I must be losing my touch if you're just 'okay.' " I use my other hand to make air quotes and chuckle. Last night was spine tingling, toe curling, fucking phenomenal. It was better than all the times we had before and anything I'd had with other women. Never in the history of us has sex been "okay," and we both know it.

"I guess we need to get in more practice so that I improve," I say jokingly. The smile on Sin's face dies so fast you would've thought I broke the secret to her that there's no Santa Claus.

"Jake," she says softly. "All the stuff that happened on the balcony and everything that went down last night... that was closure, you know?"

I study her face long and hard.

Wow. Sin's serious.

"This was a one and done. You know that, right?" She attempts to step back into the room, but I tighten my hold on her neck, stopping her retreat. "We needed that one last time. Get it out of our systems," she murmurs.

The word closure scrapes my already exposed nerves raw. Closure my ass. I don't know everything, but I know a little bit, and last night wasn't closure. It was a new beginning.

But if that's what she needs to tell herself, so be it. The train wreck that is Sin and I is my bed, and I've been lying in it for four years. It's time to buy a new mattress and change the sheets. After years of yearning for one more time, the finality of her words sucks the air out of my lungs and chill my body.

This is what hell feels like. Having everything you want, everything you desire at your fingertips, and not being able to fully grasp it. I can't help wondering if this is how Sin felt when she found Tina and me.

"I'm not asking for a relationship," I say roughly, and I'm not. At least not yet. She's skittish enough as it is, and I have the feeling if I push too hard, she'll run again. I have to give her just enough space and time to find her way back to me and I have no hesitation in using our attraction to lure her in or convolute the waters to get her to stay.

What I'm not doing is accepting this one-time bullshit.

We stare at each other. She's stiff and guarded and I'm grappling with how to scale those walls.

"It doesn't have to be complicated," I say finally, dropping my forehead to hers.

"Have we ever been anything else?"

"I think so. You don't remember? It wasn't that long ago." I move my hand into the soft hair at the nape of her neck.

"I stopped thinking about us a long time ago." Sin lets out a sad laugh. "It was the only way I was able to move on with my life."

"But have you really moved on? From where I'm standing it feels like we're right back where we started. A new beginning, if you will." I close the distance between our lips, my mouth slanting over hers. There's a moment of hesitation before she melts under my touch.

She tastes sweeter than she has a right to, and her mouth is so warm. Her tongue is beyond talented, dancing over mine in a deliberate caress. Her long fingers grip the bare skin of my waist, while she takes from my mouth like woman long denied water in a barren desert.

I fist my hand in her hair while the other hand finds the edge her T-shirt delving underneath to find warm flawless skin. Kissing Sin is more than two mouths meeting. It's a sharing of the soul. It's when she's most open. Even though she denies it.

Sin's hands trembled as she pulls me closer. Satisfied moans pour from her mouth as she frantically returns my kiss.

I pull my head back, but we continue to clutch each other. My eyes open just enough to see her sooty lashes resting above her cheek. Her eyes flicker open and she looks at me the same way I'm sure I'm looking at her—a confusing mix of love and lust.

"What are you doing to me?" she asks quietly, pulling her gaze from my lips.

"The same thing you're doing to me."

"What's that?"

"I don't have a name for it, Sin, but I'd like to find out. Wouldn't you?"

I lick my lips and fight the urge to step back over the threshold. I take a deep breath. "We don't need all the answers right now. We have an entire year to figure it out."

The dazed look lifts from her eyes and a smirk turns the corners of her mouth. "I forgot how persistent you could be."

"Yeah." I draw the pad of my thumb on her bottom lip. "But only when it comes to you."

Chapter 24

Four Years Ago
Jake

"*T*he number you have dialed is not in service, please check the *number and dial again.*"

It's been seventy-two hours. No word. No communication. I don't know who's watching our house, but every day when I come home from the office, more of her stuff is gone. I know she's been here because I can still smell the faint scent of the almond shampoo that she uses. She's fading from my life. It's understandable and breaking my fucking heart, but I get it.

I walk down the hall toward our bedroom, and I wonder what's missing this time? I never realized how intertwined all our things were until hers started to disappear. I look around the house taking inventory, trying to notice the small things that are different.

So far there is nothing out of the ordinary. The tension that's sitting like a rock in my gut starts to ease. I feel like we're finally on the other side of this thing. She'll come home at some point. It's not like she can avoid me forever. Couples have fights. People work through infidelity all the time. I know I messed up. I messed up bad.

Now I just want to get past it, fix it, fix us, but who am I kidding? I don't even know where to start. But I have to try. I'm not giving up.

And then I notice the house keys sitting on top of a folded piece of paper on the kitchen counter. That rock in my gut comes back, but this time it is boulder size. I palm both the keys and the note and continue toward our bedroom. All the pictures that used to line the hall have been taken down. She left the only one that captures us. Our intimacy. Our closeness. It's an artistic black and white of us after she won a local contest to be the opening act for a much more significant band. Her smile is huge, our fingers are threaded together, I'm leaning down to her, and she's on tiptoe reaching for me. The photographer snapped the shot right before I kissed her.

The AC kicks on and that weird suction rolls through the house, slamming doors. I force myself to keep moving toward the bedroom. I don't know what's waiting around the next corner. Call it a gut feeling or maybe instinct but whatever's coming next is going to rip me down to the fucking marrow of my bones.

The door to the spare room, where Sin stores her ridiculous collection of guitars and other instruments, catches on something and bounces back wide open. Empty pegs line the walls where guitars use to hang. The missing keyboard stands left deep indents on the carpet. The only thing left in the room is the classic Fender I bought her for her last birthday.

I place my hand over the ache in the center of my chest. Trying to hold the broken pieces of my heart together from the outside. What started as a dull ache is now a radiant, all-consuming pain. The small room appears massive without the instruments lining the walls or the cushions piled on the floor. Her absence is like a tumor eating me from the inside out. The longer she's gone, the more it festers and grows until it consumes me. At the same time, this house feels small, almost stifling without her. That's the way it feels when she's on tour, and now that she's moved out, it's more than small.

It's lifeless.

I glanced around what had been our home. There is no indication she ever lived here and only one lone picture to testify to our relationship.

I unfold the paper in my hand and quickly read her words.

"I treated you with the respect that you have not earned, and you do not deserve. I have loved every piece of you with everything in me. Today a part of

me died. And when you miss me, because you will miss me, remember I didn't walk away, you kicked me out the fucking door."

There it is. The moment I've been waiting for over the last couple of years. She's gone. There are no take backs. No big blowups or confrontations. Sin disappeared from my life the same way she came in, suddenly and with heartbreaking clarity.

For the thirtieth time in the last hour, I dial Sin's number. For the thirtieth time, I get a disconnect message. I lower the phone from my ear and stare blankly at the screen. This is crazy. I thought sooner or later Sin and I would have it out, and on that *day of judgment*, I'd be found lacking because I cheated. But of all the possible scenarios, I never considered she'd freeze me out.

I know where she's been staying. I'd have to be an idiot not to know. She's with Adam. Until I walked into an empty house, I believed, maybe stupidly, she'd be back. She had to get all her stuff, right? But I didn't bank on her making it a stealthy covert mission to do it. At the very least I thought she'd say something, anything. I thought she'd yell and cuss, and we'd have it out but, in the end, we'd still be us and still be together.

But Sin is done. She's not coming back. If our empty house didn't solidify that fact, the dear Jake letter damn well did.

Adam and Sin are closer than I've ever been comfortable with, and now I have to tuck tail, go to his house, or at the very least ask for his help. He knows Sin as well as I do, if not better, so if she isn't there, which I know she will be, he'll know exactly where to find her.

I've been prowling through the house for the last several minutes vacillating between extreme anger at how she left and who she's with, to shame for being the poster child for fuckboys everywhere and getting caught in the worst possible position. Then I go to missing her and wanting nothing more than to see her. Knowing she's in the city, but not home with me burns, and then the anger comes again. The ugly cycle's giving me emotional whiplash. I just need a sign, a clue how to fix what I broke. Something that will give me with a way out, but I can't find the silver lining. There's nothing to look forward to.

The hardest thing about this whole situation is that it was all me. I did it to myself and now I have to sit in the eye of the storm and accept responsibility. I may not be comfortable with how close she's to Adam, but are they bumping uglies on tour? Fuck, I don't know but based on the pictures, it's a good possibility. It's always been in the back of my mind. Always. But she's so adamant. So probably not.

I'm grasping at straws, trying to rationalize my fucked up self and I can't. There is no way to rationalize this. All I can say is that I missed her. I missed her, and I was angry she was gone. Jealous she was out there chasing her dreams while I sacrificed mine for a family legacy that didn't mean shit anywhere except casino floors and sketchy backrooms.

My feet move toward the door before my brain can catch up. I'm on autopilot when I get in my car. The drive to Adam's house only takes fifteen minutes, the sun is barely dipping behind the western ridge of the mountains when I pull up outside. All the blinds are open. It is the first real glimpse I've had of Sin in days, three long days. I look at my reddened eyes in the review mirror.

Get out of the fucking car, Jake. Get out of this car and get your girl.

But fuck if I know what to say or do. Saying I'm sorry is not enough and saying I love you is even worse. I get out of the car and cut across the yards desert landscaping toward the front door. From where I'm standing, I have a perfect view of Sin. Without the makeup or stage clothes, she looks more like the girl I met in college. Her coarse, dark hair is piled in a bun on top of her head, glasses perched on her nose, and her creamy brown skin so smooth and perfect I curl my fingers into a fist to fight the urge to touch her. Reluctantly I turn away from the window.

I ring the doorbell and try to calm my racing heart. I hear footsteps approach the door, and I'm pretty sure someone just looked at me through the peephole. I start to pace the small piece of concrete in front of the door, agitation making my steps short.

She's going to leave me out here.

Heavier footsteps approach the door, and instead of my soft curvy girlfriend answering and falling adoringly into my arms, I'm greeted by a pissed Adam. He's as pale as Sin is dark. His blond hair and bright blue eyes—her perfect counterpart.

She's going to leave me out here. I don't even get a fuck you or a go to hell or a chance to say I'm sorry. She's is seriously going to leave me out here and that fissure in my heart that started when I stepped in our home and saw all her things gone, it burst wide open and panic and desperation pour out.

"Look, I just want to talk to her. That's it. I just need to." I look over his shoulder and shout, "Sin. Sinclair, please!" I yell through the open door. I take a step forward, and his hand meets solidly with my chest.

"She doesn't want to talk to you."

I hit his arm with enough force that he stumbles back. "Man, it seriously is not the time."

He steps over the threshold, closing the door securely behind him. "It is long past the time." His calm demeanor amps me up even more, making me want to bum-rush him to remove this barrier between Sin and me.

"Look, this has nothing to do with you," I say, balling up fist and grinding my molars and just barely holding on to a modicum of restraint.

"It's got everything to do with me when she shows up at my house, asking for a place to stay because she walked in on you fucking her friend."

This fucking guy with the mouth and the greater than thou attitude. Yes, he knew Sin first, but somethings are between a man and his

176

woman. Sometimes the best friend needs to take a back seat and slow his row, know his place, "Look, Adam—"

"No, you look. I've stood on the sidelines for years and watched her bend herself like a pretzel, turning down gigs that could have catapulted her career, staying in Vegas when every independent distribution label in L.A. has begged us to move there. She did all that to try to keep you happy. I've had to listen to her talk about all your petty insecurities, the whole men and women can't be friends thing. The why are you on tour and away from home thing, the stalking the fucking social media pages like a fuckboy looking for evidence of indiscretions and, bro, if even half of the shit she told me is true, you're a bigger bitch than I thought."

Did the dude sporting a man bun seriously just call me a bitch? I might be a lot of things, but a bitch is nowhere in me. I roll my eyes to the darkening sky and start counting. I'm almost to five before he steps into my personal space to drop more pearls of wisdom.

"I've watched her minimize herself to make you comfortable with who she's destined to be. I've listened to her hope and pray and wish for you to step up, be a man, or at the very least, her fucking man. And she showed up here shattered. Let you talk to her? Fuck you."

His words are eating through my conscience like acid because he's right. But fuck right. My anger is beyond rational at this point. I throw a punch that connects with the side of his face. The sound of my knuckles colliding with skin is satisfying. God, it feels good to hit his pretty boy face after all this time. He's never known his place. Always coming at me with the mean mugging and shitty comments. And I'd place good money on the fact he's always in Sin's ear talking shit. All the emotion that I've held in for the last three days erupts. The swiftness of my attack may have caught Adam off guard, but then he hits me back, faster than I can block and harder than I expect.

The door opens wider behind him, and we both fall at Sin's feet. Sin is only five feet tall, but from my position on the floor she looks taller, and hurt, and broken. In that blink of an eye, we're back where we started.

"Sin, please." My voice breaks.

Adam stands, his presence a glowering figure at her back.

"Thank you, friend, but I got it from here." She's talking to Adam, but her eyes never leave mine. Those midnight pools that generally sparkle are dull and puffy. Her nose is bright with a shine that only comes from blowing your nose with frequency. She's clutching a piece of tissue in her hand. Pain twists her features like a warped mask, and even her pain is its own kind of beauty.

Adam slips inside the door but not before giving her a one-armed hug and I hear his rough voice say, "Stay strong, Sin. This asshole isn't worth your tears." Throwing me the evil eye, he says, "And he never was." I watch intently as his back retreats deeper into the house.

"Get up, Jake." I'm surprised when she offers me a hand. Our fingers intertwine, and for the first time in days, I feel the frayed edges of my world begin to knit back together. I get to my feet, and she immediately drops my hand as if the contact burned.

"What do you want, Jake?" Her arms wrap tight around her middle like she's trying to hold herself together.

I'm finally face-to-face with Sin and I've got... nothing. My brain is blank. Every practiced speech and contrite apology are gone. My eyes are glued to hers and fuck me, I can't think of one word. After holding my gaze for a little less than a breath, her eyes glaze over with tears, and her teeth sink into her bottom lip to stop the trembling.

She takes a step back over the threshold, doorknob in her hand, preparing to close the door in my face.

"Hold on." I press a palm against the door, keeping it cracked, to wedge myself between the opening. I close the space between us. The need to feel her, smell her, be in her space, and have her in mine propelling me forward. My hand slides around the back of her neck pulling her toward me. She stumbles into my arms and trips over her own feet, but like every other time we've touched, it's right.

Finally, the pressure in my chest lets up, and I breathe easy. I rest my forehead against hers and whisper against her lips, "I still want you, Sin. Only you." I close my eyes against the accusations in hers. This close, her breath is co-mingled with mine, and I can smell the faint scent of almond from her shampoo.

"Come back home," I beg. My lips move over hers, but she doesn't kiss me back. "I need you. I need us." I breathe out on a plea.

This time when I seek her lips, she yields but it's not with sweet abandon. It's stiff and tinged with regret. This kiss is heartbreak played out with the brush of lips and the slide of tongues.

And it hurts.

Our lips pull apart and I let out a shuddered breath as my heart finally rips completely apart. Instinctively I tighten my arms around her, trying to keep her close, but she pulls back. The air slips between us as easy as a knife through butter. I know what's coming. Good-bye. She going to put the final nail in the proverbial coffin. I watch her mouth move but I can't comprehend the words.

"I don't know what's worse, the idea that you think I'm foolish enough to believe you, or the fact you think I'm stupid enough to take you back."

Don't say the words. Don't say we're done. I scream in my head, but the words get stuck behind the lump of emotion in my throat.

"I get it, Jake, I really do, but loving you is tearing me apart. I can't pretend like it didn't happen, and I can't come home. I'm done… okay?"

No. It's not okay. None of this is okay. This would be a good time for that apology. Say anything. Don't let her go. My mind is screaming but I remain mute. My voice refusing to give purchase to my thoughts.

"You win. Your family wins. We should have listened to everyone six years ago and saved ourselves from this moment they all somehow predicted. In some ways I guess it was always going to end this way. Girls like me don't end up with boys like you—" Tears stream down her face, cutting off the flow of words.

I cup her cheek and swipe her tears with my thumb and words tumble out of my mouth, spurred by desperation. "I'm sorry. I just want us to be okay. Just tell me how to make us right again." I place chaste kisses on her lips, cheeks, eyes—any place that I can reach. "Just tell me what to do, Sin. I just want us. I'll fix it. I swear I will," I whisper

Her eyes flutter shut, and a tremor moves through her entire body. She takes one deep breath, and when she opens her eyes, I see it.

Those beautiful brown eyes I use to drown in have shut down. Sin is folding herself away, going somewhere I can't follow.

She takes a small step back, and cold air rushes into the space her warm body just occupied,

"This is the easy part. We were always good when it came to good-bye." Without another word, she steps back into the house.

If the look in her eyes didn't let me know loud and clear it was over, the sound of the deadbolt sliding into place does.

And then I hear it—gut-wrenching sobs on the other side of the door.

I lay my face on the cold metal surface listening to heartache flow from her in waves. "Help me," I whisper, looking up at the starless sky. This would be the perfect time for divine intervention, but no one answers back.

The overwhelming sense of loss cripples me and I drop to the ground. I didn't realize it would feel like this, a pain so sharp I want to crawl out of my skin to get away from it.

I sit there long after the door closed, praying to whatever is up there that Sin will open the door and tell me we can work it out, but that never happens. Instead I hear the first chords of a song. The melody is the same haunting sound of her tears.

And that's when the walls of bullshit that I'd hunkered down behind cave in, and I'm hit with wave after wave of emotion. Regret and shame vie for the dominance to take me down first and I can't fight it.

I give up

After minutes of sitting outside the door, I walk away. In my mind, me leaving isn't forever, it's until. Until I can figure out how to fix it. Until she's ready to listen.

Fuck this day! I just want to rewind time. Go back to that horrible moment and change my mind. I want to spit in temptations face and tell my pride to go fuck itself.

Every mistake, every misstep plays in my mind on a warped loop. It's like a scratch on record that's stuck on one cracked piece of music. As I drive down the freeway back toward our house, I fight the urge to turn the car around. Go back to Adam's house and post up until she'll talk to me. Have a real conversation about the hard ugly truth.

I try to blink back the tears that have been threatening to fall since Sin left, but this time I can't. My eyes glass over, blurring the road in front of me.

Chapter 25

"M S. JAMES, ARE YOU LISTENING TO ME?" JEANINE GLANCES UP from her cell phone. Her short hair is pulled back with a red headband the exact shade of her glasses and instead of her traditional power suit, she's wearing a black and gold T-shirt with The Hotel logo blazed across the front, black jeans, and black tennis shoes. Casual looks good on her, but only Jeanine can make jeans and a T-shirt seem *tres chic*.

I'm dragging. The eight o'clock wake-up call was super early, considering Jake left the villa sometime around five. There are bags under my eyes. The six cornrows I've plated into my hair are lopsided and lumpy. I have on the same shirt as Jeanine, but I cut a larger hole in the neck, so it hangs off one shoulder. It's supposed to reach at least ninety degrees, so I opted for jean shorts.

"Do I have a choice not to?"

"And who says that rock stars aren't bright?" She taps a nicely manicured nail against her lips.

"I didn't," Adam says, swinging his guitar around his back.

"*Et tu, Brute?*" I say, laughing.

"Brutus was a coward who stabbed Caesar in the back. I did it right to your face. Gotta respect that," he says with a wink.

"No. I really don't."

"Well, you should. You ready to roll. We're supposed to be on stage at ten and it's already eight thirty." He pulls out of his phone, confirming the time before returning it to his pocket.

We're doing a stripped-down acoustic set for a fun run downtown to support Take Refuge, the only battered women's shelter in the valley. The Hotel is a major sponsor, providing music and food alongside resources for the women that are seeking help.

According to Jeanine, it generates thousands of dollars for the shelter each year and when Jake brought it up one night in bed, I wanted to help because his passion for the project was contagious and because I wanted to see him outside of midnight and four walls. And I want to do something that helps.

Tired of waiting on us to get moving, Adam takes charge, directing the roadies that will be transporting our equipment and giving our security clear instructions. In true Adam style, he takes charge, completely disregarding the instructions Jeanine already gave the crew. Jeanine gives Adam a sidelong glance, irritation making her eyes narrow and her lips pinch

"Is he always that autocratic?" she asks, still watching his back as he leans in to speak quietly to Seth and Aiden. Adam taps a fist on each guards shoulder, apparently finished with whatever it is he had to say, he turns his back on the men, and I see Seth melt from over here. So, they're definitely still a thing.

"Adam is many things," I say, shrugging my shoulders before turning my attention completely on Jeanine. "But I've never thought of him that way. He's actually pretty chill once you get to know him."

"I have introduced myself three times, Ms. James, there will not be a fourth. He is still dismissively high-handed and excessively rude." I don't say anything because I can't argue that fact. Adam is not a fan of Jeanine's and it shows. I, on the other hand, have grown to appreciate her candor. In the words of Venetria, although she be cunty, she be good.

"Are shorts and boots a thing now? Jeanine asks, eyeing my legs and Dr. Martens. "It's almost as ridiculous as high heels and shorts."

I point at myself. "They are for this girl."

"Your fashion choices are… interesting as always, Ms. James."

"Not really. I'm more of a wear what my hands land on kinda girl, and today this is what you get. Whatever I wear is fashion. One of the perks of being me." I wink at her cheekily. The corner of her lip pulls up into a smile and she shakes her head.

"You ready to go?" I ask, already heading for the door.

We enter the garage. Our group breaks in half to fit in two SUVs. Once seated our drivers make quick work of getting out of the hotel parking garage. We roll up to one of the few vacant lots in Downtown Las Vegas. A temporary stage has been erected, news crews are already there, leaving barely enough room for the people actually participating in the fundraiser but it's tame. The reporters aren't manic or crawling over each other to get a sound bite. They're lounging around the area, drinking coffee, and eating donuts. A couple wave as Adam and I climb on stage to start the sound check.

There are groups of volunteers clustered together at various stations. Most are dressed in colorful T-shirts that have different company logos on the front and denote what task their group will perform. The people at the water station are wearing light blue. The people at the sign in table are wearing horrible Easter egg yellow. From the stage, locating our group is easy. We're the only people wearing black shirts, and in a sea of pastels, the contrast is striking.

From my perch I watch Jeanine make a beeline for a tall grizzly man with skin so weathered it looks like cracked leather. He has a full beard and a beer belly. They speak for a couple of minutes before he hands her a stack of papers attached to a clipboard. Jeanine walks over to our group, which has convened in front of the stage. She places two fingers in her mouth and lets out an ear-piercing whistle.

"All right then, listen up. Before we get started, I want to give you a few guidelines on dealing with the media. If they want to speak with you, they must go through me. In the case of Ms. James and Mr. Johnson…"

At the mention of his name, my eyes snap up and immediately

find his. *Are you as tired as I am? Maybe we should have gone to sleep after the first or second round. Did we really need to go for a third?* He nods, a knowing smirk pulling at his lips.

Jake's T-shirt is identical to the rest of us. He's wearing dark jeans with a backward baseball cap and sunglasses on the back of his neck. And for a hot second, I see him as he was ten years ago with a shit ton of swagger and no responsibility, or at least not the kind that made his shoulders heavy and crease his brow even in sleep.

"The media is here to cover the race, not the two of you. If they ask about your personal history redirect them to the foundation, if they persist, redirect them to me," Jeanine continues.

"Our team is working with Clyde. His mother founded the shelter thirty years ago when she lost her sister to domestic violence. Clyde still handles the day-to-day operational needs of the facility, and he is also the head brewer at Glitter Gulch Brewery." Jeanine looks over her shoulder at the man she was talking to earlier.

"Say hello, Clyde." He waves one hand while stuffing his mouth with a donut.

"Ms. James and Mr. Beckham will take care of the entertainment. The rest of us will function as liaisons for the various stations, ensuring that the water station does indeed have water, that the sign-in booth has swag bags and entry bracelets, and that we count and secure additional donations. You get the gist. Check with me if you are uncertain where you are needed. Make me look good, people."

The group turns toward Clyde to get started. Contrary to his appearance Clyde is soft-spoken and exceptionally well organized. He breaks them into pairs. Then hands out supplies based on assigned tasks. Jake holds my gaze for a long beat before turning away.

"You're playing with fire, Sin," Adam says in a tone so low, that only I can hear him.

"I'm sorry, what?" I ask startled at his proximity.

"Jacob Johnson was a bad choice ten years ago and he's a bad choice now."

"How'd you know?" I ask.

"I knew after the first time it happened."

Of course, he did. I knew it was only a matter of time before he would if he didn't already

"You don't hide it well. Neither of you do. If you're trying to keep this thing under wraps, maybe don't eye fuck in public."

"I wasn't—"

"You were. And so was he. What are you thinking, Sin? You know this dude, and you're still falling for his bullshit," he whisper-shouts, shaking his head like a frustrated puppy.

"Not all of us live our lives, hiding in the shadows," I snap, and his shoulders hunch forward like that verbal jab hit him square in the chest.

"That was a low blow, Sin. Real low. You know why I'm not…" He cuts off the flow of words, his fingers digging at his scalp in a way that makes me wince in pain. "Why I can't… It would be a mess—"

"And we'd clean it up and you'd be happy. Seth loves—"

"Don't say another fucking word," he growls, holding up his hand and turning his head so his face is no longer visible, and takes deep, deep breaths.

"I'm sorry," I say, placing a hand on the hard muscles of his arm. "I don't know what I'm doing with Jake. I don't. And it might end up in an even bigger disaster, but right now doing whatever we're doing is the only thing that feels right. He feels right and I want that feeling for as long as I can have it. I want my happy. And I want you to find yours too. So, if Seth—"

"We don't talk about Seth. I can't…" He swipes a tired hand down his face. "I can't go there. Not right now." He turns to face me, those oh so blue eyes red rimmed. "Be careful, Sin. That's all I'm saying."

"I will," I say, frowning as I take notice of the tired lines around his eyes. "You okay?"

"I'm not." He looks up at the sky when his eyes water. "I'm really not." I immediately pull him into a hug, the guitar stopping me from totally embracing him. He drops his head to my shoulder. *Jesus. I've never seen him like this. I'm normally the emotional one. What did I miss?* We stay in that awkward pose for a couple more seconds before taking small steps backward.

"Whatever it is I'm here. Just say the word and I'll cut a bitch," I say, moving my hand in a slicing motion. A small grin pulls at one side of his mouth.

"What if I'm the bitch that needs cutting?" His eyes travel to the edge of the stage to land on Seth before coming back to mine.

"Then we go with plan B."

"What's that?"

"I haven't figured it out yet but when I do it'll be good."

He laughs but it's a brittle sound, joyless.

"Adam?"

"What's up?"

"I'm always around if you want to talk it out."

He studies me for a long, drawn out moment before covering his eyes with a pair of sunglasses. "Somethings are better left unsaid," he says almost himself as he strums an open E chord.

We move through our sound check in silence. It isn't tense or uncomfortable, but I give Adam a wide berth. There are some subjects I don't want to broach either. We both take solace in the ritual of preparing for a show, testing chords, checking mics, adjusting the stage sound and making sure that the house, or in this case, the outdoor stage sound is at the right levels. And by the time we finish, it's okay.

We're Adam and Sin, the professional musicians, the people that play when our hearts are empty and broken, that smile through the pain, that pour every ounce of ourselves into the music and let it smooth the rough edges and triage the broken parts.

The stripped-down set goes off without a hitch. We try out the new song and the base of the acoustic chords echo in the cavern of my chest. It tells my story without the frills or fillers. It's audible sex, love-making expressed with soulful riffs and sweet melodies. After the last chord fades the crowd stays silent, suspended in the moment, before a loud applause erupts.

Adam and I share a significant look as we're bombarded by the cacophony of sound. The earlier argument forgotten. The applause confirms that "Quenched" is just as good as "Exquisitely Broken."

I catch a glimpse of Jake out of the corner of my eye. He's at the check-in station directly across from the stage, leaning on a table and openly staring with sultry eyes that say, *Yes. I want to do all the things you sang. I want you.* The sweep of his gaze is a warm caress that I feel across my skin and my body pulses with desire. We were naked in my bed a handful of hours ago but that doesn't stop me craving him again, to taste him, to drown in the sensations of his naked skin against my naked skin. Lust, unfiltered and untampered, rockets through me. I stumble through an awkward thank you, my brain foggy with obscene images. Jake on his knees, my leg draped over his shoulder. Jake behind me his big hands palming my breast. Jake in me, around me, on me. Yep obscene and absolutely filthy.

Adam and I step off center stage. Hidden behind the curtains I blow out a shaky breath.

"You good?" Adam asks, his distracted gaze focused behind my shoulder.

"I'm fine." Don't worry about me. My ex-boyfriend, who you have a profound dislike of, has a scorching, sexy stare that turns me into a walking, talking sex fiend. Nothing going on here. As you were.

"Okay. I'm gonna bounce. You'll still have..." He raises his sunglasses, his eyes narrow into slits. I follow the direction of his gaze and see Seth laughing with one the volunteers. The guy is handsy, but Seth doesn't seem to mind. In fact, he seems to be enjoying himself. Adam lowers the sunglasses, but not before, I see the flash of pain across his features.

"I can't tell you what to do, Sin, but he's not worth it," he says, turning his head away from the two men. "Maybe we only get one love in our lifetime. One passion. And for us maybe that's the music. You know? Maybe we don't get to have two passions, two loves. Maybe it's selfish to want more." He's talking as much to himself as he is to me.

"But maybe we have it all. Maybe we get everything."

"People like us don't get everything," he says with a shake of his head

People like us? People that don't have roots and makeshift families? Or people that have music as an integral part of our lives and need the validation of strangers as much as the adoration of a significant other.

"But maybe we have it all."

"Open your eyes, Sin. When you come from the places we come from, have seen the things that we've seen everything is not part of the deal." Adam walks away toward the back of the stage, irritation making his naturally relaxed gait stiff. He slips down the narrow steps out of sight.

The minute he disappears from view, the smile drops off Seth's face and his physical presence sags. His new friend, Handsy the Beard, gives him a quick hug and sidles away.

I walk across the now vacant stage and stop next to Seth.

"Seth?"

"Sin," he says in warning, blowing out a frustrated breath. I ignore the tone and keep going because I care about them both, because more than any other person I know Adam deserves to find his person.

"Adam is…" I pause, looking for the right words. "Complicated."

"No offense, but you don't have to tell me about Adam. I know him. I know him in ways that…" He sucks his lips into his mouth, cutting off the flow of words. Seth opens his mouth like he's about to say something but snaps it closed as quickly.

What is going on between these two? When you live with someone day in and day out, you learn their moods and patterns. For example, Seth knows all about Jake. Like the fact that Jake normally shows up around ten or eleven at night and is gone by eight in the morning. He knows I haven't told the guys, and even though he's doing whatever he's doing with Adam, I know with full confidence he won't discuss my private business.

Just like he sees things, I see them too. Since arriving in Vegas, he's been giving Adam a superwide berth. Not in the "I hate you, stay away from me" kinda way. More in the self-preservation "I need a break before this ruins me" kinda way.

"We done here?" He moves back to a topic that we can discuss easily. "Let's get something to eat. I'm starved."

After touring for years and going through stages where I wanted self-expression and fame and money and all the things that come with celebrity, it now seems trite. Because I showed up in Las Vegas nestled comfortably in all those things and secure in my feelings about the Jacob Johnson. Then in less than twenty-four hours, he blew all those absolutes out of the water.

He's breaking through every barrier, addressing every objection, and I'm over here rooting for him to prove me wrong, to prove Adam wrong, to prove that we can have something real and glorious because I want that. And I think I want it with him.

He has my body. God, does he have that, but my heart isn't buying it. It's still battling with my head, and even I don't know which one will win. I don't know which one I want to win. The problem with leaving the way I did is that I never got answers. On the flip side there is nothing he could've said at that specific time that I would have accepted.

I leave the stage, followed by my personal shadows also known as Aiden and Seth, and walk over to one of the catering trucks that pulled up a couple of minutes ago. The volunteers from each organization clamber for space in the lines. The two security guards create a bubble forcing most of the people to give me a wide berth. We maneuver to the back of the line because I already stand out with the guys looming over me, I don't want to look like I'm trying to cut the line. Also we'll be ordering three meals, which is a quick way to piss off someone standing in line. The line is steadily growing. At this rate, we'll need to get back to the hotel before I get food.

"Excuse me," a woman says to Seth. I turn toward the familiar voice and the past crashes painfully with the present. Tina Taylor is exactly the way I remember her—flawless makeup, sparkling blue eyes, and long blond hair that looks like a crown of gold in the sunlight. But unlike the last time I saw her, she's clothed and awake, looking at me around the shoulders of my security guard.

My feet kick in before my mind does, and I immediately take a step back, bumping into Aiden.

"You know her, Sin?" he asks. His concerned gaze takes in the panic on my face. I knew her a long time ago or at least I thought I did.

"Ah… yeah. Yeah. We were roommates in undergrad." At that explanation, Seth and Aiden fall back, allowing Tina into my bubble.

"Sinclair. It's… I… It's really good to see you." The words tumble out of her mouth and hang in the air between us, pregnant with our shared history and sadness. I just want her gone. I don't care where, as long as it's far, far away in a place where she will never be seen or heard from again. That's how it works in the fairy tales, right? The good girl wins, the bad girl disappears into oblivion.

"No. It's really not."

She winces. "I can believe that. If I were you, I'd feel the same way. I can't imagine what you must've thought."

"You were always a smart girl, Tina. I'm fairly positive you knew exactly what I would think."

She doesn't answer but the red flush creeping up her neck and staining her cheeks is answer enough.

"I just… I wanted to tell you face-to-face that… I'm sorry. For… everything. We were all so young. It seems like a lifetime ago." She clears her throat, her nervous hands fidget with the seam of her jeans.

Sorry? I almost laugh at how inadequate that word is for an apology. Sorry is what you say when you lose the remote or take the last piece of cake. Not when you played a role in destroying two, possibly three, lives. "A lifetime ago? It doesn't feel that way to me."

"Sin, please."

"Please what? Pretend that you weren't the skanky snake lying in my grass, waiting to slither into my bed? Forgive you for playing a role in shattering any dreams I had with that man? What exactly are you saying please to?" I look her up and down. My eyes settle on the big rock on her ring finger and I get it. This isn't about me. "Or do you want absolution because you're a married woman, and you're afraid of past sins coming to back to haunt your future?"

Her face pales, and I know that I hit a sore spot. Oh, how the tables have turned. Now and then I've wondered what her life looked like after she helped to destroy mine. Now I have my answer.

"Look, I know that we can never be friends again. And I don't blame you. I still want… I need… just let me make amends. If you'd be comfortable, we could meet somewhere and talk over coffee or something. For what it's worth I'm sorrier than you'll ever know." Her eyes are as earnest as her words.

And I don't care. I can't. When I look at her, I still see her naked limbs twisted in my sheets around my man. I can easily recall the scrape of carpet against my knees as I crawled down the hall and the way my heart shattered as I put my clothes on and walked out the door.

Now she's sorry. When I think about all the questions she used to ask about Jake, about our sex life, about how he was dealing with my long absences, I feel like an idiot. I gave her everything she needed to take my place. She wasn't sorry when her treacherous ass told me that a man like Jake wasn't the faithful type, or when she promised to keep an eye out. Let me know who was coming around. When it was her all along.

Of course, she's sorry now, but her sorry is disingenuous. It's a Hail Mary to the marriage gods to erase her karmic debt.

There are a couple of news reporters making their way over to our location, so I wrap her in a hug, putting my lips close to her ear, so no one and overhears me.

"You don't get to tell me when and how I offer forgiveness," I hiss. "Do you remember telling me that he could never love me? Do you?" I lean back and give her a pointed look before leaning back in, "Do you remember pointing out my lack of family and pedigree as a reason he couldn't possibly want a life with me? I remember every ugly hateful thing you said to me under the guise of being my friend and how deep those words cut. You want me to accept your apology, Tina?" My arms tighten around her.

"I do, Sin. But if you'd just give me a chance to..."

"Well, you can't have it." Her entire body jerks with a deep breath. "Maybe you were right. Maybe Jake and I were a pipe dream, but it wasn't up to you to make that decision for us. I hope it was worth it, Tina. I really do."

I drop my arms and turn my back on her. I walk the short distance to the sidewalk curb and sit down. I'm so upset my hands are shaking. What is it about this city that drags all my skeletons out of the closet? I've avoided Las Vegas like the plague for the last couple of years, hoping the people in my old life would fade into the preverbal sunset. But no, those fuckers keep popping up everywhere I turn.

Chapter 26

NOW
Jake

"MR. JOHNSON, THE HOTEL IS A COMMUNITY LEADER IN MANY charitable functions. What made you branch out into Habitat for Humanity?" A reporter shoves a microphone in my face.

"We try to assess where our money and time can make the biggest impact. At this time, the board feels that Take Refuge could greatly benefit from our involvement."

"I see that you brought along your ex-girlfriend, Sinclair James, for the run. Is her appearance here strictly professional or is this time together the first steps toward reconciliation?"

"Ms. James has a long history of volunteering her time to worthy causes. If The Hotel can act as a conduit to help her achieve her philanthropic goals, we're happy to do so."

I scan the space behind the reporter and see Sin hugging a woman who looks familiar. I can't place where I know her from until they split apart. Tina wipes hands under her eyes and Sin is walking in the opposite direction past the work site.

I've only seen Tina a handful of times since the night the whole thing went down. For as big as the city has gotten, it's still small in all the ways that count. Our families still haunt the same country clubs and restaurants. They go to the same church and are invited to the same weddings, so yeah, I see her.

She got married a couple of years after Sin left. As far as I know, she became the quintessential Vegas trophy wife. She's wife number three or four. Her husband is an older man. I think he's closer to my parent's ages than hers. From what I hear, he has more than a couple of women on the side and takes no care to hide it from his wife.

"Thank you for coming out and supporting a good cause. If you'll excuse me," I say, shaking his hand as I try to follow Sin's retreating form. When she disappears from my line of sight, I step around the reporter and jog in that direction.

It doesn't take much to find her. She's sitting on a low brick wall that separates the event from a busy street. Her feet swing a couple of inches above the pavement, and she's staring out at the cars speeding by, her two bodyguards casting long shadows from their positions on either side of her.

"Can you give us a sec, guys?" I ask as I move forward. They don't acknowledge me. They never do. Not when they see me leaving at dawn, blurry eyed and tired. Or apparently now when they both heard private details of my very public breakup.

"Sin, we'll be just over there if you need us." The bigger one says. He doesn't move until Sin nods. They move out of ear shot but are still close enough to respond if needed.

I hop on the wall next to her and bump her shoulder with mine. *Come on, baby, give me those eyes. Talk to me. Tell me what she said.* I want to demand answers, to beg her to ignore Tina, but before I can say anything, she starts talking.

"Did you know that Las Vegas is the only city that I've considered home?" she says still staring straight ahead. Okay, not what I was expecting but she's talking, not yelling or crying or telling me to go fuck myself. So, I'll take it.

"Have you lived in that many cities?" I ask. She cuts her eyes in a sidelong glance. Sometimes it feels like I've learned more about Sin by reading magazine articles and watching interviews. The fact I don't know all the places she's lived emphasizes how far the time and distance has stretched between us.

"But," she continues as if I hadn't spoken, "the day I found you with her, it was like my idea of home melted away in the Vegas heat, and I was just"—she finally turns her face to me fully—"adrift," she says rubbing the pad of her thumb along her bottom lip.

No, I hadn't known. There was so much that I'd never taken the time to understand. For as close as we've been, there was always a part of Sin I couldn't touch. Parts she held back, kept hidden. I didn't even realize she was holding out until I spent hours upon hours obsessing when she left.

I never get Sin raw or unfiltered. I get the carefully constructed persona. The driven creative. The sensual lover. I get glimpses into her depths but never the full picture. The only time she let's go? Gives me everything is when we're naked and sweaty and spent on each other.

In bed, we moved together in a syncopated rhythm that is as natural as it is powerful. We don't need words or explanations. Our bodies speak the same language. There are never questions about how good it feels or what she needs because Sin can't tell me anything that I don't already know.

There we have no limits.

Outside of bed is different. I crave her secrets because I want to be more than a good fuck. I want to embed myself so deep she'll feel me with every beat of her heart. I'm not satisfied with the facade anymore, and I don't care how messy she is underneath. I want her to let go, to give it all to me, to trust I'll hold her secrets with the same reverence I hold her body. I know I can be her lover, but what I crave is to be her best friend, I want all the things that Adam is privy to.

Let me see behind the curtain, baby. My eyes drill hers, willing her to read my thoughts.

"Did you know she was going to be here?" she asks.

I shake my head. "I haven't had a full conversation with Tina in years. I bump into her every now and again, but when you left…"

Her eyes shutter closed and when they open, my heart starts to beat a little harder. Her gaze slips from mine back to the cars whizzing by us on the street.

I move my hand on top of hers, attempting to lace our finger, but she jerks away. Her reaction lets me know exactly where her head is, and I'm not gonna lie. It stings.

"Answer the question. Did you or did you not know Tina was going to be here?" Her voice is barely audible above the drone of cars in the background, but each syllable is sharp and pronounced.

"No, Sin," I say giving her a definitive answer "I didn't know she was going to be here," This girl is tying me in knots. I may not know every city that she's lived in, but I know she's a runner, and right now she's lacing up her shoes.

I jump off the wall to stand in front of her, but she keeps her eyes averted somewhere over my shoulder. I get closer until I'm standing between her legs. My hands glide up the soft skin of her thighs settling on her hips.

"I'm not going anywhere, baby, so you might as well give it up. Look at me, Sin."

Look. At. Me. I squeeze the supple skin of her thighs until she turns her soulful brown eyes up to meet mine.

"When you first got here and treated me like some random off the street, I understood. Even though it hurt, I got it. I was all right because you were here, back in my space, close enough to touch, and I knew it was only a matter of time before I did."

I wiggled my eyebrows up and down, and her lips kick up into a slight smile, those dimples I love pop and the knots in my chest began to ease.

"I can swallow my pride and push past all the bullshit because, for me, it's you. When I thought all we'd have was one night, I took it gladly because here's the thing. I want you any way that I can have you, and if that means sneaking into your villa like a teenager afraid of being caught by your parents, I'll do that. If you need me to pretend like this is a casual fling, something to pass the time while you're in town, I'll be that. I take it as penance for my previous sins." I lean down to her upturned face and press a chaste kiss on her lips.

"I'm not that guy you remember. The one that would've done some stupid shit like invite Tina and wait for you to push her aside and claim me as yours. You're dealing with Jake 2.0. I don't lie. I don't cheat, and I won't hurt you again. Believe me." I kiss her again. "Believe in me," I say against her lips.

"Pretty words don't erase a disastrous past—"

I raise my hand up, interrupting "No it doesn't, but bringing up the past at this point is nothing more than an excuse."

"Fair enough." She shrugs. "Then how about I'm not buying it. A leopard doesn't change its spots."

And there it is, I'm surprised it's taken her this long to say it. The cliché statement that deals with broad strokes and worse case scenarios, instead of me. It is her way of erecting yet another wall between us, but this one has shoddy construction and is built on a crumbling foundation.

I own what I did. I won't insult either one of us by pretending my actions were anything other than foul. But the excuse, and it is an excuse at this point, doesn't hold water when I've been with her every night since I returned the guitar that was rightfully hers. I've had the pleasures of her body and the joy of her company. Nothing about those times have been anything less that spectacular.

It's in those quiet moments that she's vulnerable and open to me. When the singer is up on the shelf and the anger is put away. She doesn't analyze if we're possible or if we make sense because it obvious.

"Let's go to the cabin up on Mount Charleston, get away from the city, and the summer heat, for the weekend," I say, my hands moving farther up her thighs, and my fingertips edge just underneath the edge of her shorts.

She stares at me with a blank frown creasing skin between her eyebrows. "No."

"Think about it, Sin. Me"—I edge the fingers of one hand a little farther up and scrape the edge of her panties—"you. Pine trees. A king-size bed. The closest cabin a mile away." Her eyes melt just a little before she turns them to look at the guards.

"Jake," she sighed. "I can't disappear from my life. Not anymore."

"Of course, you can. It's one of the perks of being the boss. You get to call the shots." I finally wedge my hand high enough to get my fingers under the edge of her panties. Oh, hell, she's already wet. My fingers slip through the moisture, teasing her entrance. Her eyes shoot to mine and her hand curls around my wrist, preventing further movement.

"Come with me." No pun intended. "It'll be like old times. We're worth fighting for. This," I say leaning forward placing a stinging kiss on her lips, "is worth scaling the wall and slaying the fucking dragon."

"Scaling the… You're crazy? You know that, right?" But her eyes are dancing, and have I mentioned I love her dimples? Because I do. I really, really do.

"Do something crazy. Come with me," I say on a breath somewhere between a groan and a plea.

"I don't have clothes. No one knows…" I lean in and kiss her again, to stop the flow of words because her lips are so close and so soft. I do it because she's in front of me and I can.

"That's the point. No one has to know."

I ease my hands from underneath her shorts and place them around her waist pulling her to her feet. Although she comes willingly into my arms, her body is stiff. I cup her cheek in the palm of my hand and tilt her head up until I'm looking directly into her eyes. I search her depths and, yeah, I see the hurt feelings and wariness but under all of that is something else.

Hope?

Love?

Some undercurrent of emotion that I can't pinpoint or nail down, but I recognize. It's that thing that makes her soften toward me. That thing that keeps her coming back for more, and I'll be damned if I let Tina, our careers, or whatever other reasons she might conjure up take it away.

"Ride with me," I say, trailing my fingers along the curve of her cheek. "And I swear I'll make it worth your time."

Her eyes flutter closed, and her chest moves up and down, making the tips of her breast graze my chest.

"Sex was always the easy part with us," she says a little breathy.

"Get your mind out of the gutter, Sin," I chide. "Not everything is about sex. Let's hang out for the next couple of days. No expectations, no judgments. And when we get back, I want to take you out on a date, a real one. Hang out with the guys from your band. Wrap you in my arms at night and wake up wrapped in yours. I want to see you in the light of day because until I saw you sitting on that wall, I'd forgotten how beautiful you are under the rays of the sun." I drop a soft kiss on her lips.

I hear the shutter of camera in the distance and I don't care. I have no problem announcing to the world that this woman is mine. She stares up at me without saying anything. It was too big of an ask. I knew it. I fucking knew she'd say no. Shit.

"Or we can just hang out at your place. No heat, no judgment," I say, backtracking and trying not to choke on disappointment. I'm tired of being her dirty little secret. My body vibrates in anticipation of her answer. For every step that I take forward, I take two steps back, and Tina rearing her ugly head pushed me back the length of a football field.

"I can't see either one of us walking away from this unscathed. I don't know how to explain it." She looks at me with questions bouncing behind her eyes. "I hated you for so long." She sighs but continues, "All those old hurts are still there, but now I..."

"You what?" I say eagerly when her words stop because I need the validation. I need to know she wants me too.

"I..." She drops her head before meeting my eyes again. "How does that make sense? How is four years not enough time to get over you?"

If I had an answer to even one of her questions, I'd give it to her,

but I don't. I haven't even answered those questions for myself. But I zeroed in on the "not over you" comment.

Thank fuck! I live under her skin just like she flows through my veins. It still stings to hear her say she hated me, but she said hated not hates.

"That settles it," I say. "We'll keep it on the low. I just... I want a place, any place in your life. We can be friends and let the rest fall where it may."

Friends, my ass. Sin doesn't want to be my friend any more than I want to be hers. She needs me to remind her of that. Our relationship has always me chasing her, convincing her that being caught was so much better than being alone, but at this moment I'll say whatever she needs to hear.

"Friends?" She takes a step back out of my arms, holding out her hand. A smile on her lips making the lone dimple pop in her cheek.

I take a step forward reclaiming the space she put between us and stroke a thumb down her cheek. I lean forward and grin at Sin's sharp intake of breath.

"Friends," I say right before I kiss her, again.

Chapter 27

"YES, THEY'RE TOGETHER! AFTER AN EMOTIONAL
REUNION, SINCLAIR JAMES AND JACOB JOHNSON APPEAR TO
BE BACK ON SOLID GROUND."
—*Las Vegas Review-Journal*

"SECRET REUNION: EMOTIONAL RENDEZVOUS. JACOB
JOHNSON IS MENDING BROKEN FENCES."
—*People Magazine*

"BACK ON… JACOB JOHNSON, FIGHTING FOR HIS
RELATIONSHIP."
—*Entertainment Weekly*

Chapter 28

Four Years Ago

Sinclair

A SHRILL NOISE YANKS ME OUT OF A TENTATIVE SLEEP. I SLAM MY HAND over the button to silence the alarm clock and blink at the red numbers until I can make them out. The room is shades of gray, masked in the early morning fog of North London. I get to my feet only to trip over Miles's tall frame on the way to the bathroom. When I turn on the lights, I cover my eyes against the harsh glare it creates against the all-white surfaces. I quickly shut the door, so I don't prematurely wake the boys.

We arrived in England two days ago. The jet lag is kicking our butts. All four of us are once again cramped in a tiny hotel room because it's all we can afford, but it's worth it. All the seedy hotels, dirty bars, and crazy tours have been worth the sacrifice. Our music is finally getting some attention from the industry. We finally have just enough money to fly to London and make an EP at Chapel Studios .

The old church is known for its layered acoustics and the owner, producer Ray, is just as unique and special. He has an ability to hear the song through the music. He knows where the band is trying to go, and he paves the road to get you there. All my favorite albums have been recorded at Chapel Studios. For me it seemed like a distant goal. Something I'd hoped for but would never be close enough to really touch and now that we're here, it is bittersweet.

Everything else in my life is falling to shit but the music. My music is better than ever. Maybe I should thank Jake for blowing up my life because I'm better for it.

It's like the hurt spills from my heart and permeates my friendships, my music, my every waking thought, and I have no choice but to get it out. As a result, the songs that come are good, like radio quality, reaching millions of people good. That had always been the end game, but I always thought Jake would be next to me when it happened.

Some days I wake up, and I forget we aren't together anymore. I pick up the phone to sing him the new chorus I just wrote or throw some word placement his way, and then it hits me that Jake isn't my confidant anymore and he shouldn't be my muse either. He can't be the first person I call with good news or the person I expect to see cheering in my corner.

I have a million questions I want to ask. That I should've already asked, like why Tina? Why the woman who was the complete opposite of me? Why choose someone I knew? If Tina is what he likes, then how could he ever be attracted to me?

I'd been with him for years, and I didn't see it. If anyone had asked me if I ever thought Jake would cheat, I would've answered no before they could even finish the question. Now I comb through our past trying to find clues I didn't catch because I had to have missed something. This shit didn't come out of a vacuum. And I want to know why? What could I have possibly done to deserve this? How can he justify throwing everything we had away?

I jump in the shower and take my time under the hot spray of water. By the time I step out, the skin on my fingers have pruned and I feel flush from the heat. I wrap a clean white towel around my chest and sit on the lid of the toilet. We're finally recording vocals today. The last couple of days have been isolation booths and instruments. Yesterday, Ray followed the sound of a snare drum for hours because according to him, *"Something wasn't right."*

Today will be Adam and me, for the most part. It'll be singing and harmonies. It'll be living in that creative space where the ugly truth of pain transforms into something beautiful. The songs from this album do that and then some. Jake is going to hear them, and he'll know what inspired me. He'll know that, once again, he played the role of my muse.

I stand and approach the steam-covered mirror, swiping my hand across the surface. My reflection is less foggy but still blurry. I lean close to glass, staring at my face. I don't look different, same brown skin, same curly hair, same brown eyes. But inside I don't feel like me. I feel ugly and stupid, and so fucking angry I want to break something or hurt someone. No, not someone, Jake.

I open the door bathroom door and peek out into the dark bedroom. The boys are all still asleep. I tiptoe to where I placed my phone and on the bedside table and hightail it back to bathroom. Once I closed the door, I stare at the device in my hand; it's time. Well past the time. I dial a number that I have memorized by heart. The ringing is shrill against my ear. After three rings a deep voice says, "Jacob Johnson."

My vocal chords freeze. This was a dumb idea. What was I thinking? Shit, shit, shit!

"Hello? Jacob Johnson. How can I help you?"

You can't help me, Jake. Not anymore. Not with five thousand miles and a ton of hurt between us. I still can't force myself to speak.

I go to hit the end button when he says, "Baby?" on a shuddered breath. That name, coming from those lips in that tone, shreds me.

"Baby, talk to me. Please," he whispers.

I clear my throat a couple of times, but I can't do it. The moment of truth, my moment of truth when I spew every ugly thing I've thought and felt since leaving is gone. In its place is an ugly gaping question. One word with limitless possibilities. Why?

"Tell me where you are. I'll come to you. We can... We can... I'll do whatever you want, but I need to see you," he says, his voice a desperate plea.

"I'm not in Vegas anymore," I murmur, forcing the words past the lump of emotion in my throat.

"Fuck," he breathes heavy into the phone. "It's good to hear your voice. I miss all that rasp and those dimples. I miss you, baby."

My heart clinches. He should miss me. I just never thought I'd miss him too. Not after the way things ended. "I shouldn't have called, Jake. I gotta—"

"Don't go," he rushes out. "Not yet."

"I have to. This was a mistake."

"Just give me a couple of minutes." When I don't say anything, he must take that as permission. "I messed up, babe. I messed up, and I... please believe me when I say I'm sorry. I'm sorry and..."

My eyes burn with the rush of tears and a sob escapes into the phone. I hold a hand tight over my mouth, trying to suppress the next one. My throat aches with the effort and my shoulders shake as heartbreak once again pushes to the surface.

"Shhh, baby. It's okay."

"It's not. Nothing is okay right now," I say in broken, jagged words.

"But it will be. When you've done all the things, accomplished all the goals. You'll find your way back to me. Until then, spread your wings, Sin. Spread 'em wide and far, and when you're ready, if you're ever ready, I'll be exactly where you left me. Waiting for you. I'll always wait for you. I lo—"

I hang up the phone before he can finish that sentiment and I break down, crying like I did the first night. I cry until my tears are dry, until the gapping chasm in my chest doesn't ache quite as much. I cry until I'm numb.

I pull on my clothes with slow, tired movements and leave the conversation with Jake within those walls. Adam is already awake, sitting on the side of the bed, his sleep-tousled look not that different from his day-to-day. He cocks his head to the side his eyes search mine but he doesn't ask if I'm okay anymore because he knows I'm not.

"Morning," I say

"*Good* morning," he says, emphasizing the word good. His concerned gaze takes a quick inventory of my features. The tension eases slightly around his eyes when I offer a half smile. He's worried. They all are. I'm in a dark place and I can't get free.

"This is it, Sin. Today is about to change everything for us. You know that, right?" he says, practically buzzing with unspent energy.

"I thought you didn't care about the fame."

"You know how I roll, Sin. That's never been my motion." And it hasn't. It's one of the many reasons why we work well together and why we're so close. We both get just as much satisfaction playing for each other as we do playing for crowds.

"So, what's with the fame speech?"

"It was far from a speech, Sin. But we gotta be real. The new stuff is next level. It's going to draw people in. Anyone that has ever broken up with..." I see regret flash across his face. We don't talk about Jake. The night I showed up at his house an unraveled mess or the fact when we're in Vegas, I still crash on his couch. He starts over again. "Anyone that has ever experienced a loss will cling to these songs. I just think we both need to be ready for it, yeah?"

"Indeed." I chuckle.

Adam and I head out the door. Dan and Miles are still asleep. They'll record later this afternoon. Ray wants the drums to sound fuller, so he's tossed around the idea of recording in the court yard because the ambient sound will fill the bottom of the beat.

We enter the main recording studio, which is in an old church hall. It has the towering ceilings with the wooden beams and heavy velvet curtains that hang against the back wall. Plush rugs cover the scuffed up wooden floor. Drums, a baby grand piano, amplifiers, and speakers are set up at varying depths. Electrical cords run the length of the room, and the control booth is in a corner, removed from the studio, making it easy to forget that an engineer is working the boards.

Ray is already at the sound board when arrive. He absently waves before turning his attention back to knobs in front of him.

What are we doing first?" Adam picks up Hidalgo, the guitar he prefers to use when recording, from the stand.

"I'm thinking "Exquisitely Broken," but I was thinking about it in the shower this morning and I want to try something. Kay?" I pick up my own guitar and settle the familiar weight over my shoulders.

"What you got?"

"I need to hear this, hold up," I say, kicking off my shoes, I sit on the studio floor, legs crossed, guitar resting in my lap. I reach over and adjust the microphone typically used to collect sound from a handheld instrument to catch my voice.

Adam settles across from me. At first we're just fooling around with the melody. But the then I start to sing. Adam's voice harmonizing with mine, echoing my words and the more I sing, the harder it gets to force the words out.

I try to hold back the tears that well in my eyes, but I can't. I can't make them stop. My voice is thick with the tears and my natural rasp is more gravel and grit. *Hold it together, Sin. Get through this song. You have to get through this song.* My voice breaks at weird places, the pronunciation of individual words sounds garbled. I'm messing this up. I'm finally in The Chapel studios and I'm messing it all up. The tempo is totally off, because I can't rein the emotion in, can't get a harness on it. As soon as the song is over, I jump to my feet and half walk, half jog to the courtyard.

I lean on the stone wall and bend at the waist, forcing myself to simply breathe, breathe out the pain and the confusion and leave it on the ground. I need to get back in there. I rub my hands across my eyes and get the gumption to walk back inside.

"Sin... come over here for a sec, will ya?" Ray calls.

"Yeah... of course," I say. He and Adam are sitting at the sound board, heads close together. I walk the short distance and see them both staring at a laptop. A black and white video is on the YouTube page.

Ray presses the play icon and I hear my voice, shattered and tender.

I hadn't even been aware we were recording audio or video.

"I record every session. The playback helps me pick up on things like posture and vocal anomalies that might actually workout in a song. But this… my God," he says still looking at the video, rapt. "This is better than anything I could have put together." Ray spares me a glance before looking back at the screen. "This right here is what it's all about. The emotion is… Wow, Sin. I couldn't even focus on the nuisance of the song. Your voice sounds like encapsulated heartbreak." Because my heart is broken. It's broken and bleeding, and I don't know if it'll ever be right again. "And your face reflects that pain."

My eyes meet Adam's over the console, and we share a sad smile. "I checked with Adam before I put the footage up on my YouTube page and look at this." He points at the number of views. Sixty thousand views. We have sixty thousand views? We've never seen numbers like that, ever.

"How long has this been up?" I ask.

"You were outside for a couple of hours," Adam answers.

"Hours?" I repeat.

"Yeah." Adam nods. "We mixed the vocals. Added some layers while you were out there. And it's fucking fire, Sin. It's going to get big. Bigger than any of us imagined. No one has this sound right now. It's good. Really good," he says his eyes bright with excitement. "Miles and Dan will be here in a few. When they add in the drums and base line, I think it'll be…"

"A Grammy," Adam and Ray say together.

I chew the inside of my bottom lip. "You really think so? I thought it was super rough… I don't know, maybe we take a second—"

"No," Adam and Ray say once again in unison. Adam studies me for a long silent moment. I fidget with the bottom of my T-shirt, waiting for his response, but it doesn't come. And then Miles and Dan crash into the room, loud voices reverberating around the space.

"Daaaaaaaaaamn, Sin-a-sticks. You did that." Dan barrels forward, his dark hair flopping over his brow. The Mario Bros T-shirt, a couple of sizes too small, exposes his navel when he picks me up and swings me in his arms. He smacks a sloppy wet kiss on my cheek. "When I get in there with the drums, that shit will be sick."

"You've already seen the video?" I ask, looking first at Dan and then Miles.

Miles nods. "I copied the link from YouTube and put it up on our FB page. And it's blowing up, Sin. In the time it took us to get here from the hotel we've gotten thousands of likes and comments."

"Serious?" I ask because I can't believe it.

"Would we lie to you?" Dan asks, looking up at me and batting his lashes.

"Hell yeah, you would," Adam says with a chuckle.

"Not about this."

I don't know who moves first, but the four of us end up in a circle, our arms wrapped around each other, our heads bowed.

"This is the break, guys. The one that changes everything," I whisper, afraid to jinx it by saying the words too loud.

"Not everything," Adam says. "It doesn't change us. We're family. And family comes before everything else." His voice is solemn, and the weight of those words raise goose bumps on my arms.

"That's right, blood don't make family," Dan says.

Miles, a man of few words even on the best of days mutters, "Family."

The session is long and grueling, and by the end, I've been through the ringer. It's like my body relives the shock of Jake's betrayal every time I sing the words. I have to fight the spasms in my legs to remain standing, the ache in my throat as it tries to close, and the tears that have dropped every single time without fail.

Every session for the next three weeks goes pretty much the same, but at the end, we have a full album. One that everyone who participated in the making knows is a once in a lifetime creation

Chapter 29

NOW

Sinclair

"So, Sin-a-sticks, I hear you've been keeping secrets. When did you start bumping uglies with the evil one?" Dan says, falling in the chair across from me. Adam chokes on a drink, spewing the clear liquid from his mouth in a wide arc.

"You knew too?" Miles asks, looking at Adam who is wiping a hand across is mouth.

"Am I the only one who didn't know." Dan asks, a slight frown marring his brow.

"How did you know?" I ask, turning to Miles.

"I showed up late to that party opening night. I was going to stay home but you know Kisha. She was in bed by the time I got home. She was surprised when I came in and asked me why I wasn't supporting you guys. So, I got dressed and showed up at the party. I didn't see either of you jokers." He wags a finger between Adam and Dan. "But I saw you and He Who Must Not Be Named—are we still calling him that?"

"Would you get to the point," Dan yells.

Miles clears his throat. "I, ah, saw you go out on a balcony, and I wasn't sure if I should intervene. So, I followed you. The door was locked but the, um, door panel is glass and… and you were…"

"Please tell me you did not see…" I drop my head into my hands, embarrassed heat licking down my spine.

"All I saw was a man drop to his knees and…"

"Do not say another word." I stand up, holding my palms out in front of my face. "You hear me? Not one more word."

"Aw, damn, this is better than I thought. Sin was getting some roof-top, open air, public kind of loving." Dan cackles, clapping his hands.

"Both of you just shut the hell up," I say loudly, trying to talk over their words.

"On a balcony, Sin. Damn, I didn't know you had it in you," Adam quips.

"I expect that bullshit from them but you?" I glare at Adam until he throws his hands up in defeat.

"I'm... surprised, is all." Adam says on a laugh.

"All three of you are assholes. You know that, right?" I say, and this makes them laugh harder. *Grade A assholes.*

"Five minutes, guys," The sound tech says, peeking his head through the door.

I speed walk past the guys and hightail it for the stage. I love all three of those boys like brothers, but there are somethings that should never be discussed. I can't believe Miles saw me and Jake on the bal-cony and is just now saying something.

I stop walking when I get to the steps that lead up to the stage. It's dark. So dark that I can't see anything beyond the thin line of lights that lay on the edge of each step. Adam's hand is a heavy weight that settles on my shoulder, and I don't have to see to know Miles is behind Adam and Dan is behind Miles.

This is us. This is our ritual. We don't pray or drink ourselves into oblivion. We remember the kids that started this.

"Blood don't make..." Adam says out loud.

"Family," our three separate voices answer in unison.

The house lights drop, and the roar of the audience gets louder, hands claps, feet stomp, whistles blow. I still can't believe we continue to sell out night after night. This arena is a long way away from smoky bars in nowhere towns.

The lights come up, the first heavy guitar riff echoes off the walls and a thousand people push to their feet chanting, "Sin City, Sin City, Sin City"

I let the first wail travel from my diaphragm and up my throat. I coat my voice in the agony of my past breakup with Jake, allowing every tortured lyric to take me back to that place. Normally, I relive that trauma every time I sing, but tonight something is different. I can't remember the hurt anymore. When I think of Jake, I see adoring hazel eyes and full lips parted in a smile. Images of him in bed with another woman have been replace with a million mental images of us. Us kissing so deep and so long that my lips are tender and my heart is full. His body pressed skin to skin with my body, his heart beating strong under my palm. Those are the things that I think about. The sadness I feel is because I'm afraid to claim him or let him claim me.

I move from one side of the stage to the other, losing myself in the music, the crowd. Looking out into the sea of faces and trying to make that connection. But something keeps catching my eye to the far left. There's a person standing still in a sea of movement, and when his eyes lift to mine, a chill moves up my spine.

I know that face. How do I know that face? I miss a beat as I take in every part of him. The deep-set eyes void of emotion. The greasy dark hair and the too small, worn Sin City T-shirt. I hold his gaze, and I'm unable to look away because his energy is throwing me off in the most menacing way.

I keep singing but can't shake the feeling that he's different. Dangerous in a way that makes my skin crawl. Moving back to center stage I focus on my band and the music and all the other people that are here because they love what we do. After a couple of minutes, the creepy feeling fades to a low hum that I barely pay attention to.

The first song ends, and I raise the mic to my lips. "Good evening, Las Vegas!" The crowd goes wild, yelling and stomping in response. "I can't tell you how happy I'm to see every one of you. Being here on this stage is honestly a dream come true. In the words of a much better writer, there is no place like home." The audience cheers.

"We love you, Sin!" someone yells.

"And I love you back. You ready to rock?" I ask the audience. They scream in response, and I soak it in. At least until my eyes drift back across the stage and land on the stalker and it finally clicks. Of course, I recognize him. I've seen him for years, the stringy hair, and old concert T-shirt, the singular focus that makes me feel like a mouse cornered by a cat..

Dan taps out a fast tempo on the cymbal and moves rapidly around the drum kit. Adam followed his lead to signal the start of the next song and comes shredding the guitar, completely lost in the music. He leans against me, fingers working over the strings, face twisted in pleasure.

I try to lose myself in the music and meet Adam in that place we occupy. Where time and rhythm mesh and nothing matters but now. Every time I try to go under, I make eye contact with a pair of eyes that burn through me. I sashay around Adam to the other to the other end of the stage. The stalker gets agitated the farther away I move from his end of the stage. I watch him push a woman next to him down to the ground as he tries to follow my movement. Then he swings on another person standing between him and I. Security rushes to him when the audience starts to scatter. Oh my God! He has a gun! How did he get in here with a gun? He aims the gun straight at me and pulls the trigger.

I can't move. Not when the bullets knock over the metal guitar stands, and the speakers spark like fireworks on Fourth of July.

The barrage of bullets continues to hit the stage. The wood cracks and splinters, fragments flying. In the chaos I don't see Adam. *He was right next to me a couple of seconds ago. Where did he go?*

"Adam!" I scream at the top of my lungs. Panic lodges in a tight knot in my throat until I see him. He's less than a couple of inches from me.

He waves his hands, but I can't hear him above the panicked screams of the audience and the shouts of security.

"Sin, down!" he yells.

I hesitate for the briefest second before I drop down on the stage. Adam bolts to my location, throwing himself at me. I look up to see his worried blue eyes directly in my line of sight.

He's fine. Adam is fine. Where are Dan and Miles? I roll my head to the side. It's harder than it should be, but I finally see them, huddled at the back of the stage. The rush of relief is sudden and all-encompassing. I'm shaking as my brain processes. They're okay. We're all safe. What about our fans. People brought their kids to see us. What would make him do this?

"Adam?" I try to speak but my tongue is heavy and languid.

He stares down at me, his eyes glassing over with unshed tears. I try to tell Adam it's okay, we're okay. But my voice won't work. I swipe a hand over my mouth and blink at the bright red blood coating my fingers.

Am I bleeding?

I don't feel hurt.

"Stay with me, Sin, just stay... HELP! PLEASE HELP ME! SOMEBODY PLEASE..."

Adam's voice starts to fade into the distance. I try to raise my arm, but my limbs feel heavy, and I'm cold, so cold.

I close my eyes to rest, and it feels like I'm floating. The darkness is soothing.

"Sin, look at me." Adam shakes me, and I force my lids to open. "Sinclair, this is not how it ends for you, do you hear me?" he cries.

Once again, I close my eyes and this time instead of the hard stage under me and the numbness tingling through my limbs. I'm in a soft bed, warm and cozy. Jake's big body at my back and his hand resting on the curve of my hip. I snuggle into his body, pulling his arms around me. Jake presses a kiss to the back of my neck, and I close my eyes to sleep. Totally surrendering to the darkness.

Chapter 30

THE INVESTOR'S MEETING RAN LATER THAN IT SHOULD'VE. HARD TO start a meeting without the CEO and half of the board. These meetings are a necessary evil. Everyone likes money, but no one wants the details of where the money came from. After hitting on all the gains we've had this quarter, what should have taken forty-five minutes has gone past the hour mark, and that's after all the other preliminary stuff.

I stand at the head of a long table in front of the room, going through slide after slide of financial growth, current projections for the next several quarters, and the one thing everyone in the room wants to know—dividends based on shares. The chatter picks up once the numbers are out. I meet my father's pride-fill gaze and do my best to ignore the smirk from Connor. What we've accomplished in four years is virtually unheard of. As of the yesterday, all investors have received a one hundred fifty percent return on their investment in less than five years.

Things are falling into place. I finally have room to breathe and not just at work. Sin… is still a little reluctant, but every day she shows me more, gives me more. When she's asleep, her body reaches for mine, when she arrives back in Vegas after a trip to wherever she's happy to see me, and when I'm inside her she looks up at me the way she used to, with eyes full of love. We'll get there. I'd like it to be sooner rather than later, but Sin isn't ready yet. She's still boxing demons, and it's turning into one hell of a battle. I wish I could do it for her I want to, but I'm on the sidelines with this one. I've done everything I know how to do. I've told her I love her, I've been totally transparent about where I want us to go. And maybe more important than any of that is I've been consistent. I've answered every call, ever text, showed up every night.

"Excuse me, Mr. Johnson, Mr. Rappaport." Emma, the receptionist, is at the door. Her pale skin flushed and her steps quick as she all but runs to me. "We have a…" her words trail off as she looks at the curious eyes following her around the room. She reaches my side in record time.

"Mr. Johnson. Mr. Rappaport, we… there has been an incident that requires you both," she says in a hushed voice.

My phone vibrates in my pocket for the umpteenth time in the last ten minutes. I immediately hit the silence button. I see Connor do the same thing. Our eyes meet across the board table, and he stands to his feet coming to stand next to me.

"I'm sorry, Emma, you were saying?" My phone goes off again before she can speak. When the buzzing stops, I finally take it out of my pocket and look at the screen. I realize I've missed dozens of calls and text messages. I frown as Jeanine's name flashes across the screen, again. I feel the involuntary tensing of my muscles as I answer the phone.

"Hello?"

"Mr. Johnson, oh thank God." Her voice cracks. I hear a couple of sniffles. My pulse jumps, beating harder through my veins. Jeanine is a fucking bulldog and bulldogs don't cry.

"What's wrong? I ask, fighting the sudden feeling of dread.

"I don't know how to tell you."

"Tell me what?"

"There's been a shooting at the concert arena. I tried to call you earlier, but you didn't answer."

"Where is Sin, Jeanine?"

"S-s-s-she she… People have been shot and she…"

217

"She what? Where is she, J?" I've never used that nickname before but for some reason right now, I can't say another syllable.

"Ms. James, she... There was just so much blood. They couldn't get her to wake up. She was taken to the hospital a couple of minutes ago. There isn't any information, yet."

"Someone has to know something. You call Adam or Dan or Miles. One of them will know..."

"Mr. Beckham accompanied her in ambulance. I'm not... I'm not a familial relation so they won't tell me. I don't know any more than that."

"Was Sin the only one?" Shot? Sin's been shot. My fingers go numb and the phone crashes to the table surface.

"Mr. Johnson? Jacob? Jake" Her voice is a hollowed out sound, squawking at me from the tabletop.

Connor picks up my dropped device.

"J, it's Con." He nods at me and rests his hand on my shoulder. "Give it to me straight, no chaser."

I study his face while he talks into the phone, nodding through whatever Jeanine is telling him. His voice is muffled behind the pulse thumping in my ears, but his lips are moving. Connor nods a couple of more times, his eyes finding mine while he listens. I turn toward the door on legs that feel like water. I need to go but Connor grips my shoulder, shaking his head. He points to the seat. I sit because right now I need someone to take the reins. Tell me what to do.

My stomach clenches with fear, and my vision narrows. I have to breathe. Deep breaths. But the air isn't moving into my lungs. The shock is trying to shut down every system in my body.

Sin's been shot.

Shot so seriously she needs... I don't know what the fuck she needs because I'm here and she's there and no one knows a damn thing. People at my hotel who had merely been going out for a night on the town to a concert and... An unintelligible sound comes out of my mouth.

"Repeat that. You said UMC, right?" Connor repeats. "Wait a minute, did you say multiple people were transported?"

"Multiple people?" I ask.

Connor holds up a finger for me to hold on. He talks for what seem like an eternity but is probably only a minute before he hangs up the phone.

"Jake." His voice is coming at me from the other side of a tunnel. "Jacob." He snaps his fingers in front of my face. Hearing my given name from my best friend that only uses it sparingly penetrates the haze. My head whips up, and I force myself to meet his gaze.

"How bad is it?" I barely grunt.

"It's"—he runs a hand through his hair—"it's really bad, but there were no fatalities. Six people were injured. Five of the six have bumps and bruises from getting trampled. Sin was shot twice. They think in the upper chest. We'll know more when we get there."

Honestly, I didn't hear anything after "shot twice," because really, what in the ever-loving hell is going on right now?

"Let's go," he says, his long stride eating up the space toward the door. "You take care of your lady, and I'll take care of everything else."

I follow his figure through the halls leading to the underground parking garage, trusting him to get us where we need to go. We both get into his car at the same time, and Connor peels out of the garage.

I don't know how we stay on the road. Connor is setting land speed records while periodically looking at me for long moments.

"Jeanine has already set up a private room for Sinclair James, and as soon as she knows anything, I'm sure she'll be on the horn," Connor says in a low voice. "J is getting legal on it, so you'll be able to see her when she comes out."

A corrosive taste floods my throat causing my mouth to water. My mind keeps manufacturing horrible images of Sin covered in blood. Sin in back of an ambulance rushing to the hospital.

"Jacob listen to me," Connor says, his voice is hard and demanding.

I look at him dumbly.

"Dude, breathe… take a fucking breath."

"I'm trying, Con. Man, I'm really trying but she was shot. Twice. And I…" I take in a deep inhale of air, but it doesn't go down easy. Every time I exhale my chest gets tighter. The air coming out as wisps of fragile sound.

"And you what?" He gives me a sidelong glance as he pulls to a screeching stop at a red light. "You are Jacob Muthafuckin Johnson. This is what you do. You deal with shit."

"What if she's d—?"

"Get that out of your head. You understand me? Deal with what you know, not what you think. And what we know is Sinclair James was taken to the hospital."

"What if it's worse than they're telling us?" Because that's the way this works, right? The doctors tell the family and friends that everything will be all right. When at the end of a hallway behind a closed door a loved one is in a battle for their lives.

"Then we deal. But know we got this." He reaches over and taps the top of my shoulder with a closed fist as the light turns green and the tires peel rubber as he takes off. "Do what you gotta do right now in this car, but when we step out be the man I know. The one that holds his head under pressure. Be the man she needs because Sinclair is going to have a rough time. She can't worry about you too."

We fall into silence, and I'm not sure how he did it, but Connor pulls up to the hospital in less than fifteen minutes. We walk shoulder to shoulder through the Emergency entrance. The first thing I notice is that the large waiting room is teeming with humanity. Sick old people, young hurt people, and everything in between. People are clustered small groups for comfort and support. I immediately look for my people, my comfort, my support. I find them clustered near the reception desk.

A frazzled Jeanine breaks away from the shell-shocked members of the band, and the team of security that stand at attention with their eyes covered by dark sunglasses, hands clasped behind their backs, body language screaming all kinds of stay back. She hustles toward us with black makeup running under her eyes, her bright red glasses sitting askew on her face.

"Thank God, you both are here." Tears pool in her eyes and she shoves the glasses up her nose to wipe away the moisture. "Shit. They keep doing this. It's like they won't stop." She waves a hand at her watery eyes.

"What have they said? What do you know?" I ask in a burst of sound that surprises me and makes Jeanine jerk her head back. A startled expression on her face. Connor's shoulder bumps mine, and he repeats the same questions but calmer, much, much calmer.

"They've taken her into surgery. But beyond that I don't know any more now than I did when I called you."

"So, we what? Just sit here and wait?"

Jeanine gives me a disgruntled look. This I can deal with, some normalcy in the face of chaos.

"As opposed to what, Mr. Johnson, storming the operating room, interrupting what could quite possibly be a lifesaving procedure to get you answers."

"Retract the claws, J. He's struggling," Connor says.

"Aren't we all."

"Where are the police? Shouldn't they be here? Shouldn't the ER be closed?"

Jeanine takes a deep, give me patience, breath before she says, "No, Mr. Johnson, that is not how incidents such as this work. Prior to your arrival, I spoke directly with the public information officer for Metro Police. He was very clear that the police's primary function at this time is to locate and neutralize the threat and secure the crime scene. Only once they have done the other two will they begin investigations. Detectives will conduct the investigation. Depending on what the investigation turns up, the FBI, Homeland Security, and possibly the ATF may get involved.

"So, in the meantime we do nothing? Sit here and wait for the person who did this to walk through the door and try to do it again?" I say once again in a voice bordering on too loud and too angry. I can't be the only one that sees how totally wrong this is.

"Mr. Johnson," she says after a long pause. "I know how upset you must be. However, University Medical Center is the only trauma hospital for the entire state. Ms. James is more secure in this hospital than just about anywhere else.

"Those metal doors," she says, pointing at the tall, black doors that have chips in the paint and dents in the metal where they've been hit by gurneys or wheelchairs or a foot kicking the door. "Are thick and require an access card to enter.

"The hospital has been kind enough to provide additional security, so fans and passersby cannot gain access, and as you can see, Sin City's personal security and The Hotel security are here as well to assist with the task.

"The hospital assures me that after the shooting of Tupac Shakur, they put protocols in place for situations involving celebrity patients. But according to the hospital chairman they only shut down the hospital if, *a*"—Jeanine ticks off the point on her outstretched finger—"the President of the United States is in the facility for any given reason, *b*"—she holds up a second finger—"they are no longer able to adequately provide service because of the sheer numbers, or *c*"—she holds up a third finger—"there is an immediate threat to the hospital or its surrounding areas. None of which are the current circumstance. Please just take a seat, and if you believe in a higher power, maybe say a prayer. If you don't then send her all your positive energy so she knows she's not alone."

It's only then that I look at the other people in our group, the people here for Sin and understand that we're all in the same boat. They love and are worried about her too, and they are scared to death that this might be the last time, and they didn't get to say good-bye too. Miles has his arms wrapped around himself rocking back and forth, mumbling something under his breath. Dan is pacing from one side of the desk to the other and every so often stops near the doors that lead to the surgery area and stares at the entrance like sheer force of will bring the doctors out. Then my gaze lands on Adam. He's sitting in a chair, fingering the dark red spots on his shirt. It's not hard to miss the pallor beneath his natural surfer boy good looks. Blond strands hang in his face, some strands tinted dark red with what I assume is Sin's blood.

I leave Connor and Jeanine and make my way toward the one person that means the world to my world.

I settle in the seat next to Adam, and he turns his haunted eyes to me. For the first time ever, we connect as people versus rivals. Two people that share time and memories and, at present, sorrow for the same person we both love. We're each trying to make sense of this situation which is unexplainable.

Thirty maybe forty-five minutes pass with nothing. I heard what Jeanine said, but I still expected police officers to rush in, sequester the members of the band, and place the ER on lock-down but there are no loud sirens or the sound of heavy boots filling the corridors as SWAT moves in. There are only the sounds of the massive AC unit kicking on, one person on the other side of the room hacking uncontrollably, the pinging of cell phone notifications, and hushed voices that don't want to be heard in the open space.

"I couldn't stop the bleeding. I tried," Adam says suddenly. His voice a hoarse. Opening his fingers wide in a helpless motion, his eyes never leave his bloodstained hands.

"She'll be okay. You know Sin," I say instead of demanding he tell me every nuance of what happened, so I can hunt down the man or woman or persons that did this.

"I've always protected her. Always. But the one time she really needed me. I let her down." Tears leak from the corner of his eyes, leaving trails in the mixture of blood and dirt on his face. He doesn't wipe the wetness. He balls his hands into fists and rotates them almost like he's trying to see them from a new angle or locate a clean spot.

"Adam," I say, placing my hand on top of his to stop the incessant movement. He looks up at me with crushing despair. "This isn't on you. You did everything you could. No one plans for… this. How could you?" I look around at the sterile white walls and the broken, worn chairs. It's all so normal. Looking at the inanimate objects in this room, one would never know my life is tearing apart at the seams.

Seeing Adam covered in Sin's blood is a reality I'm not ready for. A confirmation that constricts my heart to the point where it's struggling to beat.

I just got Sin back. I can't lose her, not yet, not like this. I dig the tips of my fingers into my eyes, trying to staunch the tears that burn the back of my lids. If I let them fall, the thin thread I'm holding will snap, and it'll be a flood of emotion that I won't be able to rein back in.

"She's going to be okay. She can get through this," I tell him, but I know it's more for my benefit than his.

Before I can say anything else, a tall, African-American doctor walks through the doors in blue scrubs with a Kente cloth cap over her hair.

"Are you all here for Sinclair James?" We all stand and crowd in on the doctor like a pack of wolves circling prey.

"Yes," Connor says when everyone else in the group remains silent.

"She's out of surgery and has been moved into a recovery room. Once she wakes from the anesthesia, we'll get her into the private room."

My knees almost buckle with relief. I have no idea how I'm still standing. I can only imagine I've been running on pure adrenaline, and hearing Sin is alive makes every ounce I had drain from my body. Chills race down my body and my limbs shake. Sin is alive. She's out of surgery and in recovery.

The doctor clarifies further, "I don't want to set the wrong expectation. The recovery will be difficult, but I don't see any reason why Ms. James shouldn't come back stronger than ever."

"Are you all"—she peers around at our group—"Ms. James's family?"

Adam and I both walk forward without hesitation.

A frown creases the center of her brows. She looks at Adam first. "And you are her…"

"I'm her brother," he says.

The doctor looks him up and down, skepticism lining her face, but she doesn't challenge him.

"And that would make you?" She looks at me?

"I'm her…" I want to lie, tell this woman that can't possibly understand us, that I'm her husband, because in a different life I could've been, but in this life Sin is so well-known, she'll recognize the lie and shut me down. But what am I? Her boyfriend? Her jump-off? Her man? I clear my throat and start again.

"I'm her boyfriend?" I ask, frustration finally making the words hard and angry. Hospitals don't give a damn about boyfriends. If I'm not a spouse or family, she has a legal obligation to withhold information from me.

When she turns her attention back to Adam, dismissing me, I have to fight the urge to curse and demand she tells me everything she knows.

"I'm Doctor Pippen, chief of surgery." She holds out a hand to shake.

"Adam Beckett."

"Okay, Adam," she says in a quiet voice. "Let me give you the basic rundown of what we repaired, and where I think we'll go from here." She gently tugs Adam toward the doors she just exited. I can still hear their conversation although she's speaking low.

"Your sister had a significant injury to the right lung. We were able to repair all the damage and remove the bullets and debris from the chest cavity. We still have to run a couple more tests when she's awake, but while we wait for that, I can take you in to see her. As her family, you can authorize other visitors to see her, although we like to keep the number around two at a time."

The doctor swipes a card to unlock the door, and she and Adam quickly disappear behind the steel gray doors. I stand at the doors until the lock reengages. A firm hand on my shoulder guides me to sit in a chair.

"Come on, Jake. We need to talk strategy. Is Adam Beckett the only family that she has?"

"I think so."

"You think so, or you know so. If Sinclair has any other family, we need to call them and let them know what happened."

"Only Adam," I say with more conviction. "Well, Adam and the other guys from the band."

"Okay, that's easy enough because they're all here. J?" he calls over his shoulder. "Get her publicist, and anyone else you can think of on the horn. We need to get in front of the camera and address this as soon as possible."

"It's already done, Connor. Everyone is appraised and all hands are on deck." Jeanine swipes at the tears still gathering in her eyes, and with renewed purpose, she straightens her glasses and takes a phone out of her pocket. Her fingers begin to fly over the keyboard.

The energy in the room is quiet when compared to the remnant of chaos that was still hanging on when I first walked in, but I still feel crazy, like my world exploded into a million shards, and there is no way I will ever be able to pull it back together.

"You heard the doctor, Jake. She's going to be okay." Connor says his hand on my shoulder squeezes until I look at him.

He holds my gaze for a long beat before he repeats. "Sinclair is okay"

"She's going to be okay," I repeat his words letting the reality sink in past the panic and anxiety that are still bouncing around my system.

"And when she wakes up, she's going to need you."

"Sin has never needed me." Want me? Maybe. Sometimes. But need has always fallen squarely on my side of the line.

"Bullshit," he says in a weary voice. "It's time to take the blinders off, man. Everyone sees it. The tabloids, the fans. The hotel surveillance teams that have to delete footage from rooftop escapades, and unauthorized entrance into a certain secure villa that is supposed to have a nameless guest who not only doesn't pay for said villa but requested that only her personal security have entry codes."

"Shit, Con?" My mind immediately plays all the times I've shown up at her door and that first night on my knees in front of her with my mouth working her core.

"Why would I lie?" he asks. A signature smirk curls one side of his mouth.

It all makes sense now. The ease I had getting access. As the moneyman, I never had to deal with security and cameras. Cameras apparently hidden on the roof of a building that saw a mostly naked Sin and me, doing what we had no business doing, especially in public.

"Did you see…?"

"Enough to know that if you hadn't cockblocked me I would've had a lovely experience with Ms. James? Indeed." That smirk moves to a full-blown smile.

"And you never said anything. Why?"

"Because it's not for me to say anything. I told you. If you want her, then I want her for you. It would have been nice if you weren't so sloppy but I gotchu. It's that simple." Connor stands to his full height, buttoning his suit coat and smoothing a hand over the wrinkles on the sleeve. "This is going to be a long night, Jake. But by the time the sun peeks over Sunrise Mountain, I promise, things won't look so bleak."

"Right," I say and as a second thought I say, "Connor?"

He looks at me in question.

"Thanks…" for getting me to the hospital, for being solid when I was nothing more than a puddle, for taking care of stuff by yourself because I can't do it right now. I don't say all the words in my head, but he nods like he heard them.

"You know, I don't believe in all that love shit, but even I can see that you two are perfect together."

"Perfect, huh?"

"Abso-fucking-lutely," he says with a wink before he walks away and joins Jeanine on the other side of the room.

I stay parked in the seats right in front of the doors until they open hours later. Adam stands on the other side of the threshold and waves me inside. The bloodstained clothes and haunted eyes have been replaced with blue scrubs and a hopeful gaze.

"She woke up a couple of minutes ago. Just long enough for the nurse to check her vitals and shove papers in her face."

"That's huge," I say. He nods and turns to me.

"It is man. It really is. I thought…" He doesn't finish the sentence, but I already know. I had thought the same thing.

"I have to go let the boys know what's going on, but I wanted to let you know first. Seeing her like that was the worst fucking moment of my life, but I'd rather be by her side than on the other side of the door. So, I know you gotta be tripping right about now."

I was…" I say but I correct myself. "I am. I just need to see her with my own eyes."

He silently studies me as he's done so many times before but this time there is no derision, no judgement.

"She's this way." He starts down a typically nondescript hospital hallway and I follow. Sin's room is at across from the nurses' station. Adam stops at the door, bracing himself before he walks inside, and I do the same.

The room is dark. One light over the bed, illuminating Sin lying on her back in the center of the mattress. She looks so tiny and frail. Her normally rich brown skin has a grayish pallor. The woman always so full of life and passion is abnormally still. I take a step forward blinking over and over, trying to force my brain to comprehend the sight in front of me.

I stand there afraid to move forward but to too scared to go back.

I watch as Adam walks right up to the bed and leans forward until his lips are next to her ear. He speaks in hushed tones. His voice words hidden by the bleeps from machines. When he's done, he rubs a gentle hand down her cheek and looks at me.

"I was just letting her know that I'm going out to give the boys an update, and I have to check on…" He suddenly stops. "I won't be that far away."

"Oh, okay," I whisper in response as I finally step next to him.

"I'll be back in a bit," he whispers back.

Adam walks out, leaving me us alone and I stand there for minutes taking in the rise of her chest and the whiz of air when she exhales. I gingerly run fingertips down her arm, but she doesn't respond. Not a wince, no jerk. I need her to know that I'm here. I lace her unresponsive fingers with mine.

"Sin," I utter on a choked whisper. "It's me." I stare at her closed eyelids expecting them to flutter open like they do in the movies, but that doesn't happen. She doesn't move.

A lump of frustration gathers in my throat as I try again. "Baby," I say, running my hand back up her arm, moving it into her hair, and letting the curls twine around my fingers. She always loves it when I play in her hair.

"Just open up your eyes and look at me." I lean forward the way Adam did a second ago. I let my lips brush the edge of her ear with each word. "If I can see your eyes, I know everything will be okay. Please." I lean back to take in her face. "Just let me see your eyes." I know it's irrational because she's not just asleep. She's dealing with trauma to her body and the effects of anesthesia.

I soothe my fingertips over her eyebrows and down the bridge of her nose. "If you open your eyes, I'll go get you a grilled cheese from In-N-Out and a strawberry milkshake," I say as a bribe. "I'll rub your back, and your feet, and your hands. You love when I rub your hands." To demonstrate I turn her hand, so the palm is facing me and rub circles along the lines that cross her skin.

I squeeze her hand in mine "Come back to me. If not to me then to Adam, and Miles, and Dan. They're all here." I talk until I run out of words and my throat aches. And then because I can't think of anything else to say, to do. I finally sit down in the chair next to her bed and lay my head on the mattress at her hip. I hold her hand in mine and close my eyes.

I don't remember drifting off to sleep but Sin's hands pull away from mine and I immediately look up.

She blinks her eyelids open, and her normally warm brown eyes are glazed with pain or maybe the residual effects of the anesthesia, and she seems unable to focus on my face. She tries to say something, but nothing comes out. She tries again but gets the same result, and her eyes get wild with panic as she opens her mouth wide, trying to force out sounds.

"Babe, calm down. Please. Just let me get a nurse. Okay?" Eight long strides take me out of the door and to the front of the nurses' station where a youngish nurse in pastel blue scrubs with unicorns and rainbows is sitting. He looks up at me in question.

"Excuse me but Sin, my..." I clear my throat. "My girlfriend just woke up and she's not... it's like she can't... She's a singer and her voice..."

"Will return with time. She was intubated for the surgery," he says as he steps from behind the desk.

"So, the loss of her voice is temporary?"

"As far as we know. But let's go take a look. I'll page the doctor."

I follow the nurse back into the room.

Sin is staring at the ceiling, tears rolling back into her hair.

"Ms. James, my name is Craig, and I'll be your nurse for the next several hours." Sin blinks hard at his voice, but her eyes pass over him and find mine. Those wet lashes are spiked. Her nose flares with every harsh breath. Her eyes are open, and her chest is moving and she's alive.

"Your boyfriend said that you having a hard time speaking. The soreness is probably inflammation of your vocal chords that will calm with time." It takes him about ten minutes to check all the machines, provide a dose of morphine, page the doctor, add an additional blanket to the bed because she's nods to confirm that yes, she is cold. By the time he walks out the door, the tears have stopped. Sin's muscles are relaxed, and her eyes close. For the first time since I got that god-awful call, I breathe easy.

I lace our fingers and drop a kiss on her knuckles. "Relax, baby, I gotchu," I mumble against her skin and this time she holds my hand as tight as I hold hers.

Chapter 31

Sinclair

M Y HEAD POUNDS, AND WHEN I TRY TO TAKE A DEEP BREATH, IT feels like I swallowed a spike. The last thing I remember is laying on the stage with Adam scream over me for help. And blood. There was so much blood all over me.

I force my heavy eyes open in the cold room at the sound of the door opening, I turn my head to see Jake walking through the door, holding a flimsy white paper coffee cup. He rounds the bed and sits on the side closer to my head. He has a day's growth of whiskers on his face and he looks haggard and tired. He runs a hand down his face.

"Hey, baby." His voice is rough but, at the sound of something so familiar, I feel my eyes well with tears. He gently cups my cheek, using his thumb to wipe away the wetness under my eyes. I squeeze my eyes shut and lean into him, tears falling in earnest.

I try to say his name, but my voice comes out as a squeak and a huff of air.

All the memories come crashing down, the concert and the stalker. The man that I've seen countless times over the years. The one who shows up at every concert in the Sin City T-shirt from our first tour. The one I assured security would never do anything.

Then I heard the gun shots, the people screaming, and the chaos. There was so much chaos. I remember the excruciating pain of bullets ripping through muscle and bone and hitting the stage with a thud. Wanting to move but not being able to pull in enough oxygen to make my muscles fire.

Had anyone else been shot? I try to pull up something, anything from my memory banks but I got nothing. All I remember is looking into dead eyes and a gun pointing at me. Not at Dan or Miles or Adam. Not at any of the people that came to see us. But at me.

I swallow rapidly, choking on panic and pain, as a tremor moves through my body. I need answers to questions, so many questions that I'm afraid to ask. Was anyone else shot? Did anyone die? Did they get the man that did this? How could something like this happen?

"Sin," he whispers, his voice full of anguish and compassion. That compassion is practically oozing out of his pours. It feels very real. It feels warm and comforting. It feels like love and it breaks me wide open.

Tears fall hot and heavy down my face as I grip his shirt.

Jake gathers me close as full body sobs rack my frame, and he curves his body around mine, not offering words of comfort, not saying I'll be okay because I won't, not for a long time.

How could something like this happen?

The stage is one of the only places I have always felt safe, my home away from home. Now my home is bullet riddled and shattered. Just the thought of the bullets whizzing by my head and ripping into my chest causes phantom pains to ricochet through my bones.

I don't know how long we stay like that, but my arms are numb, and my hands tingle from being fisted in his shirt.

"I'm so sorry, Sin," he says.

I can't answer him, so I burrow closer to his chest. The steady pulse of his heartbeat is a soothing melody under my ear.

My eyes grow heavy, and I succumb to sleep.

"That bed is only made for one person," a nurse chides from somewhere in the small room.

I pry my eyes open and, for a minute, I'm confused. I'm still in a hospital but the room looks different. The thin curtain at the door is gone. As are the scuffed beige linoleum, thin blankets, windowless walls. The room is large for a hospital room. A love seat rests under the window and early morning light pours through the slightly open blinds, casting the room in shades of pink and orange, but it still doesn't soften the harsh overhead lights or the cool medicinal air.

The memories of last night flood through my mind, I was doing a show when people started yelling and loud explosions of sound overpowered the noise of the crowd.

Gunshots.

Someone had been shooting at us. I'd been shot.

I move my head but a head next to mine on the pillow limits the movement. I take note of the cadence of his breaths, and the rich scent of cocoa butter that coats his skin. I know it's Jake before I hear his voice rumble in my ear when he tells the nurse he'll move.

I blink my eyes open when he slips an arm from under my head. Even that small movement takes a tremendous amount of effort. The light in the room hurts my eyes, making them water and become unfocused. I cover my eyes with my forearm until the world comes back into focus and the light doesn't feel like it's burning my retinas.

"Don't go," I say. My voice comes out hoarse, but it's there! This time.

"I'm not going anywhere, babe." He drops a kiss on my forehead.

The nurse, pacified by Jake moving, smiles at me as the doctor walks in the door.

"Good morning, Sinclair," The doctor says as he stops in front of the hand sanitizer mounted to the wall and rubs a generous amount into his skin. He removes the stethoscope from around his shoulders and approaches the bed. "I'm Dr. Bennett. I'm just going to look you over real quick before we send breakfast in okay?"

I nod.

"Mr. Johnson, maybe you want to step outside while Dr. Bennett completes an exam? I promise she will be in good hands. Grab a cup of coffee. Freshen up and we'll see you in a few." The nurse shoos him from the room.

At his absence her smile grows more prominent, which illuminates her features. She busies herself with checking the machines before she pulls down the top of my gown for the doctor to check a bandage on my chest.

"No blood, hun. That's good," the nurse says.

"How good?" I ask, my voice breaking. *Please say I'll be back on my feet tomorrow, and it'll be like nothing happened. Just say that I'll be fine. That in less than a week I'll be back on stage singing and playing again.*

"Faster than you think," Dr. Bennett answers. "It'll take a little time but holding long or hitting high notes won't be immediate. However, we have every reason to believe that you will have a full recovery and be on stage again before you know it."

"What kind of time are we talking?" I ask.

"I can't give you exacts. But your lungs experienced a trauma and like any bruise or cut, it has to heal. How fast you heal depends on a lot of factors. Let's take it one step at a time. Sit up for me, Ms. James."

I sit up with surprising ease. Yeah, my body still hurts but I thought maybe that every muscle in my body would be screaming. Dr. Bennett places the cold bell of the stethoscope directly on my skin.

"Deep breath in and blow out hard." And I do it. My breathing hitches before my lungs hit full capacity. "Again," he says as he moves the stethoscope over, listening.

"Rachel, Ms. James will need pulmonary consult and rehab. One a scale of one to ten where would you put your pain level, Ms. James?"

"A four?" I rasp. He stares at me, not blinking, for a long moment.

"That's good. Real good," he says. "Rachel?"

"Yes, doctor."

"Lower the pain meds and see how she does. We have to stay in front of the pain. If we get behind, it won't be a good thing."

"Okay, Ms. James, as far as I can tell you are doing as well as can be expected. I want you up and walking as soon as possible. I'll be around later this afternoon to check in with you."

And he left. The nurse helps me tie the gown back in place. She removes the catheter. Gives me a small toiletry kit with toothpaste, a toothbrush, mouthwash, and a small comb.

"Okay, hon," she says, pulling off the latex gloves. "Press this button." She taps the red button with a picture of a nurse on it. "If you need anything. And this one"—she taps the button next to it—"is for the TV."

Jake walks back in the room and her friendly smile freezes, turning brittle enough to break. "Ms. James, I'll be on duty until four this evening. I'll be back soon with food." She walks out the room giving Jake a wide berth.

Jake and I fall into a strained silence. He studies me for a while. His eyes sweeping up and down my prone frame.

He sighs. "I think I lost fifty years off my life when I got the call that you'd been shot," he says.

"We don't have to talk about it." I try to make my voice light but between the harsh sound and the tears that fill my eyes. I fail miserably.

"We do, babe. We really do." I barely nod.

"Somehow, in all the years I've known you, it never really hit me how vulnerable you really are when you're on stage. The police came by to talk to Adam before he left, and he recognized the shooter. I guess the guy has been obsessed with you for years. How did I not know this? Adam said he used to follow the band around in the early years." There is accusation and hurt behind his words. "That's crazy, Sin, like seriously insane. I understood you had to deal with media but this… Fuck, when I thought I lost you." He walks an agitated line across the room before turning to walk back toward me. "I've never felt so helpless in my life. It put a lot of shit into perspective."

"Oh yeah?" I ask as he walks over to the bed to loom above me. I can't make out his expression since it's backlit against the sunlight. But he leans in, and his hazel eyes come into focus.

"Yeah," he says after beat. His eyes skip away from mine but when they come back, they're wet. One lone finger traces the contours of my faces and he lets out a shaky breath.

"Life is too short not to go after what I want. Who I want," he says meaningfully. "I know you don't want to hear this, and I'm probably an ass for saying it right now, but I…" He kisses me with trembling dry lips. His eyes are open too. I know because my eyes are open as well. I don't blink because I'd miss the way he's looking at me.

"I love you," he says simply, and I blink to hold in the rush of tears.

"Always have. Always will," he says kissing me between words. Jake pulls back, his thumb brushing the tears that have gathered at the corners of my eyes. "I'm done accepting the little bit you're willing to give me when I want it all, and you want it too."

I'm so tired of pretending I'm too angry to forgive and too strong to be vulnerable. With my body broken in the hospital, I can't pretend that my heart is in the same place it was when I arrived. Especially when I already know the only person who can fix it is standing in front of me daring me to create my destiny and claim him as mine.

"I love you, and if you can't say it back now, I'm willing to wait until you are. When you get out of this hospital, you're going to rock harder than you ever have before, and when you step off that stage, I'll rock you just as hard. It's our time. Ours, babe."

Deep in my soul, I feel the truth of his words.

"You love me, Sin. I know it. You know it. Give in gracefully, baby. Let me love you." He places a kiss on my forehead. "Let me take care of you." He drops kisses on my eyes forcing them closed. "I'm not going anywhere, ever." His lips press against mine. I pull back, searching his face.

"Say it again," I demand.

"I love you," he says immediately.

"Me too," I respond and this time I kiss him first. "I love you too," I say against his lips.

"I promise for as long as you live you won't regret saying that. Never again," he says, staring into my eyes. For the first time since I slapped him, what seems like forever ago, I believe every word coming out of his mouth.

Every time I close my eyes to settle into sleep, a nurse walks in to check something or ask a question. Every single time I've opened my eyes, I feel a little panic bubble in my chest until I see Jake.

Sometimes he's on the phone pacing back and forth, a worried frown creasing his brows. Other times he's sitting in a chair staring out the window, giving me an opportunity to study his profile. This time when I open my eyes, Jake is lying on the bed at my hip, head resting on folded arms finally asleep. I tried to get him to go home to at least to take a shower, but he refused, saying he'd leave when Adam came back. God, he's stubborn.

At my movement he wakes up, stretching his neck and blinking up at me with sleepy eyes.

"Hey, baby, you good?" He runs a hand over his face.

No, I'm not good. Every time I blink there's another explosion of pain behind my eyes that travels down my throat and into my chest, making it hard to breathe. The pain is everywhere, but I don't want to worry him.

So instead of telling him how horrible I feel I say, "I'm okay." I don't think I've been admitted to a hospital since the day I was born. Being here now is scary. Not being able to breathe easy or force my vocal chords to make even the simplest noises terrifies me.

Adam, Dan, and Miles all pile into my room around midmorning. Jake is sitting in a chair close to the bed. One leg crossed over his knee. Gold rim glasses that I've never seen before rest on his face. He's reading through emails on his phone. I use one hand to cup his chin and gently shake his head. He turns his face into my palm, kissing the center before he turns his eyes to the three men that just entered the room.

"The boys are here," I say.

His features lose their softness and he sits up, eyeing the boys with weary irritation. Jake pushes the chair away from the bed and stands in front of the group. I expected yelling and shouting about the lack of security at the venue or the over protective big brother act, but to my surprise, they pepper him with questions about what the doctors have said and how I'm feeling.

The four of them talk about me like I'm not here in the bed a couple of feet away. When did this happen? But Jake gives them the run down.

"The shooter was apprehended within minutes of the shooting. Seth"—at the mention of his name, I turn my eyes on Adam, who refuses to meet my gaze—"actually jumped off the stage and grabbed the guy until the police arrived."

"It turns out the shooter actually got a job working in the arena and was able to bring one piece of the gun in at a time and hide the parts in multiple restrooms inside the facility. So, the night of the concert. He collected all the parts and yeah. You know the rest."

"I know I heard some of this yesterday, but I can't remember shit. So bottom line is the cops nabbed the douchebag and Sin?" Adam asks Jake.

"The bullets nicked her lungs but she's okay. The surgery was completely successful. They were able to repair the damage. A plastic surgeon was brought in to close the wounds, so there should be minimal scaring. She will need physical therapy and a voice coach, something about retraining her lungs to move air over her vocal chords."

Adam collapses in the chair Jake vacated and bends over with his head between his legs, taking deep breaths. Jesus, I must look like death warmed over. When he lifts his head, his eyes are mournful, and his lips are pressed into a thin line.

"Sin, I'm sorry. I tried to get to you, but everything happened so fast. I just couldn't get there fast enough. I—" He looks devastated and so guilty. But this guilt isn't his cross to bear.

"Last time I checked you aren't psychic or on my security detail. You didn't know this was going to happen, and it's no one's fault but the idiot who was shooting." I somehow manage to get all of that out without wheezing but my chest feels like it's on fire.

I look at Dan and Miles to gauge their reaction to my speech and both nod in agreement. Adam has always been the "parent" figure. The one with the rational head planted clearly on his square shoulders. He's been the one who gets things done, who takes care of us all, but this is too much even for his shoulders. I won't let him tear himself to shreds for something he could do nothing about.

"You should listen to Sin-a-sticks, Adam. It's not that often that she makes sense."

"Nice Dan," Miles says.

"What? You didn't think she'd get a pass because she's lazing around the hospital, did you? If you ask me, one of us should've gotten shot a long time ago. We need the street cred." A boyish grin breaks across Miles's face, but it doesn't reach his eyes. I know this little show is Dan's attempt to get us back to normal.

And it works. We all laugh at the insanity coming out of his mouth and it feels good. I'm going to be okay. My band is going to be fine. We will face this just like we've faced everything else, and we'll overcome it because that's who we are.

Jake has disengaged from the group, watching us with wearing eyes. Conflicting emotions flit across his face going from jealousy to concern to fear so fast I'm not sure if I imagined it. I try to catch his eye, but his gaze shifts around the guys.

I can tell by his weary gaze and his twitchy muscles he's about to make his escape. But before he makes for the door Adam stands closing the space between them. He holds out his hand, palm up to Jake.

Jake stares at the hand for a couple of beats before he drops his hand to Adam's.

"Thanks for being here," Adam says.

"You don't have to ever thank me for being here for Sin," Jake replies.

"I was thanking you on my behalf, not hers."

Jake's shoulders deflate a bit before he utters, "Welcome."

"Lookee here. It's a Christmas miracle," Dan quips, his gaze bouncing back and forth between Adam and Jake.

"It's nowhere near Christmas, asshole." Miles grumbles but there is a smile pulling at the corners of his mouth.

I can't help the giggle that escapes my mouth and, before I know it, all five of us are laughing. It's in this moment that I truly know everything will be okay.

Chapter 32

NOW

Sinclair

THE LAST WEEK WAS ROUGH. I'M GOING ON DAY FIVE IN THE hospital, and I'm so ready to go that I almost run out the doors before the doctor can change her mind.

I walk out of the hospital with four prescriptions, two appointments, one for a pulmonologist and the other for a counselor. Rachel, the nurse from my first day, gives me detailed instructions before she goes to get the final signatures on the release papers. After the papers are signed, the release moves quickly. I gingerly walk into the bathroom and change into the clothes Adam bought me yesterday. A nurse shows up with a wheelchair and pushes me out a side entrance to a familiar white Audi.

Jake stands by the open passenger door with the engine idling and a worried frown creasing his brow. I follow his gaze across the parking lot and see multiple paparazzi congregating toward the front of the hospital. They've been like circling vultures. One even went so far as to dress in scrubs and carry a chart, trying to get into my room.

"Thank God they don't know what exit you're coming out of." He nods toward the group that has almost doubled in size in the last couple of minutes. When I stand, it's hard to put one foot in front of the other. My legs feel weak, and just that little bit of effort has my breath coming in huffs, making it hard to breathe. I thought I got shot in the chest. Why are my legs not working? Jake helps situate me into the seat. He's treating me like I'm made of porcelain. I don't pay attention to where we're driving until we pass the Strip on the freeway.

"Where are we going?"

"To my place." He drums his fingers on the stirring wheel, his nervousness becoming more apparent with every mile. "I just thought it would be more comfortable than the hotel, you know?"

"Oh," I utter because I don't have any other words. I've been trying to keep Jake in a special little box, and pull him out to play every so often, but we're so past that. He told me in the hospital to let him love me.

I want that.

"Sin, look at me," he demands. My head jerks up. I didn't even realize that I wasn't looking at him. We're stopped at a red light, and he waits for me to lift my eyes. "Stop running, baby, because I'm never going to stop chasing." He hand caresses my cheek before moving into the hair at the nape of my neck.

"I'm not running."

"Yeah, okay."

"I'm not," I insist.

"It doesn't matter if you were because You." Kiss. "Belong." Kiss. "With." Kiss. "Me." He punctuates the last word by dipping his tongue between my lips.

We stare at each other until the light turns green and the car behind us hits its horn. It doesn't matter to Jake. He holds my gaze and I keep my eyes on his. He's the first to look away as he steps on the accelerator and eases back into traffic. We're on the road another fifteen minutes before he turns into a driveway of a modern house that sits on an elevated lot. As we wait for one of the garage doors to open, his face is turns toward me, but I keep facing forward trying to ignore him, or maybe I'm ignoring us. I don't know anymore. I've been playing this game so long I lost track of the projected outcome.

I haven't let myself be curious about Jake. It felt a little too much like a commitment. A little too much like history repeating itself.

I blink as Jake drives into the garage, parking next to a sleek black Porsche and a huge SUV that probably cost more than all my guitars combined. He turns off the car and steps out. I watch his figure round the front of the vehicle before walking to my side and opening the door. He reaches for my hand and laces our fingers, helping to stand. Hand in hand we walk to the door that leads into his home. Jake hits a code on the lock and pushes the door open, gently pulling me into the house.

My eyes get bigger as I step farther inside. This house is stunning.

"You like?" He places his keys on one of the hooks mounted on the wall of the mudroom. He guides me through the warm and inviting kitchen, down a hallway, and into a massive bedroom dominated by the king-size bed with the heavy curved frame upholstered with black leather. One wall has oversized glass doors that overlook the red-tinted mountains of Red Rock Canyon.

"This is... wow... It's exquisite," I say. Inwardly, I wince wondering if that came out as stilted and awkward as it sounded in my head.

"It is," he says, but he isn't looking at the room. He's looking at me. With our fingers still interlaced he walks me to the bed. He lets go to pull back the comforter and bed sheets and fluff the pillows.

"Get in."

For the first time, maybe ever, I follow his order. I'm tired. No, I'm exhausted. I toe off my shoes, untie the loose-fitting sweats, let them fall to the floor, and slip between the cool sheets.

"I'm tired. Just going to take a little nap"

"Whatever you need, Sin," he says before kicking off his shoes and dropping trou. He leaves on his T-shirt and boxer briefs and crawls into bed. His heavy weight dips his side of the bed and he gently eases behind me. Being in his space and feeling his body in bed next to mine, I feel safe, protected. The even sounds of his breathing lull me to sleep.

I jerk awake. My body is slick with sweat. The sound of bullets and screaming echoing in my ears.

"Shh... baby. It's okay. You're okay," Jake croons in my ear. His strong arms wrap around my waist.

But I can't. I can't move past the panic. It feels like ash in my mouth. I raise a tentative hand to my chest fingering the edge of the bandage. Jesus Christ, he shot me. I make to sit up, but Jake's arms tighten, holding me in my position.

"I—"

"Sleep, baby. I promise anyone coming in here will have to go through me to get to you. You're safe. Everything else can wait until we wake up." He pulls my prone body next to his and, second by second, I succumb to the warm heat of his chest pressed into my back and the steady whisper of his breath against my ear.

For the second time in the history of us, I do exactly as I'm told.

Chapter 33

NOW

Jake

I AWAKE HOURS LATER TO FIND THE ROOM DARK. THE MOON SHINES through the window in muted silver light across the hardwood floor. Sin is lying on her back. The bullet went clean through her upper chest, but it wreaked havoc and rained misery on its way out.

The surgery to repair the damage was minimally invasive. Along with closing the bullet entry and exit points just below her shoulder, she has two small two-inch incisions on the side of her chest right between her ribs. Thick white gauze and tape cover the area and after seven days of watching nurses treat, clean, and bandage the wound, I know it's easier for her on her side because it shifts her weight and removes the pressure from the area.

What I didn't expect was the satisfaction I feel at having her here. Call it possessive or obsessive, but I love that she's in my house, wrapped in my sheets, her body soft and relaxed against mine.

I've never had this burning desire to own any other woman. Sin breaks me down to my baser self. The man obsessed with claiming, owning, and fucking his woman. At all times. In all the ways. It's a Neanderthal impulse. It doesn't look pretty when analyzed, but it feels certain and final.

I slip from behind her, tiptoe into the bathroom, and shut the door with a soft click, careful not to wake her. I turn on the shower, and hiss when the hot water pelts my skin. After a quick wash. I brush my teeth and wash my face.

I'm drained. Even after the five or six hours I just slept.

When I open the door, I find Sin sitting up her back resting on pillows against the headboard, big brown eyes assessing me.

"I'm sorry. I didn't mean to wake you," I say as I walk across the room to the dresser, dropping the towel to the floor right before I grab a pair of boxer briefs, and pull them up my legs.

"No, you didn't," she says in a sleepy voice. Every day her voice is getting stronger, the husky timbre now more prominent than the scratchy whisper that was coming out of her mouth on day one.

Holy shit, she's beautiful. And she's in my bed, waiting for me. My dick stirs at the sight of her, unaware that we're here to take care of Sin not fuck her to our heart's content.

Sin watches me as I, approach the bed. Her lids at half-mast, making it difficult to read her eyes. I settle on the bed next to her.

Turning my head to the side, I study her profile for a few long minutes before she turns and meets my stare with a combination of fierce defiance, and something I think might be love. Its right there. I see it in her eyes when she looks at me, and in her body when she touches me.

She takes in a deep breath through her nose and lets it slowly ease out of her mouth.

We're at a crossroads. Our proverbial moment of truth, and I want Sin to go my way. I want her to choose me. Love me. I want it so bad it's become an ache in my chest and an unfettered longing in my heart.

"I know when you got back in town you thought I was an itch that needed to be scratched, but here we are all this time later and we're still not done. I've told you since day one what I want, but what do you want? Do you want me?"

Sin's drowsy eyes drill mine. And for a long minute I she doesn't speak. *She not saying anything because she doesn't want to hurt me? It's no. She's actually going to say no.*

"You know I want you but that doesn't mean…"

"Baby, it means we're in this together. We'll figure the rest out. Up until now I've been asking you for a chance, but I'm done asking. This is it, our opportunity at forever. Maybe our last one, and I'm taking it."

Sin grips the comforter, pulling the fabric taut. "You don't get to do that. You don't get to make all the decisions." Her voice is soft, almost pleading.

"I know I'm probably asking for the impossible, but if you give just a little, just an inch, have the smallest bit of faith, I swear from this moment on your life will be magic."

"I want that."

"Reach out and take it, baby. It's right here and it's yours."

Sinclair

The last vestiges of the wall that had fortified my heart over the previous four years crumbled under the weight of his conviction because I believe in magic, the magic composed of us. When I think about giving in, letting it all go, and giving everything that I have, I'm terrified.

I drop my eyes from him, unable to hold his gaze. I pick at a loose thread in the comforter before I turn my eyes back to his. "I don't know how, Jake. I want to put the past to rest, but every single time things are going good I expect the other shoe to drop, you know?"

My throat aches with the tears that have started rolling down my cheeks. How can I write a whole album expressing my feelings and thoughts about this man, but when he's right in front of me, I become a stammering mess?

"Don't cry," he whispers. "Please, don't."

"God, I'm so bad at this."

I barely get the last word out before he cups my face in both of his hands and kisses me, stealing my breath only to replace it with his own. His hands skim down my body, careful of wounds in my chest and ribs. And he wraps both around my waist, gently lifting me to straddle his lap, one thigh on either side of his.

Jake deepens the kiss, taking deep pulls from my mouth. The tears come hotter and faster as my tongue tangles with his.

"I love you," I say into his kiss. "But I'm still me. My life right now is the stage and the road. Even after all of this"—I gingerly touch the bandage—"for me it's going to sleep in one city and waking up in another. You don't want that life Jake. You never did."

There I said it. Poked the elephant standing in the middle of the room and gave voice to the one thing we've both been afraid to address. In less than seven months I'm leaving. Our history says that our relationship won't survive the ravages of distance or the lapse of time.

He breaks the kiss, pulling his head back, his eyes roving my face. He brushes a thumb over my bottom lip, and his voice sounds like gravel when he says, "So, give me now. Give me the next seven months." He releases a long breath. "And when the show ends…"

"So, do we," I finish.

I stare into his eyes and they're clear. No deceit. No hint of indecision. The only thing there is love. It illuminates his hazel irises but there is also grim understanding. The knowledge that sometimes love isn't enough. That even the best of intentions fall prey to absence and loneliness.

I lean forward, holding his eyes until my lips meet his. Jake opens for me, his hand fisting the hair at the back of my head, and this kiss… it's dark chocolate, bitter and sweet, and heartbreaking in a very different way. Jake breaks the kiss, leaning his head back against the headboard eyes squeezed tight.

"It'll kill me this time. Watching you go will break something that…"

"Will never be repaired?" I ask.

He nods. Eyes still closed.

"Then come," I say, giving voice to my secret desire. The wish I've never admitted to myself let alone anyone else. Leaning forward, I kiss him again. "Come with me, Jake. Me and you, right?"

"Sin, my life…" He opens his eyes to stare at me "Is here. My family… is here. Connor and I are buying another property directly across from the MGM Grand at the beginning of next year. I can't just walk away from that."

"But you can walk away from me, from us?" I try to move off his lap, but his hands settle on my hips, keeping me there.

"It's not that simple. Would you give up singing and touring to stay here with me?"

"Our careers are totally different. You're trying to compare apples and oranges, and it's not fair."

"Exactly. Nothing about this is fair, Sin. I have people depending on me just like you have people depending on you. Both our hands are tied," he says, tilting his head, looking up at me. "Tell me you see that."

"I get it, Jake. It's…" I lick my suddenly dry lips. "It's reality or at least our reality."

"Yeah. So, we have the next seven months. You came back to me once. Maybe lightning will hit the same spot twice."

We both move at the same time, and we kiss until our lips are tender and our breath is short. We kiss like we have a small allotment of time and our number will soon be up.

Chapter 34

Jake

It's been seven months since the shooting. I've watched Sin bounce back and recover as if nothing happened. When she hit the ground, it was with a vengeance. I thought she'd have more of an issue with getting back on stage, but she conquered that with the same ease she's over come every other obstacle in her life.

The Hotel offered to let Sin City out of its residency, but they insisted with Sin being the loudest that they were not letting anyone, especially a crazy man like the shooter, Ian Foster, scare them away from doing what they loved. So, we doubled down on security. Fully vetted every new hire. There are four nightly sweeps conducted before and after each show to ensure there are no nefarious pieces or parts left to hurt anyone.

I've been dreading the last night of Sin's residency. Just when everything between us is finally in perfect accord, she's leaving. I swallow around the lump in my throat, rapidly blinking my eyes. I watch from the sidelines as Sin works the stage for her final show, and I'm ten seconds away from barreling out there and begging her to stay.

Sin talked about leaving my house after she was better, but it just didn't make sense. So, she moved in with her security in tow. Pretended as if this was our forever. Even though we both knew the end would come sooner than either of us thought.

When I woke up this morning, Sin was already out of bed. She had two large suitcases laid open on the floor. She was strategically placing items inside. I walked up behind her and wrapped my arms around her waist.

"Morning," I whispered, dropping a kiss on her neck.

"Morning." Her hands come over my forearms. She squeezes both before gently pulling my arms open and stepping out of my reach.

Knowing she has to go and letting it happen are two very different things. For days I'd been trying to figure out how to ask her to stay, hoping she'd stay on her own accord, and solve the problem for both of us. At the eleventh hour, I'm trying my damnedest to be the good guy. To lean on the knowledge that this time the end isn't a shock and good-bye doesn't mean forever. It's more like until. Until the fucking stars align, and all the green and black ducks have made their way back into a row.

When we started this thing, it was rocky. Hell, the middle was rocky too, but then we found our groove, it became home wrapped in a single intention.

Sin is back, but she isn't mine to keep, Not yet. Sin City is releasing a new album and the publicity tour is starting in New York the day after the lights go out for the last time in Vegas. I make no bones about how far gone I am for her. She knows it. Everyone in the casino knows it. The fucking world knows it. But this is history repeating itself. My place is here in Vegas where it's always been as much as hers is on the road.

"Sin, you're not gone yet. You don't have to…" I let out a sigh, cutting myself off. For the last couple of days, she's been withdrawing, locking pieces of herself away from me, freezing me out. I've been trying to put on the happy face. I told her seven months ago that it would kill me when she left. And it is. But what's the alternative? Ask her to stay even when I told her that I wouldn't go? Ask her to give up her dreams for me when I can't walk away from my business, my responsibility for her.

I have to let her go when it feels like I just got her back after mourning her loss for years. And unlike the last time. Neither one of us is pretending like long sporadic flights, stolen moments in between shows, disjointed phone calls, and frozen FaceTime screens will be enough to sustain us. I watch her for a couple more minutes as she moves back and forth between the suitcases and other rooms in the house.

Her stride is choppy, and when she finally lifts her eyes to mine, they're swimming in unshed tears.

"Baby, no…"

She places hands over both her eyes completely blocking her face from my view. I close the space between us and pull her hands from her face and see my own misery reflected back. I know it's fucked up to revel in her suffering, but it's the ultimate validation. Sinclair James still loves me. She still hasn't said it, but it's right there in her eyes clear as day. I feel it when we're in bed when she fusses over sheets and pillows before wrapping her body around mine.

It's taken me one year to regain her trust. A year of taking everything she could think to throw at me. I did the one thing I thought was impossible: I made Sin love me again. In that sense, our mutual sadness was a beautiful thing.

I brush my lips across Sin's and her breath shudders past her lips to ghost over mine. I take the minuscule space she offers to dip my tongue into her mouth, growling as her flavor floods my senses. Sin is the most decadent dessert, sweet, vibrant, addictive. One taste is never enough.

"I'm leaving, Jake," she says, tearing her mouth away from mine. "This time tomorrow I'll be in New York at a listening party for the new album. And two days after when the new album drops, I'll be in London for the first leg of our international tour and after London we hit Paris."

"And you're not gone yet, Sin." I invade her mouth again, this time with more force, rolling her tongue with mine, fisting her hair tight so she can't break away. "I need this," I whispered against her wet lips. "We need this." I didn't give her a chance to answer. I licked my way back into her mouth, breaking the kiss only to kiss down her neck.

She doesn't protest as I walk her to the edge of the bed, dropping to my knees in front of her. She kisses me again, her thighs spreading wide, and her body curving to cradle me against her. I brake the kiss, and with a gentle push to the center of her chest, she sprawls in front of me. My lips move across the sensitive skin of her inner thighs, only stopping when I hit the fabric of the tiny black Spandex shorts she wears to bed.

My fingers curl into the waistband and peel them down her legs. "So pretty." I run a finger down her slit. Her hips buck at the contact, and an involuntary shiver runs through her legs. I cover her pussy with my mouth, my tongue sliding over her sex, lapping at her juices, dipping into her tight hole. She's strung so tight.

Sin wraps her hands around the back of my head, drawing me in tighter. I suck her clit into my mouth, and her back arches on the bed. She gyrates her hips against my face.

"That's right, Sin. Get it. Fuck my face."

I plunge one finger into the first knuckle, and her tight sheath grips my finger like a vice. I add a second finger, and she lets out a high wail that is in perfect pitch. I kept going, teasing her lips before moving back to her clit, making her ride my fingers like she rides my dick. It doesn't take too long before she breaks apart under my hands, and her thighs squeeze my head most satisfyingly.

I kissed my way up her belly, stopping momentarily to tongue those dark brown nipples pebbled and begging for my mouth. Her back arches in a sharp bow. I wrapped my arm around her waist, pulling her in close and grinding my still covered dick against her wet core. Her legs come up around my hips as her hands push down my sweats. Her movements become frantic, almost desperate. I raise my head up to meet her eyes, but they're squeezed shut with tears running down her beautiful face. I dropped my head to her neck, taking in big deep breaths, willing myself not to fall apart. I pushed my sweats down enough to free my dick and fill her to hilt in one stroke. I'm home.

Back in the only place that matters. Back in Sin. Her mouth opens in a soundless cry and her eyes finally snap open to meet mine.

"God, you're beautiful," I mumble against her lips. I pull my hips back only to tunnel in farther. I want to go so deep inside her that she'll feel me long after she's left, long after she's replaced me with someone else.

"Harder, Jake," she breathes against my lips.

I take her mouth in a wet and sloppy kiss unable to maintain the smooth finesse when the world around me is crumbling to rubble.

"Make this last time count. I need to feel all of you."

Last time. Those words hit like a boulder to the chest. Goddammit, it hurts. I funnel all that emotion into raw animal fucking. I turn into a savage, pounding Sin until the only sounds are wet skin and our combined breathing. Sin's eyes roll into the back of her head, eyelids shutting as she comes for the second time. Her pussy is so tight and pulsing around my length. I only last another couple of shallow strokes before I fall over that edge right behind her.

I run a hand up her back bringing us chest to chest, our heartbeats syncopated in the rapid rhythm.

"Sin."

She hides her face in the crook of my neck.

"It's okay." But it's not. Nothing about any of this is okay. I kiss her salty lips. "We'll find our way back to each other. You believe me?"

"Promise me," she says through her tears. "Promise me that you won't forget me as soon as I get on that plane. That if I decide to come back after a week or a month or a year, you'll still be here."

"You're thinking about coming back?"

"Promise me," she insists.

"I promise."

We stay together in the bed until she has to get ready for her last show and we make love. It's deliberate and poignant. Both of us aware that this is the last time for a long time

Sin is center stage middle of the spotlight for the last notes of the closing number. The countdown is over. We have no time left. A limo is picking the crew up right after the show to take them to the executive airport. They have to be in London for a show in two days.

The arena goes dark. There is no encore and when the house lights come up Sin is no longer at center stage. The applause is deafening even from where I stand. It's over. She's done.

At this point, I'm just going through the motions. Trying not to break down when it's the only thing I want more than Sin right now. She quickly changes into tight sweatpants and one of those sweatshirts that hang off one shoulder. Her dark skin still glistens with sweat, giving her a glow maybe only I can see because she shines to me. She threads our fingers and guides me through the back hallways toward the limo waiting outside a secret entrance used for celebrities.

We settle into the back of the car with Dan and Miles, and it's abnormally quiet. The postconcert excitement dimmed by the pain of two hearts breaking.

Chapter 35

Sinclair

THE LIMO PULLS DIRECTLY ONTO THE TARMAC NEXT TO A PRIVATE JET. The stairs are already down. The pilot ducks his head out to wave at Adam who arrived shortly after us. I take note of a million little nuances of the airfield like the metal fence hanging by a screw and the sliding glass doors to the private terminal that keep opening even though no one is walking through them. I stare out the window like my life depends on it because anything is better than looking at Jake. I barely even register Adam getting out of the car until the door snaps shut.

I knew leaving would be hard, but I didn't expect to feel regret or this pit in my stomach because I'm making a bad decision, the ultimate wrong choice. I can't pinpoint the exact moment I fell back in love with him. God knows it wasn't something I purposefully cultivated. But it happened. Part of me wants to rest in that glow, in the knowledge that from the ashes of our first relationship we started something brand-new. Jake wasn't a devil spawn spewed from the pits of hell and sent to earth with the sole intention of destroying me. He was a guy that made a mistake, a mistake that exploded in his face and shattered my world, but a mistake just the same.

I turn in my seat to take him in, keeping distance between us. I can't touch him. If I touch him, my resolve will melt into a puddle on the floor of this car. Once upon a time, I thought Jake was my personal brand of kryptonite, but this last year he's proven he can be so much more.

"Jake..."

"No." He lifts his shadowed eyes to mine. "I know what you're going to say, Sin, and I don't want to hear it."

"I… I'm trying to do this right."

"Is there ever a right time to rip somebody's heart to shreds?" A heavy breath leaves his lungs.

I finally look at him, and he's staring back at me. His eyes are begging where his lips are silent. If he says the words, I'll figure out a way to have both, him and my career.

"So, this is it," I say dumbly.

"Looks like it." Jake clenches his jaw, grinding his teeth. The truth an anchor between us. Love isn't always enough to make a relationship work. I can't bring myself to say another word. Not when his eyes beg me to change my mind and emotion making my throat ache.

He closes the space between us. His hands grip either side of my neck, and his forehead dips forward to rest on mine. "Come back to me, Sin. Find your way back to me."

"I will," I whisper, searching his eyes. Taking a mental picture of this moment.

Jake tries to pull away, but I place hands over his forearms holding him in place. "I love you."

"I love you too," he says. I can't stop the tears from falling down my face fast and hard, or the fact that they increase when he swipes his thumbs across my cheeks. We stare at each other for several beats.

"Say it again, Jake," I whisper.

"I… I," he starts, his voice hoarse with emotion. His lips brush across mine in a chaste kiss. "I love you, Sin." His hands tighten on either side of my neck.

"I love you too," I whisper into his mouth. With those words, I break contact and open the door. I wipe hands across my wet face and slip out of the seat. When my feet hit the asphalt, I turn back to Jake for the last time. "For what it's worth, I wish things were different." I walk toward the stairs of the plane, and by the time I settle in my seat and look out the window, the limo is gone.

Chapter 36

NOW
Jake

"Thanks, Adam."

I palm the key to Sin's hotel suite as I leave his room. When I called him this morning, I wasn't sure if he'd help me, but true to form he had no qualms with doing what he thought was best for Sin.

He gave me their hotel info and asked if I wanted him to tell Sin I was on my way. I wasn't sure she wanted to see me. She'd been so adamant back in Vegas. Her certainty made me question myself and my resolve. The truth of the matter is I do want a home that is ours. I want to wake up to her face on the pillow next to mine every morning and go to sleep with her warmth beside me every night. I want little brown babies that have her big doe eyes and bright smile.

There's never been a time I didn't want Sin. That's the thing that finally got my ass on the plane after a two long miserable weeks. I don't care what I have to do to have her or what compromises she needs me to make. Sin is mine, and I'm hers. I'm not going another day without her.

I walk down the narrow corridor until I stop in front of the numbers Adam scribbled on a small piece of paper. I think twice about using the card. Sin doesn't know I'm here. I'm not trying to scare the hell out of her.

I knock on the door, the tap loud in the seemingly silent hallway. After a minute she still doesn't answer. So, I knock harder, the thud echoing off the metal door across from hers. This time I hear movement on the other side of the door. I take a deep breath, shore up my confidence and wait. The door opens a couple of inches hindered by the metal security flap on the top. And there she is. A barefoot Sin, wearing no makeup. Her natural curls pulled up into a curly puff on top of her head. The short black sleeping shorts she prefers showing inches and inches of smooth brown skin and an old tank top I recognize as one of my own.

"Is everything okay." Sin's raspy voice falls off and sleepy brown eyes widen as she takes me in.

"It's good now. All good."

"Jake? How did you…"

"Open up the door, baby, and I'll answer all your questions." The door immediately closes with a snap. I hear the metal piece at the top flipping before the door opens again. Sin steps back giving me room to enter.

I move into the narrow space as she lets the door go. We stand with about three feet of space between us. Cloaked in darkness and silence. Each taking the other in.

"I can't believe you're here. Let me turn on a light." She runs her hand along the wall until she hits a switch. The overhead light shines down and my eyes have to adjust to the brightness, but when they do, I have never seen a better sight.

Sin leans against the wall, her fingers toying nervously with the edge of her shirt.

"Come here, baby," I whisper, holding out my arms. She walks forward until the side of her face is resting against my heart and her arms come around my waist.

"I can't believe you're here."

Believe it, baby. I'm here and I'm never going anywhere again. My arms tighten around her so tight that she squeals with laughter.

That laugh? It's everything.

Confirmation that it's not too late.

That I'm not too late.

I walk us back toward the king-size bed in the middle of the room. Our movements are uncoordinated as we stumble over clothes in the center of the floor before we fall onto the mattress in a jumble of limbs and smiles and kisses that land off center. I lean back and just stare at her in awe that after everything we've gone through, it's finally our time.

This right here is all I want, all I've ever wanted.

Sin's arms come over my shoulders and her legs widen to accept my weight into her body It comes as natural to her as breathing. She feels it too. That her place is with me, in my arms, in my bed, in my life. I cuddle into her body, my head dropping to her neck to breathe a sigh of relief. I touch my tongue to the base of her neck, moving down to dip into the line between her breasts.

"Shouldn't we talk… ahhhh." She lets out a sigh, moaning, her head moving to give my mouth a better path.

"Not yet," I say.

I move lower and sucking her nipple through the flimsy material of her shirt. Sin's hands move to my head, her back arches leaving a gap between her body and the bed. I roll her under me and her thighs immediately part and her hips pump against my rigid length as her breath begins to come in short burst.

I move back up her body finally taking her mouth

"Jake," she whispers against my lips right before my tongue pushes against hers in lascivious motions that mimics what I wanted to do with other parts of my body.

I quickly make work of removing my clothes. I toe off my shoes, which land with a thud on the floor and quickly strip my pants and shirt. I can't be the gentle lover she deserved, not after weeks of not seeing her. I'll make it up to her later. Right now I need to be in her, a part of her.

"I need this," I say against her lips. "Please." I press her knees wide pulling those barely there shorts to the side. My thumb slicks up and down my already slippery flesh. "Fuck, baby, you're already wet," I say as I position the swollen tip of my dick at her entrance, sliding my length through her silky folds.

Sin sighs as I tap the crown against her clit. "Now, Jake," she moans.

She doesn't have to ask twice. I plunged into her in one swift movement and then I still. The significance of this moment bears down on me, and I need Sin with me.

"Hey, baby," I whisper against her lips, my hands skimming her face and the sharp turn of her collarbones. My arms shake as I hold myself above her fighting the urge to pound into her.

She rocks her hips, working her pussy up and down my length, anchoring her legs over my ass to get leverage. It takes every shred of control I possess not to move. I give her more of my weight slowing her movements making it more difficult for her to move. I lean in close, dropping kisses on her lips.

"I miss you so much," I say.

Sin stills.

"Actually," I start again, trying to ignore how good it feels to be back inside her. "Since you got on that plane and flew out of my life, you're all I think about."

Her eyes turn watery at my words, but she holds my gaze. In their depths, I see a heart as fractured as my own and the other half of my soul. Behind all our broken and jagged parts is a love more significant than our combined existence and more profound than our past mistakes.

"I know I agreed that when you left, we'd be over. Here's the thing. I barely existed when I knew that you hated me, and now..." I thrust slow and languorous into her body, drawing out a low moan from deep in her throat. "Without you, I'm nothing, less than zero."

Sin shifted under me, her legs pulling me in, holding me tighter.

"Jake, I—"

"Shhh, baby, let me say this..."

A fat tear slips past her long ashes, rolling down her temple toward her hair.

"This distance thing sucks," I say after kissing the corner of her eye. "But I'd rather have you, any part of you than nothing at all."

"What exactly are you saying, Jake? Because last time we tried…"

"We didn't try, or at least I didn't," I say, dropping my forehead to hers. My body was straining over hers, but I needed to get it out, and say what I came here to say.

"I know all the things I'm not. All the reason why we didn't work, why we shouldn't work. Let me tell you what I am. I'm so in love with you. If you don't believe anything else about me, believe those words. I. Love. You." I accentuated each word a thrust.

"I loved the girl that I met at eighteen, and I fell even harder for the woman she became at twenty-nine, and I'm here. I'll be here when the tours are over, and the call of the road has lost its luster. I'll still be here when you're ready to put my ring on your finger and tell the world I'm yours. And I'll be here every day looking forward to the day when my baby grows in your belly, and we're a family in all the ways that count. I want it all, Sin, and I want it with you. Marry me"

Tears roll from the corners of her eyes back toward her temples.

"Say yes, baby" I beg. A fresh waves of tears fill her eyes as she looks up at me with first shock and then disbelief. *Please, please, please, say yes.* I don't know what I'll do if Sin doesn't say yes. The ring is still in my pants on the floor. Maybe I need to say the words?

"Are you asking me to marry—"

"Say yes," I rush out.

"Yes," she says, smiling up at me.

"Really? Don't answer that." I crush her lips with mine. "Thank fuck," I say, slamming my eyes shut and taking my first deep breath in what feels like an eternity.

I fuse my mouth to Sin's in a sensual kiss that communicates every ounce of longing I've felt in her absence and every single hope I hold for our future.

"Who do you belong to, baby?" I open my eyes to find her staring up at me. I cup her cheek with my hand, and her she turns her head to kiss the center of my palm.

"I've only ever been yours, Jake," she whispers.

Those six simple words have a severe effect on me, and before I realize what I'm doing, I'm pounding into her, over and over, trying to spill the last couple weeks of loneliness into her body.

I've only ever been yours, that's what she said, only ever been mine. I pray to God she means it because I'm never letting her go again.

The End

Epilogue

Two Years Later
Sinclair

"WAKE UP BABE. WE'RE HOME."

A smile pulls at the corners of my mouth as I peel open my tired eyes. Jake, is already out of the driver's seat, walking around the front end of his new Audi Q7. He finally gave up the sedan that carried him through college for something bigger with more room. I watch sleepily, as he makes his way to my side of the SUV, opens the door unfastening my seatbelt, and lifting me in his arms.

"Put me down before you hurt something," I say even as my arms twine around his neck and my head drops to his shoulder. "It's tradition to carry your wife across the threshold the first time you enter the home as a married couple."

"I thought that's what we were doing when you 'carried me over the threshold' of our cabana in Mexico on our wedding night."

"Nah." He says with a shake of his head. "That was horny and tired. I needed my wife, naked, in my bed, to consummate our marriage, and I didn't want to listen to another toast or take another round of congratulations. But this…" He balances my weight while he twists the doorknob. "Is us. In Las Vegas, starting our new life, in our new home. You ready baby?"

He doesn't wait for an answer as he carries me into our home. The one we purchased together while we were still on tour. The one that is empty except for the bed in the master bedroom because we didn't have time to furnish it before leaving for our wedding.

Jake carries me into the bedroom carefully placing me on the bed. I move further on the mattress, dropping back on the fluffy pillows. Exhaustion making my limbs heavy, and my eyes itchy with the desire to close.

"Sin?" Jake says laying down next to me. We roll toward each other. His arms coming around my back, my head moving to his shoulder, our legs intertwining.

"Hmmm?"

"You're happy right?" He moves his hand, fingers spread wide on my rounded belly. Earnest hazel eyes bore into mine. Am I happy that I married the only man that I've ever loved? Am I happy that I finally have a much-needed break from touring and living on the road? Am I happy to be pregnant with his baby and finally get the one thing I have wanted more than music and fame, a family? I place my hand on the sharp curve of his jaw. The whiskers from his five o'clock shadows scrape against the pads of my fingertips as I lean in and kiss him. It's slow and sweet and the sensation almost pulls me under before I pull away.

"Absolutely babe. You've made me happier than I ever knew I could be."

About the Author

M. Jay Granberry is first and foremost an insatiable reader.

Among her favorite things are classic fairy tales, smutty books where characters have heart, old lady sweaters (preferably chunky knit), gift baskets (giving not receiving), and charcuterie trays (green olives, smoked cheese, and Genoa salami).

She is a true Las Vegas native, the one in Nevada not New Mexico, and to answer the most frequently asked questions about growing up in Sin City...

- No, she doesn't live in a hotel.
- No, she has never been a stripper although she does know some.
- Prostitution is absolutely illegal in Clark County (Las Vegas)!
- And what happens in Vegas does indeed stay in Vegas.

M. Jay earned a degree in words and stories, and after fifteen plus years of doing everything other than writing, she penned her first novel.

Acknowledgments

It's the end of the book and here's the bizness...

The last year as been a world wind! *Exquisitely Broken* was a farfetched idea for years. In the middle of what I refer to as my "midlife crisis" I made the commitment to follow my dream and write a story about imperfect people, that didn't always make the best decisions, that hurt each other in horrible ways, that messed up again and again but in the end, were perfect for each other.

And I finally did it!!! I love these characters hard y'all and hope you do too!

That said, let me get on to thanking some folks.

Erick P, who read multiple drafts, talked me off the ledge, and believed in me when I doubted myself. You are the f*ckin' MVP and I don't know where I'd be without you! Makidad (hand claps)

Control Freaks, each and every one of you, thank you for humoring my sullen moods and thoughtful questions. For listening to me go on and on about this project, and for being the best co-workers a girl could ask for.

Lauren Schmelz, editor extraordinaire, you were tough girl! At times I had to close my laptop because I couldn't stand reading ONE MORE COMMENT but your critiques made me a better writer. They made my story complex and my characters better developed. You were exactly what I needed. THANK YOU!

And to the AWESOME readers who took a chance on a new author THANK YOU for giving me the chance to entertain you! BIG hugs!

That's it for me.
Mjay out!
xx

Made in the USA
Monee, IL
03 September 2019